CRIMEU

Say It Again

A Murderous Ink Press Anthology

★★★★★★★★★★★★★★★★★★★★★★★★★★★★★★★

Murderous Ink Press

CRIMEUCOPIA

Say It Again

First published by Murderous-Ink Press

Crowland

LINCOLNSHIRE

England

www.murderousinkpress.co.uk

Editorial Copyright © Murderous Ink Press 2024

Cover treatment and lettering © Willie Chob-Chob 2024

All rights are retained by the respective authors & artists on publication

Paperback Edition ISBN: 9781909498549

eBook Edition ISBN: 9781909498556

To those writers and artists who helped make this anthology what it is,
I can only say a heartfelt Thank You!

And to Den, as always.

Contents

Brandon Barrows — What Goes Around — first appeared in *The Dark City Crime & Mystery Magazine Vol. 6 issue 4* (July 2021)

Anthony Regolino — Who is Elliott Harbinger? — first appeared in *The Dark City Crime & Mystery Magazine, Vol. 6, issue 3* (April 2021) under the title *Elliott Harbinger*

Madeleine McDonald — Machinations in the Museum — first appeared in *Strife and Harmony* (S&H Publishing, 2019)

Nikki Knight — Owl Be Damned — first appeared online at *Tough Magazine* (Aug 8, 2022) and in the *MysteryRat's Maze* podcast series (Jan 10 2023)

Michele Bazan Reed — Sweet Revenge — first appeared in *The Big Fang* (Harbor Humane Society, April 2022)

Lyn Fraser — Death by Discussion — first appeared in the Spring 2017 web pages of *Mysterical-E* (2 May 2017)

Michael Wiley — The Best of Times — first appeared in *Ellery Queen Mystery Magazine Vol. 158 No. 5 & 6 Whole Nos. 962 & 963* (Nov/Dec 2021)

Eve Fisher — Time to Mourn — first appeared in *Alfred Hitchcock Mystery Magazine Vol. 56* (Jan/Feb 2011)

John Floyd — Wanted — first appeared in *Mystery Weekly Magazine* (Feb 2021)

Michael Cahlin — Killer Advice — first appeared in *Down & Out Mystery Magazine Vol. 2 issue 2* (Dec 2020)

Kevin R. Tipple — Visions of Reality — first appeared in the self published anthology *MIND SLICES* (2012)

Martin Zeigler — Wave to Me — first appeared in an unamended form in the self-published anthology *Hypochondria And Other Stories* (2020) This version (2023) has minor cosmetic amends, but the main remains the same

Lev Raphael — Lost in London — first appeared online in *Bewildering Stories* (Jan 2023)

Andrew Darlington — Photographs of Falling Objects Blur — first appeared in *SCI-FRIGHT no.6: First Year Anniversary/Millennium Issue* (UK – March 2000)

Nick Young — Smooth — first appeared in *Half Hour to Kill* (August 2022)

John Kojak — Going to California — first appeared in *Switchblade Magazine Issue 9* (April 2019)

Andrew Welsh-Huggins — A Smith & Wesson with a Side of Chorizo — first appeared as a stand alone novella from *Down & Out Books* (Dec 2021) as part of the *Guns + Tacos* series, Book 18

Ever Get A Feeling Of Déjà Vu?

(An Editorial of Sorts)

There are many things which can be said of the Modern World, and one of those is the amount of 'noise' when it comes to finding something - anything - that makes you sit up and say *I like that*. And sometimes, by the time that happens, the 'item' has passed by and gone, washed out of sight by the riptide of The Next New Thing to surf across your attention.

Which is why, whenever we open the doors to new projects and submissions, we also see pieces passed to us with the offer of reprinting them.

Some may only have a paper history, some may only have been up on a webzine site – placed for a short period of time before being archived into the depths of an ISP's hosting server.

And there are also those pieces which, quite rightly, authors may have a fondness for – the joyful offspring of their creative minds, regardless of how twisted they might be (the offspring that is, rather than the minds of their creators), and which they feel are deserving of a second read.

So we kick off with two from *The Dark City Crime & Mystery Magazine* from the pens of *Brandon Barrows* with *What Goes Around*, and Crimeucopia new name, *Anthony Regolino* who asks *Who is Elliott Harbinger?* — where only the title has been slightly changed to protect the guilty.

From there we step into the darker part of Cosy Country with *Madeleine McDonald's* tale of *Machinations in the Museum*, Nikki Knight ruffles feathers with *Owl be Damned*, *Michele Bazan Reed* tells us about *Sweet Revenge*, and *Lyn Fraser* explains about the dangers of sofa beds in her *Death by Discussion*.

From there we have a short break for a touch of modern PI humour from *Michael Wiley*'s Sam Kelson in *The Best of Times*, before we move back in time to the American West of the 19th Century, with *Eve Fisher's A Time to Mourn*, and *John M. Floyd*'s pedigree piece, *Wanted*.

Next up is another new Crimeucopian, *Michael Cahlin*, who offers up some *Killer Advice*, before *Kevin R. Tipple* gives us a *Vision of Reality*, and *Martin Zeigler* sort of eases us into a different section with his *Wave to Me*.

From there the rollercoaster drops us rapidly into *Lev Raphael*'s off-kilter *Lost in London*, which takes us around the bend and into *Andrew Darlington*'s mind-twisting, deceptively titled, *Photographs of Falling Objects Blur*.

From there we timeslip into *Nick Young*'s mid-1950s wise-cracking world of Drummond and Doris, in *Smooth*, which swings us into *John Kojak*'s quick-paced tale about *Going to California*.

From there, we then have our third and final new Crimucopian of this closing triptych, in the form of the *Andrew Welsh-Huggins* novella *A Smith & Wesson with a Side of Chorizo*.

Hopefully by presenting these pieces here, you'll start looking at various magazine and webzine archives, in search of something that may have passed you by, or that you missed the first time around.

And, as always with all of these anthologies, we hope you'll find something that you immediately like, as well as something that takes you out of your regular comfort zone — and puts you into a completely new one because, in the spirit of the Murderous Ink Press motto:

You never know what you like until you read it.

What Goes Around

Brandon Barrows

The phone rang – the landline, not my cell. I figured it was another robo-telemarketer, pretty much the only calls that phone got, but it was almost eleven, so I climbed out of bed to answer. The number was in the book and there was always the chance it was some sort of emergency. "Hello?"

There was silence on the line for a few seconds, then the sound of labored breathing. I slammed the phone into its cradle. First robots, now perverts. If the phone didn't come bundled with the cable TV and internet, I wouldn't have it at all. It was just a pain in the ass.

I was halfway across the room, headed back to bed, when the phone rang again. This time, I looked at the caller ID before I answered, but it was just a local number I didn't recognize. "Hello," I said, putting irritation into my voice.

"Bobby, I'm comin' up." There was a click and the connection was dead. It was a soft, whispery voice that somehow carried a note of sickness. Something in it was familiar, too, something that put an icy finger against the base of my spine.

I went back into the bedroom, moved to the dresser, and took from it the .25 automatic I carried sometimes when I worked late nights and had a lot of cash around. I popped the magazine out to make sure it was loaded, pushed it back into place, then went and sat on the edge of the bed.

I wanted the gun because the voice reminded me of John Rill and he was the very last person I ever wanted to see again. Why? Because he was dead. More than two years ago and almost a thousand miles away, I put two slugs from my old .38 into John Rill and left him for dead in a New England snowbank. That gun was long gone and Rill should have been, too.

There was no way it could be John, I told myself. He was dead, I was sure of that. But who else ever called me Bobby? Nobody around here knew me as anything but Rob Lewis, part owner of the King Street Laundromat. The gutter days were behind me and I was lucky to get out with no record and a little money to start over. It cost a man's life, but it wasn't much of one and he'd have done the same to me if I let him.

I stood up, went to the cabinet over the sink in the kitchenette. There was a fifth of half-decent bourbon in there. I took a pull straight from the bottle, trying to calm some of the thoughts racing through my head.

It couldn't be Rill because Rill was dead. So was the old me, the Bobby Lewis who grew up on Zeigler Street, rolling drunks and shoplifting beers. That guy was a punk, a loser who never did himself or anyone else any good. His first step into the big-time was his last, and nobody knew about that but me and John Rill. It was a spur of the moment kind of thing, the sort that comes up out of nowhere and is too good to miss.

We pulled it, got away clean, and were at a rest-stop somewhere in Vermont when John must have decided the whole fourteen grand sounded a lot better than just his rightful half. He started some beef with me, I don't even remember what about, but we argued, it got rough, and then his hand went under his coat. He was going for his gun. I was just a little faster. I put two slugs through his belt-buckle, then dug a hole in a huge pile of plowed-up snow at the edge of the parking lot, rolled him in, and collapsed it on top of the body. It was the middle of the night, so nobody was around, and there was enough snow that nobody would find him 'til spring. Even when they did, it wouldn't matter, because I'd be long gone and there was nothing to tie us together.

After that, I turned the car south and left New England several states behind me. A few months later, I found a nice little town and a business glad to take on a partner with some ready cash. My life's been pretty boring since, but I wasn't complaining.

There was a knock on the apartment door, soft but insistent. Shoving the gun in the waistband of my pajama pants, I moved to the door and put my eye to the peephole. Whoever was outside was too close; the light from the hallway threw their shadow across the lens, keeping me from seeing anything but a black blob.

"Who is it?" I asked, afraid of the answer.

"Bobby, open the door." Even muffled, I recognized the same whispery, sick-tainted voice from the phone. Something in my head started screaming, convinced already that it was Rill – that I was talking to a ghost.

A shudder went through me. I didn't want to open the door, but I couldn't help myself. I had to know. I undid the chain, flicked the lock and stepped back. "It's open," I called.

The knob turned, the door opened, and the shape shuffled from the hallway into the apartment. I stared, mouth open, unable to say anything or even make any noise to express the shock I felt. My breath was frozen in my chest and I was afraid I'd never be able to get it moving again. My lungs started to hurt and I forced air into them, making a sort of gasping sound that was loud in the stillness of the room.

It *was* him. It was Rill. He was changed, wasted away, his clothes hanging on him like a sack, but it was him. Two years ago, he was a chunky six-footer who must have weighed two-thirty if he weighed an ounce. Now, he probably wasn't half of that. Skin hung in loose folds from his jaws and his face was the color of a long-dead fish's belly. It was obvious that he was sick as hell. I felt more than a little ill just looking at him.

There was a gurgling noise and it took me a moment to realize Rill was laughing. "I guess I don't gotta ask if you're surprised, Bobby."

"It's Rob," I said stupidly. "Nobody calls me Bobby."

"Sure," Rill agreed. "Rob Lewis, small businessman."

"How do you know that? How did you find me?" My hand went to the butt of the gun, but Rill patted the breast of his jacket. "Ah, ah, ah..." he said. "I learned my lesson about you and guns... Bobby."

I put my hands down at my sides, clenched them into fists. "How are you even alive?"

"One question at a time," Rill rasped, deep in his throat. "Let me sit down somewhere, will you? I'm a sick man."

I didn't know what else to do. I stepped back, made room, and gestured towards the couch. Slowly, Rill crossed to it and sank down onto the cushions. He closed his eyes and sighed, sounding grateful for the rest. After a moment, he looked up at me. "Internet."

"What?"

"*Internet*," he repeated. "You can find damned near anything on the internet. You weren't exactly hiding, you know, and I had a lot of time to search for you, layin' in that hospital bed."

"Hospital?" I didn't know what to say, it was all so overwhelming. I spent the last two years of my life trying to forget the worst thing I ever did and now, here it was, staring me right in the face.

Rill smiled and it wasn't pleasant. "Hospital. You got me right in the belly, sure enough, but you didn't kill me. I was in no shape to fight back, so I played 'possum. The snow gave me some trouble, but once I was sure you were gone, I dug myself out and started crawling. Eventually, someone came by and got me to a hospital."

I backed up until I hit the wall and leaned against it for support. "So you're okay?"

That gurgling laugh rattled his thin chest again. "'Okay,' he asks me." He laughed some more. "I look okay, Bobby? You know what they did to me in the hospital? You know what they had to do, tryin' to fix what *you* did?"

I shook my head, not trusting my voice.

"You shot too low to kill me, Bobby. You tore up my intestines real good, though. Doctors had to take out almost four feet of 'em and stitch 'em back together. I spent two months in the hospital that time. The doctors wanted to know how it happened, the cops wanted to know. Those boys rode me hard, but I never said a word about you, no matter how they pressed me. You know why?"

"Why?" I asked, but I didn't want to know the answer.

"It wasn't out of the goodness of my heart, I'll tell you that. No." He shook his head and it was clear the effort that took. "It was because I knew, even then, that you killed me and I decided that if it was the last thing I did, I was going to take your life away from you, too."

I licked dry lips and stared at him. The sight of Rill sickened me, not just the way he looked and sounded but the guilt that he stirred up inside me. But I was almost getting used to it now – enough, anyway, that my brain was starting to work again. He said he was going to take my life, but how the hell could he do that? He wasn't any older than I was, not even thirty, but he was a sick old man who could barely move. He could have told the cops everything two years ago, but he couldn't prove anything then and the trail was long cold by now. Suddenly, I wasn't scared of him anymore.

"Get out of here, John. I'm sorry for what happened, but I'm not that guy you knew. I'm different now."

Rill's laugh echoed in his throat again. "Sure, you are. Me, too. But my story ain't done yet. The least you can do is listen, right?" He didn't wait for me to respond before he went on. "That was just the *first* time I went into the hospital. The next time I went in, they took out another three feet of my guts. The time after that, it was only about a foot and a half. You know you got like thirty feet of intestines all coiled up in your belly, Bobby? Well, you know how much I got? None. After the last time in the hospital, practically none at all."

"What do you want from me, John?"

"I'm dying, Bobby. You get that, right? It took you two years, but you killed me. Before I go, I want to make sure you get what you deserve. I hope that fourteen grand was worth it."

It was the last that drove me over the edge. Sure, I shot John Rill, but he'd have done the same to me if I let him. As guilty as I felt taking his life, I always tempered it with the knowledge that I was saving my own. Now, knowing I didn't actually kill him after all, it was all burning away in a mixture of disgust and anger.

I took the little gun from my waistband and pointed it at the other man. "Get up, Rill. Get the hell out before I finish what I started."

The smile was back on Rill's face. "You won't use that, Bobby. You got twenty, thirty neighbors all around you. You fire that thing, you'll have the cops on you in minutes."

I shook my head. "You got a gun, too, John. You already threatened me with it, remember? Leave or I'll put another slug in your belly. All I have to do to get out from under is say it was self-defense. That's what I should have done last time."

Rill gurgled deep in his chest again, smiling and shaking his head. The movement dislodged big fat drops of sweat from his hairline that ran down his forehead. He seemed to be getting even paler. All of this effort was really costing him. I knew he wasn't kidding about how close he was to dying. "You think so, huh?" He said it so quietly I almost didn't hear it.

When he looked up, there was pain in his eyes and something else, something I thought might be insanity. "I got maybe a couple months left, Bobby..."

I couldn't imagine how bad the last two years had been for him and, thinking about it, I let the gun's barrel dip for a second,

Louder, Rill said, "I might as well use 'em all at once!" and his hand disappeared into his jacket, faster than any move I'd seen him make 'til then.

My hand came up and the .25 bucked, the hard snap of the shot bouncing off the walls of the room. A red-purple splotch appeared on Rill's shirt. He sighed and fell back against the couch cushions as the light went out of his eyes. Silence returned to the room, but I knew it wouldn't last. A dozen neighbors were probably calling 911 even then. I'd have more company soon.

I moved to the couch and bent down over Rill, planning to get his gun, to make sure it was out and in his hand so when the cops showed up, it would look right. I opened his jacket, careful to avoid the blood spreading across his shirt. My jaw dropped. There was no gun in Rill's pocket. Where I expected to find one, there was a black plastic TV remote wrapped in wads of tissue to give it more or less the right bulk and shape for an automatic.

I stood stunned for long minutes. Then there was pounding on the door and a voice that was used to authority calling for me to open it. Without any warning, I threw up, splattering the couch, my pajama bottoms, and my feet. I barely noticed. I was still too sick and dazed to move when they finally broke the door in and found me staring at the man who made me kill him not once, but twice.

And this time, there was no place to put the body and no way to call it self-defense that anyone would believe. Rill was just a frail, dying man. I was never in any danger from him. As they put the cuffs on me, I tried to laugh at the irony of it, but it came out a sob. For two years, I thought I killed John Rill and got away with it. He crawled out of his grave just to make sure I didn't.

Who is Elliott Harbinger?

Anthony Regolino

As I await my sanity review to see if I will be allowed to finally leave the Cherryville Home for the Unwell (formerly the Cherryville Insane Asylum), I am asked to look over and present the following text, which I had initially written years ago prior to my entering this establishment. I look it over and make notes or slight alterations, additions that either had not occurred to me at that time or may benefit from further explanation. It would not do to present something that does not make me look my best. In fact, let me read you what I had written. I would love to know what you think.

*****

It all began with my passion for the works of Elliott Harbinger, someone whom I had no reason to doubt actually existed. After all, his debut novel, *What Would I Be Without You*, placed him on the Times Bestseller List and made him the most sought-after author by editors and agents alike. The film adaptation deal that followed was only agreed-to by him on the provision that he be allowed to offer the first draft. And newspaper and magazine interviews offered his personal responses to the questions submitted to him. They were even accompanied by a photo. Does this sound like someone who isn't real?

I was one of those early admirers, the ones that instantly recognized his talent, long before the blockbuster movie garnered him scores of additional fans. It was when that first book first came out that I attempted to ascertain his whereabouts, in the simple hope of sending my first edition copy out to be autographed.

I had done so before, and it was never any great feat to find out where an author lived. It was not like they were movie stars, in constant need of keeping their home addresses secret to stave off stalkers. Often, the publishing house itself had some helpful information for how to contact an author, even if it was just the contact info for an agent. But, as of his first book's release, Mister Harbinger didn't yet have literary representation in the form of an agent or manager. And since this was back in the eighties, there was no such thing as Internet to help ease my search efforts.

Reclusive. That was how the media described him. And he wasn't the first. Nothing special or exclusive there. Just another of those odd-bodies who shun attention and produce art for art's sake, and not for the notoriety that often accompanies it. It just made him that much more admirable in my eyes.

I waited for his mask to slip. Somehow, as more and more of his work was published and subsequently produced as a film, there would have to be some slip-up. Someone somewhere would give something away. They had to! And I would wait, watch, and catch it.

My first lead came when I was watching an old movie on a channel devoted to classic films. In a minor scene where the main character was shown around a fifties' studio interpretation of a newsroom, the camera settled on the last of the background workers once the principal performers crossed in front of them and exited for their next scene. It was not in close-up, but it didn't matter. The food tray I had been picking from fell to the floor with a clatter, but I hardly noticed. All I could think about was that image on the screen.

In the room where I kept the stacks of books, videos, and other Elliott Harbinger memorabilia I had collected, I searched furiously. It took literally an hour and a half to finally find it, that now-four-year-old article that introduced the rising literary star and included his picture. Except it wasn't just his picture; it was a shot from an old movie!

"Nailed him!" I thought, as I tried to recreate the set of circumstances that could have led to this curious situation. An early foray into Hollywood in the hopes of becoming an actor. A failed career that perhaps turned out a few bit parts like the one I had just seen. Years of struggle and frustration that fueled the creative side of his brain until he had to set it all out in pen! Yes, that must be it.

I returned to the other room, where the film was just about to wrap up. The main character was having a light moment after all his escapades were neatly tidied up in preparation for the fade-out and final credits. He was back in the newsroom with his arms resting in camaraderie around a couple of background actors, and he addressed the one whom I now knew to be Elliott Harbinger, calling him "Charlie." Charlie!

The character had a name, perhaps even had lines in the film—which I had missed as I searched for the old article. If he did speak, he would be included in the credits! I knocked the nearby snack tray halfway across the room as I bolted to the television and kneeled in front of its giant 27-inch screen the way I used to when I was a kid in front of my 13-inch one.

As the cast listing scrolled upward, my eyes darted from name to name. Toward the end I found it: Charlie. And across from it, at the end of a string of dots: Melvin Oppenheimer. To the library!

For those of you not old enough to recall a time when we didn't have all the world's data at the tip of our fingers, looking up a person was not the simple matter of typing in a name and hitting Enter. The right type of tome must be discovered, say perhaps a *Who's Who* for a particular field. And then there was the possibility of it not being up-to-date with current addresses. The Melvin Oppenheimer I was looking for did not rate an entry in any text that revealed actors' info, but I was lucky enough to find someone with his name in such a book for Hollywood crew techs, his apparent specialty being "key grip"—whatever the hell that is. The birth year it provided seemed to be about right for my guy, so I took down the last known address for him—which was from a dozen and a half years ago—and set off for home to decide my next move.

The address was a good four hours away—not unreasonable—so I decided to drive out to the place on the weekend. I would have loved to be able to call first to see if he still lived there—to see if he still *lived,* for that matter—but no phone number was provided, and I didn't have access to any phone books from out-of-state. When Saturday arrived, I was out of the house by 5:30 A.M.

I got lost several times along the way (no GPS, of course), so I didn't arrive at the house until noon. It was a farm house with very little land around it, and what there was of it was in shabby shape, neglected. I pulled open the screen door gently, as it looked like it was only being held on by the grace of some well-positioned twine, and knocked firmly on the solid wood door behind it.

After five full minutes, I could finally discern movement on the other side of the door, and when it opened I could not believe my eyes. It was him! Older, of course—well into his sixties—but definitely the man from the photo and the fifties' motion picture. Thinner, balding, and quite feeble, his movements painfully slow, as if he were another decade or two older than he actually was. "Mister Harbinger?" I inquired.

"No, Oppenheimer. Don't know any Harbinger." He was about to swing the door closed but stopped when I continued.

"Yes. Melvin Oppenheimer, the actor. You used to be in movies. And now you're a writer. With the pen name Elliott Harbinger. Unless Oppenheimer's a stage name and Harbinger is your real one."

He was obviously confused, taking several more seconds than should be necessary to process what I had just said. "No. Like I said, I don't know any Harbinger. You got the acting part right, though. Never much took to stage names, so I used my own. Oppenheimer. They didn't like it, they could shove it."

"No, but I mean now," I explained, "with your writing career." To which he replied derisively, "What writing career!" I took out the magazine article and showed him his own picture, in the magazine where his interview answered questions about his writing technique, but never any personal information. What he saw incited him. "My likeness!" he exclaimed. "They're using my likeness without my permission!"

He ran off with my magazine and headed straight for the phone hanging on a nearby wall, no doubt to call a lawyer. Since I had a few more copies of that particular issue, I decided not to attempt taking it back, so I closed the door, dismissed and probably already dropped from the mind of this failed onetime bit actor.

There was no reason for me to suspect that he was putting on an act; it made sense that he would not be aware of the deception. Whoever was behind it would want as few people as possible to know the truth—whatever that was—and so they found a likeness that seemed to fit the author's image, belonging to someone whom they figured nobody would recognize or question. And then I just happened to get lucky and stumble upon their hoax.

I must admit I took it rather poorly, almost as if it were personal and the deception intended just for me. Over the next year, I refused to participate in the pretense. I bought no book of his, attended no movie based on one of his stories, and changed the channel whenever he was mentioned in the news. I wanted none of him. I even had a bonfire in my yard and kept it alive well into the night by feeding it all the things I had collected of his.

But it was not enough. I realized I could not ban him from my mind the way I had banned him from my apartment, and so I was back on his trail once again, exactly one year to the date that I had met the man whose face he stole.

I concentrated on the publishing house, both because they were the most likely to be involved in it and because I had no other leads to follow. I applied for—and got—a lowly position within the company, forsaking my own job where I earned nearly twice the salary, and from there I began learning all I could about who was involved in Harbinger's books being published.

There was one editor—the man who supposedly "discovered" Elliott Harbinger—who was responsible for all of them. Ben Parker. As a reward for his intuitiveness, and the continued accumulation of wealth he garnered for the company, he was given his own office, unlike the rest of the editors who simply had cubicles in a shared space. Because of this, and the fact that he always kept his door closed, I could not spy on him or the contents of his desk. But the jealousy and resentment he earned from his coworkers meant that others would freely speak of him (usually disparagingly) and spill all they knew about him and his—in their mind—unorthodox approaches.

I watched and learned Mister Parker's routine: his work schedule, including meetings and what days he stayed late; when he would announce a new Elliott Harbinger novel, and what events seemed to transpire around it; even what foods he liked to eat—liverwurst especially—and whether he was seeing anyone. As for that last one, there seemed to be no one, unless there was something more to that odd fellow who would stop by once a week right before quitting time, the one day of the week Ben Parker chose to work extra hours.

I hung around the office late on one of those days, which wasn't easily justified because my position was not one that offered any opportunities for overtime. So after faking a gastrointestinal problem all day, I remained sequestered within the men's room nearest Parker's office until I was sure everyone else has left, and I snuck up to the office door to see what I could discover. But their excited conversing filtered through as insensible whispers and mumblings on my side of the door, and I could learn nothing more, other than that they spent a good three hours behind those closed doors.

Repeated spying confirmed that they did this on a weekly basis, convincing me that something was going on in there that would answer some, if not *all*, of my questions about the elusive Elliott Harbinger. So when they had left one evening, I slipped inside and inspected the office. Parker kept his desk drawers locked, and nothing was left lying about that could offer any clues, but I did see a dusty side closet that didn't look used. A quick look inside confirmed that it wasn't—except perhaps by a few well-meaning spiders—and a new plan formed in my mind.

It took me several weeks to proceed to my next step—mostly due to a wait for a handgun permit to go through—during which time I made sure that the two kept their usual weekly assignation and never strayed from it. When the time came when I could advance to the execution stage of my mission, I must confess that I actually balked. Fear overwhelmed me, and weeks went by where I continually failed to work up the guts to put my plan into motion.

Eventually, my undying curiosity got the better of me. I HAD to know—finally!—for once and for all!—WHO is Elliott Harbinger! I loaded the gun as I had been instructed.

I called in sick, leaving a message on my supervisor's messaging system, then showed up at my job earlier than everyone else. I entered the abandoned closet in Mister Parker's office, and settled myself down for a long day of waiting. Parker himself called in sick that day as well, so I had wasted a sick day for nothing.

I scheduled a vacation day for the following week, once I knew that Parker's illness was of the non-serious, twenty-four-hour variety, and repeated my actions of early arrival and waiting in the closet in silence. This time Parker arrived on schedule, and as I listened in to his daily calls and meetings the name of Elliott Harbinger would pop up time and again, causing me to stir and pay closer attention. But nothing revealing was mentioned on those instances, and I was practically asleep from boredom when his end-of-workday visitor finally showed up.

I perked up my ears to listen, but the words they used triggered no recognition on my part. Whether they were business terms or expressions for some highfalutin computer technology, I could not tell. The jargon kept going; it was as if they didn't speak English. I finally got so fed up with it all that I burst out of the closet with the gun held out for them to see.

They nearly jumped three feet in the air, but landed back in their seats to stare at me with open mouths. No point in wasting time with explanations that I felt they didn't deserve anyway; I demanded that they tell me who Elliott Harbinger is immediately or I would shoot. I wouldn't really shoot, and I hoped that they couldn't tell that I had neglected to slide off the safety, but I counted on my hyper-agitated state putting them off guard.

It seemed to be working. The pants fabric at Parker's lap was instantly stained from the urine that flooded out of him, and his guest was frozen in terror, clutching an attaché case like it was a life preserver. Since Ben was perhaps the more sensible of the two at that moment, I addressed him, my gun swinging along with my head at whomever I was looking at. As it was aimed his way and remained trained on him, a squeaky sound and a pungent smell revealed that his bowels had failed him too.

Realizing that I expected him to speak, regardless of the state he was in, he stammered and kept looking over at his visitor for assistance. A futile effort.

"I don't know what to say," he finally exclaimed, and if there were another way to expel waste from the body he would have done so just then. Oh, right, there is a third way. He suddenly leaned over the arm of his chair and vomited.

With all the bodily functions taking place in that room, my own bladder suddenly realized how long it had been forced to hold everything in while I was stuck in the closet in hiding, and I wished I could get this over with so I too could go to the bathroom and relieve the growing pressure to pee that I began feeling.

"Elliott Harbinger. Tell me all about him."

"Well there is no Elliott Harbinger," came the response from the visitor, who had finally found his voice. I swung my head his way, the gun moving with it. "No, really!" he added emphatically, one arm straying from his clutched case as if to ward off a blow. "He's a fabrication."

"Fine," I continued, "then who's been writing his books?"

Ben Parker's arm jerkily moved out till he was pointing over at his guest. When I looked over at the guest, his eyes bulged and he tossed his briefcase onto the desk table between them, pointing at it with stabbing motions. "Not me! That!"

"What the hell are you talking about?" I asked, moving over to the table and unzipping the case with my free hand. Inside was a thick, sturdy laptop, nothing more.

"I developed a program that utilizes formulas and statistics taken from all the greatest bestsellers of the past fifty years," the stranger explained, and despite his terror a hint of pride was evident in his voice. "Others have tried, but no one has ever accomplished what I have, and no other program has attained such an impressive track record as this one has achieved. It even worked with screenplays. It'll be the future of publishing! Writers—with their inconsistent hit-or-miss results—will never be needed again!"

I stood staring at the abomination on the desk, and I know the two of them never moved, but apparently a janitor had overheard what was going on and peeked in. All I know is that police had been summoned, and when they arrived they found me unresponsive. I couldn't stop staring at 'it'. Elliott Harbinger. I had finally found him. Sort of.

I landed in a prison cell, where I was to remain as I awaited my first court appearance. A jury of twelve Elliott Harbingers, good men and women, were selected to decide my fate, with the Honorable Judge Elliott Harbinger presiding. My boss Elliott Harbinger was called upon to act as a character witness, while Elliott Harbinger, whose office I broke into, and his computer tech, Elliott Harbinger—the two men I held at gunpoint—were the prosecution's witnesses.

I shared my cell with another, a convict named Elliott Harbinger, who bore a striking resemblance to the actor I had tracked down thinking him to be the infamous, mysterious author. What was that actor's name again? Elliott something?

I finally got my chance to take the stand. To set things right. To appeal to those twelve good and true peers of mine that what I did was rational and that any of them would have done the same in my shoes. I hoped they would see things my way.

"State your name for the court," I was asked.

I replied "Elliott Harbinger" of course.

*****

So there you have it. A perfectly able-minded recount of a legitimate misunderstanding, with forgivable actions that were utterly justifiable.

Don't you agree?

Machinations in the Museum
Madeleine McDonald

Charlotte scowled at the brightly lit display cabinets. Why had she agreed to this? Replacing his pottery with something made of torn-up T-shirts was a betrayal of Gramps and all he stood for. Gramps had put his soul into crafting the stumpy little figures, and soul was something a vulgarian like Mavis Chirk would never understand.

The previous night, the trustees and volunteers of the Congar Museum of Local Life had met to prepare the annual summer opening. The museum shut in winter, when few visitors braved the rain-lashed Welsh coast. It struggled on, from one government grant to the next, its collection of objects increasing as elderly miners and farmers died off, and their heirs donated tools rusty with disuse.

The old farmhouse which housed the museum had never been modernised. To American visitors "doing Wales" on a coach tour, that was its charm. They enthused over the uneven brick floors, low ceilings, tiny windows, dark corners and steep, narrow staircases. They cooed over the black-leaded range, the washtubs, dollies and mangles, the cast-iron fireplaces, the tables draped in yellowing, hand-embroidered cloths, and the mannequins in period costume.

The meeting had been held in the activities room. In contrast to the mock-up of a forbidding 19th century classroom with scratched desks and wooden-framed slates, the activities room was brightly painted, with communal tables offering plentiful supplies of worksheets and felt tip pens. The volunteer guides always breathed a sigh of relief once parties of bouncy schoolchildren were corralled in a room devoid of exhibits, for the old tools could be dangerous in reckless hands.

The overhead lighting in the activities room was unflattering to the mainly elderly volunteers. They were barely a dozen in number now, despite regular appeals to the town for new blood. Charlotte's youthful face marked her out.

"Item 3 on the agenda, the gift shop," the chairman announced.

Mavis, self-styled manageress of the gift shop, marshalled her papers. Around the table, people stared at their hands.

"As noted in the treasurer's report, in our first year of operation, the gift shop exceeded expectations," Mavis announced. "If we double our floor space this summer, I expect to quadruple our turnover."

"Hold on a minute, Mavis. We're a museum, not an emporium. Why do you need extra floor space?" Derek Jones asked.

"A failing museum," Mavis snapped back. "A dismal collection of moth-eaten clothes and antiquated tools. It was my retail skills that kept us going last year."

"Why don't you open a high street shop then?" Derek countered.

Charlotte hid a smile. With his untidy hair and well-worn anorak, Derek reminded her of Gramps.

"A shop lowers the tone of the museum," Derek continued. "Before you came and turned us upside down, we offered a selection of books reflecting our ethos and purpose." As the author of two self-published books on the lost railways of Snowdonia, he had particular reason to dislike Mavis, who had moved books to the back of the gift shop.

"I agree with Derek." That was Ann Poole. The oldest trustee, she walked with difficulty after two hip replacements, yet insisted on taking responsibility for dusting fragile exhibits. "You're not interested in our work, Mavis. You're using us to get your name and photo in the paper as often as possible. We all know your husband wants to be the next town mayor. And you want to be lady mayoress."

"Ladies, please." The chairman took a handkerchief from his pocket and began to polish his glasses, acknowledging that he had temporarily lost control of the proceedings.

Ann and Mavis took no notice. Miss Roberts, in charge of the minutes, laid down her pen for the duration of hostilities.

"I will not resign, Mrs Poole, I will not give you that pleasure." Puce with fury, Mavis delivered her parting shot. "And, in case any of you have forgotten, it was my Arthur who secured us grant money from Europe." She glared round the table. "You don't get money just for being a worthy cause. You need to know the right people as well. You should all be grateful to my Arthur."

The mention of money silenced the dissenters. It was true the European Union had awarded the museum a substantial sum under some coastal regeneration programme, although the extra money had been diverted to repairing the slate roof. The chairman suggested placing on record the trustees' appreciation of Mrs. Chirk's diligence. Reluctantly, Charlotte raised her hand along with the others. Miss Roberts made a note on her shorthand pad.

Mavis gave a gracious nod and steamrollered on. "Now that we are agreed on the extra floor space, I can show you two new lines we will be introducing this summer." Mavis bent to extricate items from her shopping bag. Coming up, she breathed heavily and Charlotte had the irreverent thought that chains of office were designed for ample bosoms. Mavis would carry hers well but, standing beside her, Arthur would be weighed down by Congar's municipal regalia.

Born into a family of self-employed farmers, Charlotte had been out of sync with the clamorous left-wing views of her fellow students. At the same time, she nourished a visceral hatred for the Arthurs and Mavises of this world, festooned with chains of office and frothy Tory hats. Soft-living incomers like the Chirks had never known the precarious life of the hill farmers or the slate miners. She, Charlotte Davies, might be a shining example of social progress, having attended Art College in Liverpool, but solidarity with her ancestors' existential struggle was bred into her bones.

After handing round an example of the new line of love spoons featuring the fire-breathing Welsh dragon, Mavis unrolled a bundle. She smoothed the bright colours flat. "And these are the rag rugs."

"No way, Mavis," Derek Jones said "My grandma's rugs never looked like that. She didn't waste money cutting up clothes until they were worn to threads."

"Aye, Derek's right." A couple of ladies with tightly permed grey hair voiced agreement.

Charlotte's only knowledge of rag rugs was seeing grimy rectangles set in front of the fireplaces in the various rooms. She rarely had occasion to step over the ropes that cordoned off the tableaux of village life, and could not recall having handled one.

Mavis bridled. "These are a modern version. Designed and made in Wales by Felicity Williams. Well, the originals are. I ordered one hundred."

"Without consulting us?" The normally emollient chairman bristled with indignation.

"I used my discretion. Made in China, they cost £5 each, and we can sell them for £25 each in the shop.

Around the table, heads jerked up. Even Charlotte did the mental calculation of £20 profit on a hundred rugs.

"Of course, if we want to encourage people to buy them, we'll have to find a place for Felicity's originals. I suggest we move the Duckfeathers Pottery pieces into one display case, instead of two."

"But Duckfeathers was Gramps' business," Charlotte wailed. Heads turned to look. "His pottery is part of Congar's history. He employed lots of local people."

"Quite, dear. And since you inherited his artistic talent I nominate you as the best person to make a selection of his pottery pieces." Mavis smiled at the table, not at Charlotte.

"Agreed," the chairman said, and Miss Roberts made a note. "And Charlotte, can you write something on Facebook? Those bright colours will make a good picture."

Charlotte could not refuse. Her degree in fine art had not led to a job, even at dogsbody level, and voluntary work at the museum was something to list on her CV. She had also taken responsibility for the museum's Facebook page, allowing her to claim *excellent social media skills* in her numerous job applications.

Derek Jones left the museum alongside Charlotte, chuntering discontent. "That woman is a vandal. I'll kill her if she pulls another trick like that. Plastic love spoons made in China! Time was a young man carved a spoon for his sweetheart with his own knife and only the two of them knew what the carvings said. Know what I mean?" His throaty cackle embarrassed Charlotte.

*****

The next morning, Charlotte still seethed. Instead of kicking something, she scuffed the soles of her trainers across the wooden floorboards, producing an unpleasant sound in the small room. She did it again.

You'd hate it, wouldn't you, Gramps, fake Welsh culture. Another part of her brain snorted in contradiction, for Gramps had never turned up his nose at making money. Charlotte turned her back on the display cabinet and stared out of the window.

The anger she felt since last night's meeting intensified when Mavis arrived and suggested that she remove the sheep and ducks. "Leave the cups and saucers, dear, the colours are quite pleasant. But you must agree those 1950s ornaments are beyond kitsch. I'm not saying anything against your ancestor, he did well for a self-taught man, but I'm sure your art degree has given you a sense of perspective."

Shrouding the despised ducks in layers of bubble wrap, Charlotte dreamed of being in a position of power in the art world and refusing to renew the museum's grant. As a revenge fantasy, that was as puerile as the various Facebook posts she had composed in her head following last night's meeting.

She'll pay for this, Gramps.

Objectively, she conceded that Gramps' sheep and ducks lacked taste. She held one of the pottery figures to the light, examining its unnatural blue plumage. The duck stood upright, in a defiant pose. As an object it was so hideous you had to smile. Yet Charlotte recalled Gramps explaining the nineteen forties and fifties to her, when she was a child and Gramps was unimaginably old, for Gramps was Grandpa Tom's dad. "It was a grim time. We'd won the war, but conditions were hardly better than before. Our houses were always cold, and food was rationed." He'd ruffled Charlotte's hair. "You and your little friends wouldn't recognise it for the same country. So when the good times came back and people got a bit of money in their hands, they wanted things that were bright, and shiny and new. Think on it. If you lived in a cold, damp home, with a fireplace that smoked, you'd want something new to put on the mantelpiece and cheer the place up. That's what I gave them, little ornaments that put a smile on people's faces."

Throughout art school, Charlotte had defended Gramps' homely philosophy of giving people what they wanted. Now she was complicit in sweeping him aside. Rage seethed and roiled as she packed the ornaments.

There was nothing she could do. The discussion of the previous night swilled through her brain, underlining her spineless complicity.

She'll pay for this.

The museum was almost empty. Out in the courtyard, a portable radio was set to a local station as Andy Perkins sawed and hammered, working on a new bench for the garden. A jingle cut across the radio chit chat to announce the traffic news. Somewhere Ann Poole was progressing from room to room, feather duster in hand, removing every speck of winter's dust from the jumble of display items before opening day. Mavis was in the small office on the top floor.

Charlotte made a quick foray upstairs to find one of the genuine rag rugs, noting with satisfaction that it was almost invisible against the black-painted floorboards at the top of the precipitous back stairs. Downstairs again, she headed for the alcove where the electric kettle was kept. "Ready for a cup of tea, Andy?" she called on the way.

*****

The trustees and volunteers agreed that the grand summer opening should go ahead, in tribute to Mavis's sterling work, with Councillor Arthur Chirk invited to perform the opening ceremony. "It's what she would have wanted," they told each other. The plastic love spoons and mass-produced rag rugs arrived from China, and were stored in the gift shop cupboard, thus offering the volunteers further opportunity to dissect Mavis's conduct.

Mavis had fallen down the unlit back stairs when Charlotte had called her to come and share the morning tea break. The tragic accident was blamed on her high heels. "Quite unsuitable for a woman of her age," was Ann Poole's verdict, and her cronies agreed.

The Duckfeathers Pottery display had been reinstated. The genuine rag rug was also back in its place, for Charlotte was tidy by nature.

Owl be Damned

A Jaye Jordan Vermont Radio Mystery

Nikki Knight

Everybody loves a snowy owl.

At least everybody I want to know. Nobody I want to know loves murder, though, and that sure took the joy out of Blanche's visit to Simpson.

But in January in Vermont, you take what you get.

January's pretty ugly here. Figuratively, anyhow. Literally, it's spectacularly beautiful, with thick, deep snow, shimmering blue skies, and flaming sunsets. As long as you don't mind being reminded of why some cultures believe in a Hell of Cold.

Ugly is exactly the right word for two big storms in a week, followed by a cold snap. Uglier for me, since I had to sweep that snow out of the satellite dish on the roof to keep my little radio station on the air.

Just another fun day of running WSV, the tiny operation I bought and took live and local again when my husband survived cancer but our marriage didn't. My daughter is happy here, and the station is getting by…and that's about all I want to say about it.

I'm Jaye Jordan, by the way. Yes, my real name – people always wonder with DJs. Western PA country girl made good as a New York City jock before my life unraveled. I'm the one who just keeps going, no matter what.

But January is wearing.

Which is why pretty much everyone went nuts when the snowy owl showed up near the WSV transmitter shack out on Quarry Road. Anything at all to break up the monotony of shoveling, sweeping and scraping. Especially if it's something as magnificent as a snowy owl.

Blanche, as we inevitably christened her when birdwatcher Willard

Collier pointed out that her gray-barred markings meant she was female, was the toast of the town within about fifteen minutes.

And my usually deserted stick (radio slang for transmitter) was the most popular hangout around, with folks driving and hiking up, coming close enough to see her — but not to scare her away.

That Saturday afternoon, my pals and I had finished our weekly yoga class at the Community Center, when Sadie Blacklaw waved the keys to her Hummer. "C'mon. No one else will be there right now because the Patriots are the early game."

None of us really wanted to ride in the Hummer, a genuine military surplus one that Sadie had gotten through her many connections as Town Clerk and legendary local leader. She drives like Speed Racer on meth.

But, Maeve, Alicia, and I definitely *did* want to see Blanche, and that was worth the risk.

Too bad she wasn't the first thing we saw when we wobbled out of the Hummer, crunching into the slushy tire and boot prints, an indistinguishable mess now two days after the latest storm.

No, while Blanche was perched on the corrugated-metal roof of the shack, her feathers fluffed up by the breeze, her vivid orange eyes glowing with something that sure seemed like annoyance, but the attention-getter was the guy on the ground.

He was crumpled onto a drift at the edge of the lot, half on his side, one hand reaching toward the shack. It was Willard Collier, the birdwatcher, who'd been hiking up every day from his house a half-mile away. And I was pretty sure he was dead.

"Call George!" Sadie said to Alicia, referring to her husband, Police Chief George Orr. "You're still current on CPR, right, Jaye?"

"Yeah." I kept up my certification because of my tween daughter. Mom thing. If you have it, you won't need it.

I've never been so glad that it was her weekend with her dad.

"Good. Me too." Sadie gave me a shove. "Let's go. Two-man is better than one."

"What about me?" Maeve asked.

"Reverend, you do *your* thing."

Maeve, the Reverend Collins, is indeed a duly ordained Episcopal priest, despite enviable skills with profanity, makeup, and drinking. I'm Jewish, but I'm pretty sure she has a direct line to Whoever's up there.

As Sadie and I turned the guy over, his camera fell out of his hand, skidding over a patch of frozen coffee to smack into the thermos.

First time in history coffee didn't make things better.

Something about the camera didn't look right to me, but it wasn't the time.

"I'll start with breaths," I offered.

"No, you're stronger. You do compressions."

Without even a blink, Sadie reached in and cleared the airway, and got down to it.

I started compressions. I'm not just stronger. I'm bigger — a lot taller than most of my friends, at six feet.

We reached the first pause, where you're supposed to check the person and see if they're breathing on their own.

"Nothing." Sadie shook her head.

Maeve, who'd been quietly watching from a few feet away, moved a little closer as we started again.

I heard her soft, clear voice beginning the prayers for the dying just before the siren's wail tore through the cold, still air.

*****

That evening, I was back in the studio, finally warm again thanks to double layers of fleece and most of a pot of coffee. I'd just finished a break and started the standard nightly spin of "You're the Inspiration," this time for a milestone anniversary couple, when Alicia Orr appeared.

Many weekdays, she drops by for a coffee after working late at the local bank, where she's a vice president. Sometimes weekends, too, especially when her husband, Police Chief George, is busy, as he sure was tonight. But her troubled expression was different.

I didn't remark on her new coral down coat and harmonizing striped fleece, which made her ebony skin glow. She'd wear it again – and it's better to give a compliment when people will hear it.

With the coffee poured, another pot brewing, and the next song (overwrought Celine Dion for a depressed dump-ee) started, we settled in for a talk.

"Nasty thing today at the shack," she said neutrally, though her expression wasn't neutral at all.

"Sad."

"Probably just sad, yeah."

I waited.

"Did you sense anything off?" she asked.

"Um…" The camera hadn't looked right to me, and we'd all been a little bothered by the way Willard Collier's daughter had so coolly said she was glad her dad died doing what he loved.

Everyone grieves differently, and it's not necessarily a sign of anything.

That's what I had very firmly told myself.

After all, some people can't understand how I can joke about getting my husband through cancer only to get dumped, but humor keeps me from harming anyone. Probably myself. So I wasn't going to judge.

Still, I'd never seen anyone's eyes light up at the sight of their relative on a gurney, and I'd spent enough time in the chemo suite to see a whole range of reactions.

Alicia watched me, and nodded.

"Here's the deal, Jaye," she said, speaking slowly and carefully. "I know something that makes me suspicious. But I know it because I work at the bank, and I can't break confidentiality."

"And the Chief…" I started.

"Will very rightly do nothing on the basis of his wife's gut." She shrugged. "I'm not thrilled with him, but he can't open a criminal case because I've got a bad feeling and the daughter acted like she'd won the lottery."

"True." I took a sip of my coffee, thought about what I'd seen when Sadie and I started CPR. "What if there was something inconsistent in the scene?"

"Like what?"

"Like the camera was not set up for what he was supposed to be doing."

Her eyes lit up. "Really?"

"My uncle's hobby is wildlife photography, and I know just enough to be dangerous. He explained his new camera to Ryan and me when he was up here at Thanksgiving."

"And poor Mr. Collier's camera?"

"Didn't look right to me. But I'm not the expert. Why don't I call Uncle Edgar and run it past him...and then get back to you?"

"I like it." She drank a little more of her coffee. "Thanks, Jaye."

"Glad to. It's always good to have an excuse to talk to Uncle Edgar."

She smiled, knowing I was telling the absolute truth.

Alicia stayed for a bit more coffee, and a little relaxing talk of moisturizers and long underwear, the two main topics of discussion for women in Vermont this time of year. Once she left, I picked up the phone.

"Jacks!" Uncle Edgar roared. He's the only person on earth allowed to call me that, as the closest thing I have to a father. I'm the closest he has to a daughter, since he had two sons with Aunt Mellie before she ran off with the urologist. (Don't go there.)

"Hey. How are you and Mom liking January in Palm Fountains?" He and my mother retired at roughly the same time, and they're now enjoying a very late adolescent rebellion as a brother-and-sister act in their Florida senior development.

"A little chilly. Only seventy yesterday."

"I think I hate you."

"Well, I envy you. You have a gorgeous snowy owl up there. And you've only sent me one picture?"

"I'll get some more." I am not the family photog, but I absolutely did owe him pics.

"You'd better. Maybe Judy and I fly up for a quick visit."

"We would love that." Mostly. I didn't even have to cross my fingers. "But I wanted to ask you something. A man collapsed and died near the shack earlier today, and-"

"Oh, that's too bad, Jacks. You all okay?

"It was sad, but we're fine. It's just…"

"You think there's something hinky?" Uncle Edgar did thirty years with the Mineral County Sherriff's Department. I could practically hear the click as his cop radar came on.

"Well, I'm not a hundred percent sure, but his camera looked wrong to me, and I think I know why."

"Tell me exactly what it looked like…"

I did. He agreed with me.

Alicia was glad to hear it…and so was Chief George.

*****

Sunday afternoon found us once again at the shack. This time, it was Maeve, freshly changed from vestments to fleece, picking us up in her old green SUV for a much safer trip, even if Sadie groused a little about it having less power on the hill than the Hummer did.

Blanche was back to the front of the shack, enjoying a patch of sun.

Enjoying more than that.

"Get the pic, Jaye!" Sadie called from the backseat. "She's eating!"

I'd had my cellphone ready because you never know when you might get a good shot of Blanche. I didn't really want one with a rodent tail sticking out of her beak, though – that was more Uncle Edgar's speed.

As we got out of the SUV, Blanche finished her meal and shot me a glare.

I'd have to apologize to her later.

Everyone who wasn't a vole had more serious things to worry about just then. The Simpson cruiser was on the other side of the little gravel parking area, and Chief George was leaning against it, just watching Blanche and observing the scene with his usual former NYPD cool and intensity. It's always fun to watch him, and reactions to him, since most Vermont towns do not have a six-foot-three Black guy in a leather trenchcoat as their top cop.

This appeared to be pretty much the usual owl fan club: a small knot of local folks at the back of the parking area, standing and observing, or occasionally taking a picture, all trying to be as unobtrusive (to Blanche) as possible.

Except for the woman at the front of the lot.

She couldn't be unobtrusive if her life depended on it.

Standing by her white SUV, wrapped once again in her urban-fashionable silver puffer, her expensively highlighted brown hair wafting lightly in the wind, Jennee Collier (two N's and three E's please, she'd said yesterday as Chief George asked her whether her late father had been in poor health) was placing a bouquet, down on one knee in the chunky slush.

I was honestly surprised that she was willing to get parking lot slop on her expensive yoga pants. Jennee was off in a lot of ways: that stupid white SUV that showed every bit of slush and muck, clothes always expensive and impractical, and hair and makeup far too much for Simpson. I'd always idly wondered how she afforded it on a teacher's aide's salary, and just figured there was family money around somewhere.

Now I suspected something else.

"What's going on?" Maeve whispered.

"Wait and see," Alicia replied, sending her husband a glance and getting a nod. "Must have gotten his warrant."

Sadie's eyes widened a little, and she smiled. "Looks like Blanche's lunch isn't the only show."

Jennee stood, and glanced back at what had probably been an appreciative, or at least neutral, audience when she knelt. Not so much now. Her carefully sad face changed at the sight of Chief George and Alicia, hardening into something else for an instant before she snapped back into reality-TV mournfulness, complete with quivering lip. Maeve probably recognized the brand and color of the shimmery nude lip gloss; I just knew it was better than the usual drugstore stuff.

"Ms. Collier." Chief George didn't raise his voice; it just carried across the parking lot in the chilly air.

"What?" She tried for innocent. "Is there something else? I'm just paying tribute to Dad where he had the heart attack."

She carefully wiped an eye. There was no actual moisture that I could see.

A little too obvious, I thought.

"About that, Ms. Collier." Chief George took a step toward her.

She stepped back. "I didn't do anything."

Her brittle voice gave her away.

"I've seen the bank records, ma'am. Your father found out what you'd been doing, didn't he?"

"No! He said I could use the money for whatever I needed." She looked at Alicia, with a snort. "Shows what you know."

Alicia shrugged, not taking the bait.

"He collapsed from a heart attack while he was out taking pictures," Jenee said, nodding firmly like a determined toddler.

"Not with that camera, he wasn't," I snapped. I'd had enough attitude.

Jennee's eyes widened.

"It probably looked good to you when you put it together. But it was the wrong lens. That was a big zoom lens. It's for distance shots."

She made a flapping wave at the shack. "That's a distance."

"Not that kind of distance," I said quietly. "Any decent photog wouldn't even bring that lens out for this."

"Well, he wasn't that good-"

"He was amazing," Sadie said. "I have one of his pictures of a great blue heron in my living room. Jaye's right. He would never have used the wrong lens."

Chief George unclipped the cuffs from his belt.

Jennee let out a howl.

That was enough for Blanche.

The giant owl took off with a bloodcurdling cry, and strafed toward us.

Everyone ducked.

Jennee shrieked again, and didn't duck far enough, because we all heard Blanche's talons ripping the back of that silver puffer as she flew past.

For the next minute or so, most of us were busy: the Chief helping

Jennee up – and then hooking her up, Alicia watching them, Maeve making sure Sadie didn't fall on the slick parking lot, and Sadie trying to shake free. I was the only one who got a good look at Blanche as she landed.

The owl was maybe twenty feet away from me, and she shot me a sharp glance with those big orange peepers. I managed to whip out the phone in time…and clicked off a couple of pics. Who knew if they'd be good, but she was so close I had to try.

As we all straightened up and dusted ourselves off, Alicia elbowed me.

"Thank you for being a friend."

"Blanche too." I grinned. "Love the *Golden Girls* reference."

"Just don't sing it."

*****

Back at the station, a couple of hours later, I sent my hard-won shots to Uncle Edgar.

"Nice pics."

"Nice info on the lens."

"So what was it?"

"Money. Seems she'd been quietly stealing from dad for a while, and when they went to move money from savings into a joint account, dad found out. He covered for her, but it was obvious to Alicia."

"And, of course, Alicia couldn't tell you."

"Nope. Confidentiality."

"But the lens was enough to get a warrant for the records, right?" he asked.

"Yep. And run a quick tox screen."

"Fentanyl?" he asked.

"That's the one. Apparently fed it to him in his breakfast and dumped him at the shack." I sighed. "Too many opioids are too easy to get around here."

"Everywhere, Jacks."

We were both silent for a moment, as I thanked the Lord that he'd gotten out before the worst of it, and I suspect he did too.

"Good thing you've got an eye," he said finally.

I laughed. "I just remember stuff."

"Got a pretty good shot of your owl, too, Jacks."

"Guess so."

A few minutes later, after we hung up, I looked at the picture again. I'd caught her with one eye closed. Winking.

As usual, Blanche was smarter than the rest of us.

Sweet Revenge
Michele Bazan Reed

The sparrows were chirping, and the late-April breeze brought the scent of bluebells, as I settled in with the *Burlington Free Press* and a steaming mug of coffee. I was savoring the moment, when my morning's peace was shattered — literally — by the sound of breaking glass mere inches from my Adirondack chair.

I lowered my newspaper just in time to see Kara Sampson roaring away in her red pickup, shaking her fist out the driver's side window. "I'm done with you, Jake," she shouted. "You can't pawn that swill off on me. You're gonna ruin my reputation!" The truck vanished in a haze of dust as she gunned the engine and headed out toward Route 7.

I looked down and saw a bottle of Jake's Reserve, my finest, lying near a pile of window-glass shards glinting in the late morning sun. The top had come off in the impact and a pool of amber-colored liquid was forming on the plank floor.

With a sigh I swigged down the last of my coffee and scooped up the bottle of precious liquid. With maple syrup going for more per barrel than crude oil, I figured I could salvage what was left of this bottle to use in my own coffee. I flashed back to hours in the sugar house tending the kettle, stung by Kara's comment about "swill."

After cleaning up the sticky pool so it wouldn't draw ants and flies — or worse yet that pesky raccoon that was hanging around making Sacha crazy — I swept up the broken glass. My rescue Plott Hound was on high alert inside the house, leaping up toward the window and barking for all she was worth.

"It's all right, girl. Go back to sleep." If there's one thing Sacha hates more than that raccoon, it's anything that disturbs her slumber. And Kara's well-aimed missile had certainly done that.

I squeezed through the screen door without letting Sacha out, scratched between her ears, and set the bottle on the kitchen counter. Time to go find out what Kara was upset about, I guess. I pulled on a clean T-shirt, the one with a cow appliqued in flannel. Since Kara had sold it to me when I first came to town, I thought it might mollify her. Checking in the doorway mirror to be sure I was presentable, I ran my fingers through my spiky sandy-colored hair and assessed my trim figure in profile. Dark bags under my eyes attested to long nights in the sugar house, but now that the season was over, I might just get a little rest.

Sacha had seen me grab the car keys and was already at my side, glancing from the door to my face and back again, calling shotgun with silent eye commands.

Settling into the driver's seat, I glanced over at my copilot. Sacha already had her head out the window, barking for all she was worth. That's my girl! The family from the ritzy suburb who left her at the shelter said it was because she barked too much. So did the other two families who adopted and returned her. When I got her, she'd been at the shelter for six months and had a bit of an attitude. But I didn't care. With her sleek black fur and huge dark eyes, I thought she was the most beautiful girl at Helping Hounds. And now, out here in the Vermont woods, she could bark to her heart's content, with no one but me and that dang raccoon to hear her. I loved her "singing" voice and, frankly, I didn't care what the raccoon thought.

On the short drive to Kara's, I thought about her comment on the bottle of syrup, and what this might mean for my business, but most of all, for our friendship. Not that there was anything much there yet. But a guy can hope. Kara's Kitchen was why I settled here. Little more than a pitstop for tourists heading south from the ferry crossing over Lake Champlain, Kara's served up a helping of Vermont hospitality with every slice of apple pie, chunk of cheddar or stack of maple-drenched pancakes. It was a dog-friendly place, too, with an outside tap, water bowls, and tables where guests could enjoy the company of their furry friends with their own meals.

I had stopped on my way up Route 7 from the bridge at Crown Point, having left New York behind with only my clothes, my laptop, and my canine best friend, after my girlfriend Amy's constant jealous fits had gotten too much to bear. I hadn't known where I was headed when I stopped for a break at Kara's. A cup of coffee and a piece of apple pie, along with the warm welcome she gave Sacha, and I knew I had found my own little slice of heaven.

It was on Kara's bulletin board that I'd seen the sugarbush for sale. I knew nothing about maple syrup, but how hard could it be? And I figured the secluded setting and once-a-year production schedule would give me plenty of peace and quiet to write that mystery novel that had been percolating in my brain on the long drive north.

Once Jake's Maple Heaven was up and running, Kara offered to serve my syrup with her pancakes and sell it in her gift shop alongside the marble cheese boards, pottery mugs, aged cheddars, and maple wood trivets. It was a great budding partnership, and I hoped it might blossom into a partnership of a different kind. Now, something had happened to put it all in jeopardy.

I arrived between the breakfast and lunch rushes, although out here that word took on a whole new meaning. I could see Kara through the pass-through from the kitchen, prepping veg for lunch. Even with her wavy auburn hair pulled back in a sloppy ponytail and a big green apron over her T-shirt and shorts, she looked beautiful as she concentrated on dicing carrots and onions for the soup du jour.

She glanced up as the bell on the door rang, then looked back down quickly. "Go away, Jake. I have nothing to say to you. That was a dirty trick and I expected better from you."

My head reeling, I plunked myself down at the nearest table. "Kara, please. Can we talk about this?" I must have sounded a little desperate, because she looked up then. Seeing my face and slumped shoulders, and Sacha whimpering as she stared up at me, Kara relented. Wiping her hands on a dishtowel, she grabbed two mugs, filled them with coffee and came over to my table.

"You have a lot of nerve showing up here." Her lips barely moved;

her teeth clenched tightly. If the mug hadn't been good Bennington Pottery, she probably would have snapped off the handle with her grip.

"Kara, trust me, I have no idea what you mean."

"I'll just bet. Pawning off colored sugar water as pure maple syrup, and your best grade at that! That's just big-city sleazy."

That stung. I'd struggled to be accepted here where the locals had a healthy distrust of strangers. I'd made some inroads. But I'd always thought I was safe with Kara.

"Sugar water? What are you talking about? And you've had my syrup here for months, enjoyed it yourself, you said. Why now?"

"You couldn't even face me with it, could you? Dropping it off at my kitchen door before opening last Thursday? I should've been suspicious, but no. I never suspected your switcheroo until a local returned a stack of pancakes as inedible." She drummed her fingers on the tabletop. "You know some people around here even carry their own jugs of syrup to restaurants. Not in my establishment. They've come to trust me. But if word of this gets around..." She twisted strands of her ponytail between her fingers as she stared off over my shoulder, avoiding my eyes.

"Kara, you know me. I'd never just leave a case of syrup at your door without delivering it to you in person. For one thing, it's too valuable to just leave out where someone could steal it." For another, I silently admitted to myself, I'd miss a chance at seeing Kara.

She stared down at the grounds in the bottom of her cup. "I guess that's true. But then, why does it have your label on it? And why does it taste like that garbage they sell in the supermarket, the one they have to label 'pancake syrup' because it doesn't have any maple at all?"

I knew the kind of junk she was talking about, created from high fructose corn syrup and artificial flavors and colors. The shelves at big chains were lined with it. People snapped it up because a quart could be had for $3 or less, while pure Vermont maple syrup went for $15 a pint. Worth every penny, but that wasn't the point right now. Or maybe it was.

"If word of this gets around, people will stop eating here. And they won't buy the stuff I sell in my shop. If the syrup is fake, they'll believe I import the cutting boards from China or repackage grocery store cheese as real aged cheddar." Her fist was starting to clench again, and I could see she was biting back tears. "I'll be out of business in no time. And you will, too."

"Say, do you have any of the new batch around? Could I see it? Taste it?"

"You're lucky. It's in the garbage bin, but hasn't been collected yet." This time she managed to meet my eyes. Maybe she was starting to believe me.

Kara brought over a familiar maple leaf-shaped bottle with two shot glasses. The label read "Jake's Reserve" in 20-point Bookman Bold over a picture of Sacha's smiling face. I'd spent days working on that label. If anyone could resist the sweet lure of Vermont maple syrup, they'd be hard-pressed to turn away from my pup's gorgeous mug.

As Kara poured a little in each glass, I could see at once it wasn't Jake's Reserve. My prize syrup had a rich, amber color that marked the syrup from a late-season tapping, when it becomes darker and tastes more caramelized. I put many a sleepless night into stirring that batch, hiring a couple of trusted neighbors to take turns with me so we could all get some shut-eye. The kettles couldn't be left untended for any length of time or the syrup would burn to the bottom of the vessel, and the batch would be ruined.

See. That was Number 1 of the five S's needed for syrup judging, followed by *swirl, smell, sip,* and *savor.*

I swirled to release the bouquet, like a fine wine, and sniffed it. Again, it lacked the depth of aroma that signaled a really good batch of syrup. I sipped and instead of savor, my fifth "S" step was spit.

"Ugh! You're right! That is swill." Now I was the one with clenched fists. "And it's not mine."

Kara had stopped at swirl. Looking down at the table, she dragged her fingers through the rings left by our coffee cups.

I thought of that smashed bottle on my porch, something niggling at the back of my mind. "Can you bring me an unopened bottle? I want to check the cap." I used a distinctive gold-colored screw top on my bottles.

It cost a bit extra but made my product stand out on store shelves as a little more luxe.

"You can have the whole darn case back for all I care." In a minute she was back and slammed the box down, causing my mug to rock slightly on the wobbly table. Sure enough, the caps were all standard-issue black ones.

"Bingo!" My shout made the dozing Sacha jump and bang her noggin on the bottom of the pine tabletop. "That's not my cap. Check the old stock in your shop — you'll see I use gold tops."

Her eyes lit up. "You're right, Jake! But why would somebody do this? Why fake a bottle of maple syrup?"

I was studying the box. It was from a delivery of lettuce to a local grocery store. No clue there. Whoever did this had obviously grabbed it out of a dumpster behind the store. There was no handwriting sample anywhere on the box, and Kara had already told me it was just dropped off, with no bill or note.

"I don't know why, but more importantly, who? Who would want to hurt my reputation, and yours? We've got to get to the bottom of this."

"Knock yourself out. I've gotta go finish prepping for lunch." I looked over the box of faux syrup. Despite her brusque words, Kara was grinning at me and gave a conspiratorial wink.

Who, indeed? I wracked my brain but could think of no one who would have it out for me. Sure, some locals were a bit stand-offish, but I expected that, as a newcomer in a tight-knit New England community. Yankees weren't all friendly on the outside, but once they got to know you and trust you, you could count on them till the end. I knew it would take time to earn that.

As I walked out through Kara's gift shop, I glanced at the shelves. Sure enough there was my Jake's Reserve with the familiar gold cap in a place of prominence. There were also a couple of bottles of Peterson's, relegated to a lower shelf. Walter "Pete" Peterson was my biggest rival. He'd practically cornered the maple syrup market in our little part of the world before I came along. His syrup was in similar leaf-shaped bottles and topped with a black cap. I'd be suspicious, but I knew there were only so many suppliers and a lot of us favored the glass bottles that showed off the color of our syrup, even though the popular plastic jugs weighed less and kept the syrup from light, enhancing its longevity.

"Hey, Kara! What's up with Pete's syrup? Didn't he have any for you this season?" I had to shout to be heard over the whirr of her immersion blender pureeing the soup.

"Yeah, funny thing. When folks got a taste of Jake's Maple Heaven, sales of Pete's fell off, and I mean dramatically." She switched off the blender, so she didn't have to shout. "When I reordered for this year, I cut his numbers way down. I felt like I had to stock some, of course, with him being local and all. I can tell you, he was not happy about it. Said he'd get you for this, or words to that effect."

I took the offending bottles out to the car and headed for Triple C's, the local printer. Brothers Chris and Craig Carpenter printed all the flyers around town, wedding invitations, even the local weekly newspaper. It's the only game in town, and where I'd always had my labels made, along with my advertising flyers.

Craig looked up as I entered, his smile turning to a puzzled look as I slammed the bottle down on his desk. "I take it by your frown and the forceful way you placed that bottle on my desk, that's no free sample as thanks for a job well done?"

"What can you tell me about that label, Craig? Where did it come from?"

His brow furrowed and he looked at me like I was speaking Martian. "Came from the order you placed last week." He picked up the bottle and squinted at it, studying the label. "You stuck a note on my door before opening, said you needed 100 more labels in a hurry, but you were too busy with sugaring to come and get them, so to just put them in your mailbox and send you the bill later. Figured you were anticipating a higher than usual level of production."

Must be the prankster had been watching my mailbox and pulled out the labels before I checked my mail. I did a little quick math. One hundred labels meant whoever did this could make 8 cases of 12 with a few labels left over for error. I did a quick run through of my local clients.

I explained to Craig what had happened. "So, this isn't genuine Jake's Reserve, but I'll bring a bottle of the real stuff when I come in to pay the bill. I've got to run and see if I can find out who did this before he dumps them on any more of my clients."

In the parking lot, I nearly bumped into Pete Peterson, exiting his black SUV, parked nearby.

"Morning, Pete," I said. Hoping he'd stop and chat, I angled myself to get a look in the back of his SUV. I could see two boxes crammed with glass bottles topped with black caps, but I couldn't make out if the labels on the bottles were his or mine.

"You've got your nerve, New York, being all friendly." Pete seemed more interested in his shoelaces than my face. When he looked up, the glint in his eye told me all I needed to know. "Kara cut my order and so did June. I don't like rookies coming in and taking away my business."

Sacha moved protectively between me and Pete, growling ever so softly. I knew that growl. Pete didn't want to know what came next, if he were to threaten me physically.

I knew it wasn't wise to antagonize him, but I couldn't help myself. "Well, Pete, when people taste a superior product, they just naturally want it. What can I say? I expect as word gets around, my syrup will get even more fans."

His laugh was more of a bark. "We'll see, Jake. We'll just see about that." Pete turned on his heel and headed for the main business district.

Making the rounds of my customers, I called on Grandma June's Gift Shop, Maple Artisans Gallery, Tom's Ice Creamery, and two local hotels which stocked Maple Heaven products for sale to guests. All had suspicious deliveries, and all were glad to get rid of the offending bottles. I promised fresh stock of the newest vintage in the next few days and finished making my rounds.

All but two of my regulars had been scammed. Beckett's B&B and Aunt Rita's Bake Shop were probably due to get their deliveries tonight or tomorrow. Rita thought I may be right with suspecting Pete. Based on the pattern of deliveries, we both figured her shop was next on his list. The baker dusted flour off her hands onto her apron and took me around back to show me a good spot to hide behind her freestanding brick oven, with a clear line of sight to the back porch.

"With his MO, I suspect the perp will leave the counterfeits by the back door." Rita loved her mystery books and obviously relished doing a little sleuthing of her own. "He'll be lured in by the fact that it's dark back here, but the motion-detecting lights will come on as soon as he gets to the top step and you'll have a clear view of the bad guy's face."

"Sacha and I will be out there shortly after sunset and stake the place out," I promised, as she handed me a paper bag of apple-maple muffins and homemade cheddar dog biscuits to sustain us in our vigil.

*****

The night wore on, and even a thermal mug of coffee wasn't enough to keep me awake. Crouched down with my big dog for warmth, I dozed. I don't how long I'd been asleep when a soft growl from Sacha woke me up. Her superior hearing and sharp hound nose had alerted her to the intruder. "Hush, girl," I whispered and peeked around the curve of the brick oven. A dark SUV, with a silhouette like Pete's, had coasted to a stop in the alley leading to the back of the bakery, its lights switched off. Must be he didn't want to alert anyone who could identify him.

Sacha had great eyes, having been bred for night hunting, and she saw something that had her riled up. She was straining to get at the intruder, despite my tight grip on her collar.

I heard the clang of thick glass bottles banging against each other as the driver crept up the uneven cobblestone path, punctuated with a whispered "Oof!" as he stubbed his toe and nearly lost his grip on the carton. With the box safely delivered, he turned and as the security lights came on, I had a clear view of a face that made me suck in my breath.

I had to put my hand on Sacha's neck to calm her from barking, and bite back an expletive of my own. Despite the baggy overalls and ball cap pulled low, I recognized that driver. It was none other than my ex, Amy.

*****

The next morning, at a table at Kara's Kitchen, I laid out my findings. Kara, June, Rita, Leslie and Craig were gathered around with mugs of their own and some of Rita's best maple-walnut cookies. Sacha chomped another of Rita's biscuits with a bowl of fresh water.

"I don't get it. Why is she doing this?" Kara shook her head, her lips set in a grim line.

"It's hard to explain about Amy, but she's into revenge. It's why I had to leave." I told them about her volatile temper and her penchant for getting even — sometimes when she only imagined an offense.

"I was a reporter in New York, so my cell was filled with strange phone numbers — my confidential sources. One day, Amy called one and a woman answered. I had to do a lot of work to get that city council member to even talk to me again. Amy plotted revenge, and poured a 2-liter of Mountain Dew into my gas tank." Heads nodded around the table. "Joke was on her, though. Mike down at the dealership told me I was lucky. I'd filled up the car the day before. If it had been near empty, that little trick would've ruined my engine."

I paused for a big gulp of coffee. "Then there was the time she threw all my clothes out in the rain and mud, because she found a receipt for lunch for two at a fancy Manhattan restaurant in my pocket. I'd been meeting a source for a secret exposé of some industrial espionage. Amy wasn't buying my explanation." I shook my head at the memory of my stained shirts and ties.

"But this is the worst she's ever attempted. I'm convinced she's out to destroy my new life here, in retribution for leaving her. If I don't stop her now ..." My voice trailed off leaving their imaginations to fill in the blanks.

My new friends agreed that Amy had crossed the line and were eager to help me teach her a lesson.

"I've got to stake out the B&B tonight. It's my last chance to catch her sticky-fingered, as it were."

"We'll help. What do you need?" Good old Rita, always ready in a pinch.

Leslie, the owner of Beckett's, was as mad as I was. A retired teacher, she was used to taking charge. "If anyone knows how to deal with a bully, it's a teacher. Leave it to me. I've got a plan." If I were Amy, I wouldn't like the look of that grin Leslie flashed just then.

The B&B was in an 18th-Century inn converted for the tourist trade and a popular stop on the Vermont ghost tour. It was reputed to be haunted by the wife of a Captain Otis, a Revolutionary War soldier who came home and found her, clad in a nightgown, in the arms of another man. She protested that the man was just comforting her as she grieved what she thought was a report of her husband's death in battle. Unconvinced, the enraged soldier strangled her then and there. To this day, it is said, the wronged wife walked the grounds of the inn in her nightgown, weeping.

Although some guests reported strange noises in the night and objects moved from their usual spot, Leslie swore she'd never seen the ghost. But that didn't stop the tourists from flocking there in the hopes of being the first to catch a glimpse of the spirit.

"You, know," Leslie said. "Legend has it that Mrs. Otis had a beautiful hound dog, much like our Sacha here. When she was killed, her loyal hound howled his grief to the heavens. It is said that he lived out his days curled up on his mistress's grave." She stooped to scratch Sacha between the ears as we all digested the tale of the wronged wife.

Ever the teacher, Leslie passed out assignments for each of us. We clinked our mugs, broke the huddle, and agreed to meet in Beckett's kitchen at sunset.

*****

At 8:30 that evening, the mood in the kitchen was giddy. June cut tags off one of her special "Colonial Lady" nightgowns, a flowing white gauzy number with a matching robe that she promised would flutter nicely in the evening breeze. She fussed about as Kara slipped the gown over her shorts and a white T and helped the younger woman let her hair out of its ponytail, tousling her locks to enhance the wild look.

Rita chuckled as she sprinkled flour over Kara's hair, face and hands. "You look like a credible specter," she told her as they all surveyed the results in the mirror hung by the back door.

On her cell phone, Leslie keyed up the app that she'd found to play horror movie noises. "Listen to this one!" She broke into a guffaw as the sound of wind and moaning filled the kitchen.

"That's perfect! I can't wait to see her face." Rita snapped the top back on her flour canister.

Leaving Kara in the kitchen near the back door with a quick "Break a leg!" the three women headed to the living room to find a good place to hide with a clear view out the window to the front porch.

I crouched down behind the stone wall Leslie had built with good Vermont slate, Sacha on a tight leash at my side, to wait for our mark.

Once it got good and dark, I heard the now-familiar sound of Amy's rented SUV, followed by the clinking of bottles. She grunted as she hoisted the box of syrup and headed up the slate pathway. Soon, she was right in front of the porch steps.

I started to worry. Where was Kara? Our plan depended on perfectly orchestrated timing. At this rate, Amy would be gone and we'd miss our only chance. Why was Kara dawdling?

Suddenly the air seemed chillier than it had before, and I wished I'd brought a fleece. The forecast on my phone said it would be a low of 50 degrees, but this seemed like early winter weather. A breeze picked up, and I could hear the sound of wind in dry branches followed by a low moaning. Well, at least Leslie was doing her job.

Sacha set up a howl fit to raise the dead. The hair on my arms stood on end. Amy stopped in her tracks, her head twisting from side to side, obviously shaken.

Suddenly a figure appeared around the corner, white nightgown flying out behind her in the breeze. Her sleeves fluttered, and her hair streamed out behind her. Her mouth open in a silent scream, she pointed directly at Amy with a shaking finger, her arm at full extension.

Oh, man! Kara was playing it to the hilt!

Amy gasped, a sharp intake of breath. "Stop! G-g-go away!" Her voice shook as she started backing away from the "ghost" advancing on her. This was getting to be fun!

Soon, Amy was in full panic mode. She shrieked and threw her arms up in the air, bottles flying out of the cardboard box and shattering on the slate pathway. My ex was drenched in faux-maple syrup, and she was scrambling on the slippery paving stones, going down on one knee, then recovering her footing as she ran for the vehicle. I could hear her swearing as the engine misfired, but she finally got it going and peeled out of there, laying rubber and causing lights to come on in houses across the street. I figured that was the last I'd see of my ex.

Rita, Leslie, and June ran down the front steps, laughing uproariously. We were all high-fiving and patting each other on the back. Sacha was jumping up on everyone, tail wagging and tongue hanging out in glee.

"Weird, my phone's battery died right as I went to press 'Play' on the sound effects." Leslie looked sheepish. "But I guess we didn't need them after all."

"Not with Kara's awesome acting job!" Rita sounded full of admiration.

"Great job, Kara," I said, turning to where I'd last seen her, to give her a hug. But my arms encircled empty air. She wasn't there.

"Hey guys, sorry! I heard that vehicle backfiring. Was it Amy?" Kara was just coming around the corner of the house.

"I hope I didn't ruin everything, but I couldn't get the back door open. It stuck, almost like it was locked, and for a few minutes I couldn't budge it for love or money. Almost crashed to the ground when it did give way a few seconds ago." She looked down at her white gown, the hem now trailing in sticky syrup. "Why is it so cold out here? And where did this syrup come from?"

She searched our faces, one by one.

"I guess Miss Sacha really does have a voice that could raise the dead," said Leslie. "And that earns her a pancake. C'mon in, everyone, I'm cooking breakfast — with *genuine* Jake's Reserve."

Death by Discussion
Lyn Fraser

"Folded up in a sofa bed?" Ginny stared. She bent over, leaned in, and reached under a cushion.

"Tidy ending, don't you think," Charlotte nodded her own answer. "Innovative. Never would've thought of it as a weapon, actually, a sofa bed. I mean a Murphy bed, maybe. I could see rigging one of those in a way it would fall out of the closet and knock someone senseless if you knew when they were coming. But a fold-out from actual furniture? Never would have considered the suffocation angle. Or the mangling."

Ginny frantically threw cushions on the floor and tugged at the metal apparatus of the bed. "It's Raymond," she said.

"So like him," Charlotte said. "Raymond. Since his wife died, he makes his bed up every morning while he's still in it, slipping out with the final tuck."

"How do you know stuff like that?" Ginny asked, looking up.

Charlotte flushed.

Ginny knelt on the floor to get a better angle on the sofa.

"Fiona will be pleased," Charlotte said, remaining aloft. "We're right on schedule. Victim down, clues unfolding."

Ginny sputtered as she pulled at the bedding and reached inside. "Raymond's dead."

"Right, just like he's supposed to be," Charlotte said. "Our pseudo-murder victim. Must have drawn the short straw, so to speak."

"Drew a lot more than a straw," Ginny said in a barely audible voice.

Charlotte screamed.

*****

They met one another as the only attendees of an early evening event at the Rutland Free Public Library, billed as a discussion of why mystery novels have their own section in libraries. Instead, it was a lecture, *Mystery Fiction vs. Literary Fiction*, set up like an athletic competition with brackets and seedings, but actually a somewhat snooty look at why reading mysteries is sometimes referred to as a 'guilty pleasure' — mystery fiction not quite measuring up as *real* literature.

The entire presentation was so off-putting that they left en masse and introduced themselves to one another in the parking lot, hastily agreeing on the need for recovery libations at a downtown bar and grill. The boisterous conversation and bonding over murder had led quite naturally by the end of the evening to the formation of a mystery book club.

They called themselves the Scurrilous Six:

Fiona Graham: redheaded Golden Age mysteries junkie, ran her own business as a landscape architect.

Rina Lubovik: short, stout, roughed cheeks, professional artist, originally from Romania, had learned English by watching detective shows on American television.

Leo Moreno: semi-retired investment consultant, was a devotee of Marilyn Stasio's *NYT* crime column and had thought the library lecture would be useful as a betting matrix for the NCAA basketball tournament.

Charlotte Pace: divorced real estate broker with brassy humor, had gravitated to thrillers because her profession provided the perfect plots: a cutthroat business, houses to die for, paying the price, killer listings.

Ginny Skinner: retired nurse, white hair mostly in a bun, had started at the age of ten on Earle Stanley Gardner's *The Case of the Lame Canary* because she owned one.

Raymond Sutter: attorney and widower, had begun reading mystery fiction during the hours he spent at his dying wife's bedside and welcomed the group's companionship.

For a year they met at members' homes once a month, rotating the choice of books, frequently pairing different types of mysteries such as a police procedural with a psychological suspense, a classic with a Scandinavian noir, hard boiled with over easy.

Wanting to do something special to celebrate the group's first anniversary, Fiona came up with a suggestion: "Let's murder someone." They were meeting that evening in Rina's home, and Fiona proposed her idea with such vigor that Ooster, Rina's English Beagle, jumped onto an end table with his front paws, barking and spilling Raymond's glass of burgundy.

Rina rushed over with sopping cloths. "Sorry, sorry," she said, wiping energetically. "Ooster naughty. He prefers full-bodied malbec."

She patted Ooster down.

Rina's living room was furnished in faded-elegance. One of her own massive canvasses, a painting of a steel blast furnace, hung on the wall beside fragile wooden icons. Worn Oriental rugs on the polished hardwood floor competed with Target shags, and delicate china figurines rested on the plastic end tables.

"So. Let's take a whole weekend and live out the experience of committing and solving a murder," Fiona said.

"Whose?" Ginny asked.

"One of us," Fiona said.

"I don't think that's legal," Raymond said. "*Just*, perhaps, but not legal."

"No, this is really possible, I'm serious," Fiona said. "We find a place for a weekend retreat, like cabins or a conference center, a setting with woods and water and plenty of creepy things and hiding places. We did it once for a bridal party I was in, you know, the girls-before-the-wedding thing, and it was fabulous. Killed off the bride-to-be's disapproving mother-in-law-to-be."

"Killed the mother-in-loo?" Rina asked.

"Yes, the in-law, though loo works too. Murder committed by the female priest who was officiating," Fiona said. "Whacked her with an altar candlestick. Should have seen the glint in her eyes."

"Who caught her?" Charlotte asked.

"Solved by a bridesmaid channeling Jane Marple, sneaking around the premises and listening in on conversations," Fiona said. "Helped that we were all semi-smashed, including the victim — made her seem almost human."

"The *dead* woman was almost human?" Leo asked.

"No, she wasn't really dead. We drew cards for who'd be the murderer, who'd be the victim. Jack of diamonds, ace of spades. They acted it out. The two who'd drawn those cards. The rest of us were the detectives. Somehow, though, the possibility of having been murdered woke the woman up to what a shit she'd been to the bride."

"Well, **okay** then, I'm seeing the possibilities," Leo said.

"But how would we actually do the deed, and who'd get killed?" Charlotte asked.

"We'd draw lots for the victim and the murderer, then let it play out," Fiona said, "unknown to the rest of us. The two of them would figure out how to carry it off. Drowning, strangulation, disemboweling. Nothing too messy."

"Sure," Rina said.

"The victim pretends to be dead when we find him or her, and we spend the rest of the weekend solving the crime," Fiona explained. "Because it's *one of us*, we'd actually have the murderer among us, working against us."

"What fun," Charlotte said.

"The only one who gets left out of the crime-solving is the victim," Fiona said. "But he or she could do red herrings and such."

"I can see means and opportunity," Leo said, "but what about motive? What was the motive of that priest?"

"Interesting," Fiona said. "The bride was an immigrant, and the groom's mother wanted to block her path to citizenship. Really."

"Some of you, quite frankly, I could imagine killing," Ginny said, looking slowly around the room. "But not *all* of you."

"That's the point of the investigation. To *find* a motive," Fiona said. "And the point of the killing, to have one. All of us are outspoken on a few things, right, pisses somebody else off. Quite frankly, I've thought some of our conversations about books might lead to murder."

"How could the victim and murderer possibly make a plan without the rest of us knowing about it?" Raymond asked.

"We can work on details, but my thought is that we'd start the retreat with lunch on Friday, if everyone could get there," Fiona said. "We'd draw the lots, which would all be blank except the ones designating killer and victim. Their slips would include a time and a meeting place, somewhere in the vicinity of where we're staying," Fiona said, "We'd have the rest of the day and evening to move around freely, getting together for dinner, but allowing those two the space to meet at their allotted place. We'd all have to agree not to try and watch or follow someone to figure it out. The murder would be committed by breakfast on Saturday, and we'd have until brunch on Sunday to solve it."

"Who'd make up the lots? That person would know the meeting time and place too," Raymond said.

"We'll find an objective third party to set up the draw," Fiona said.

It was obvious from the silence that wheels were turning with evil intentions.

Leo went around the room, quietly offering refills. When he returned to his seat, a wide-bottomed upholstered chair with wooden arms, the right arm fell off the chair as he sat down.

"Sorry, sorry," Rina said, flustered. "I can fix."

"No problem," Leo said, sliding to the other side of the chair. "I'll rest only my left arm."

"That arm would make a good weapon," Charlotte said. "The chair arm."

"Or the blast furnace," Ginny said, admiring the large watercolor of Rina's on the wall. "Now that could do a major singe."

"Well, sure," Raymond said. "The arm would be for a female killer and the blast furnace for a man. The choice of weapon is going to reveal the gender of the murderer and narrow the field right off."

Rina stood up, clapping her hands firmly together. "All a continuum, masculine and feminine. Where we are, here or here, not from what we do or even what we see. They don't always divide." She pounded her bosom.

Ooster barked.

"So, guys, really. We're getting a bit sidetracked here," Charlotte said.

"Not totally," Fiona said. "Those are exactly the kinds of issues we'll confront in solving the crime, especially given the capacity for deviousness of everyone in this group. To whom do the clues point and why?"

"You know," Leo said, "I think this thing could work. My former company has a cabin up in the Green Mountains that they use for entertaining customers, employee gatherings, officer doings. Three stories, plenty of bedrooms, isolated, on one of the lakes. Just what you're talking about, Fiona. Smell of pines, trails through the woods, wildlife scat, lake water lapping, misty mornings."

As they began to divvy up assignments, it became official that the group would celebrate its first anniversary by staging, committing, and solving a murder, one of the few times they had agreed on anything.

Ginny stayed a few minutes after the meeting to help Rina clean up. As they were walking out to Ginny's car, she complimented the lavish red, yellow, and white tulips blooming along Rina's sidewalk. Rina proudly pulled a large yellow tulip out of the ground and held it up.

"You see, they are plastic," Rina said. "You know, just, I put them out for my friends."

Ooster squatted and peed.

*****

The retreat began at high noon on Friday, mid-May, with Leo delivering, as promised, a secluded three-story log cabin near the Green Mountain National Forest. The property offered mountain and lake views from every room, high-end furnishings, five bedrooms plus an enclosed sleeping porch, three and a half bathrooms, industrial kitchen, requisite rustic fireplace, 70-inch wall mounted television with DVD and XBox, horseshoe pit, and side sheds stocked with canoes, bikes, balls, nets, rackets, and wickets. The cedar walls in the massive den held a taxidermist's dream of horned animal heads.

Spontaneously, most of the group, not knowing in advance what their roles would be, had brought along relevant props—bows and arrows, red dye, rope, cuffs, chains, bottles with crossbones, fishing hooks, duct tape–to supplement the natural assortment of tree limbs, kitchen tools, power trimmers, and other prospective weapons readily available on the cabin's property. Charlotte unloaded a bag of cement from the trunk of her car.

Each person had a separate bedroom except Raymond, who had chosen the sleeping porch. Leo took the third floor loft, Ginny and Charlotte bedrooms on the second floor, Fiona and Rina each a room on the ground floor at the opposite end of the cabin from Raymond.

While eating lunch, a buffet sandwich and salad bar provided by Rina, Fiona reviewed the agreed-upon activities. Lunch would be followed by the lots drawing, supervised by Emma Rae Spradling, Fiona's business partner. The afternoon was free to enjoy the retreat and/or plan a murder. In the evening, the guys would grill and there'd be a DVD offering, *The Name of the Rose*, honoring Umberto Eco, who had died the previous year. Ginny and Charlotte would organize Saturday's breakfast at 9, followed by the retreat's focus: *And Then There Were Five*.

"Is it too early for a gin and tonic?" Charlotte asked.

Ignoring murmurs of interest, Fiona pressed on with the introduction of Emma Rae Spradling for the drawing of the lots. Emma Rae resembled Julia Child and sounded a bit like her, cheerfully but assertively issuing directions in a high-pitched, lilting voice as the group assembled before her in the kitchen, glasses empty. Fiona explained that Emma Rae was present with the sole purpose of supervising the lots-drawing and would leave immediately afterwards to survey markets for high altitude plants.

Emma Rae lifted a wicker basket above her head like a priest preparing for Eucharist. She intoned, "Form a line, file by the basket, collect one envelope, and return to your room to open it."

"Lord have mercy," Ginny said.

As the line formed, Emma Rae shuffled the envelopes. "Murderer and victim are designated by colored dots on the lots, red for murderer and purple for victim," she explained. "Those two lots include a specific time and place for the relevant parties to meet, concoct the crime, and leave clues for solving it. As Fiona has explained, the murder is to occur before breakfast on Saturday morning, and you will have twenty-four hours to solve it. Are there any questions?"

"What if the murder isn't solved by then?" Raymond asked.

"Then you'll all get belladonna berries in your cereal," Fiona said. "Sherlock's favorite poison."

"But that would mean we'd all die," Charlotte said. "And the victim would get killed twice."

"Step along sharply," Emma Rae instructed, raising the basket again above her head and motioning the line forward.

*****

Charlotte's piercing scream attracted the remaining group members

No cereal was served, with or without belladonna berries, because there was no breakfast on Saturday and no brunch on Sunday. A massive spring snowstorm had arrived during the night on Friday, accompanied by freezing temperatures. When Charlotte and Ginny had met in the kitchen to begin Saturday's breakfast preparations, they felt an icy draft coming from the sleeping porch and had gone to check on Raymond.

Rina vomited, Charlotte transitioned to hysteria, and Ginny, who'd served twenty of her R.N. years as an emergency room nurse, calmly took charge.

"I was able to assess his condition," Ginny said. "Deceased. I won't go into the details at this point, but his neck was involved."

She made the 911 and necessary follow-up calls.

"At least an hour before emergency services and law enforcement can get here," Ginny said. "No cell phones or texting or any communication. Please. What I told them, you heard. We're a book club, meeting on a weekend retreat. Someone apparently walked onto the porch and snapped the sofa bed shut with Raymond in it, we presume asleep."

The snowstorm at a 4,500-plus altitude had blanketed the highway and subsidiary roads, leaving the already isolated location barely reachable.

"Would anyone like to say a prayer?" Ginny asked. No one did. With help from Leo, she covered the entire apparatus and its contents using several bedspreads.

Gathering in the den, Fiona offered hot beverages and toast, Rina built a fire, Leo passed around blankets, and the snow resumed. Ginny encouraged the group "to talk, to go over things, debrief, express our feelings, have a wake for Raymond. What's absolutely essential is that we remain together, in one space."

Someone in this room is a murderer, no one said.

"Let's begin with who drew the dots," Ginny said.

"I was supposed to be the murderer," Fiona said in an unusual voice for her, subdued. "And Raymond, the victim. I'd brought a baggie of blueberries, which do resemble belladonna berries. They're lethal as hell."

Fiona shook her head before continuing, now speaking rapidly. "We concocted the plan in about a nanosecond when we met at the canoe shed by the lake. Raymond keeps a bottle of pure cranberry juice at bedside that he sips to ward off chronic urinary infections. I mashed the berries, pretended to put in the liquid while you all watched the video, and hid the baggie in his fishing tackle box that was in the corner of the sleeping porch." She pointed to the porch.

"That was your clue," Fiona said, "plus the empty bottle turned over, and my absence during the film. I went back to the porch later, to confirm everything. He said he was taking an Ambien and calling it a night. About eleven." Fiona grabbed at the neck of her sweatshirt. "It's gone badly wrong. I'm so sorry."

"Shit," Charlotte said.

Rina wrapped an arm around Charlotte. "Good for you to say. Ginny told us. Say how you feel. Like shit."

"No, not me," Charlotte said. "Raymond. Raymond's a shit. Was."

"Tell us," Ginny said, with a hint of enthusiasm.

"He left me in bed," Charlotte said, "his side made up, spread tucked over the pillow, just leaving me naked on the other side, and off he went, as if I wasn't even there or if I were, he couldn't care less. Got me to his house to start with under false pretenses. Claimed he wanted to put the house on the market. God, what a fool I was. I'd planned to drop out of the group, then the retreat idea came up, and I wanted to do that before I resigned. Silly me. I wanted to be Nancy Drew and solve the murder."

"You still can," Rina said. "Sure."

"Motives for murder," Ginny said, speaking slowly. "Love... lust... lucre... loathing."

"So I have three of the four," Charlotte said. "No love lost."

"Don't beat yourself up, Charlotte," Fiona said. "Raymond was slick, a consummate philanderer."

"You slept with him too?" Charlotte said, surprised.

"No, not in bed, but seduced, yes. God, I needed the job, my business has sunk in the economy. He was the fiduciary for an endowment that supports beautification projects in the state. I'd bid on a new series of riverside parks, a million and a half project. More than a year's work. But I lost. To one his construction cronies."

"Isn't it possible you'll still get it?" Charlotte asked.

"No, I think it's a done deal. Sure as hell didn't want to spend a weekend with him, but we'd already put plans for this retreat in motion."

"State connections, he has, yes," Rina said. "My paintings, the blast furnaces, for the traveling exhibit, to all state capitals. Important history of our country. How they looked, what they meant to people, for jobs, for steel industry. At my opening, you all come, Raymond too, for reception. You are nice. Committee comes, from Montpelier, they choose the canvasses that will travel. They like. But I hear, him, Raymond, he talks to head of committee, he lies, he says work reviewed by critic from New York, 'Powerful, yes, but Rina Lubovik's work is derivative. American artists were doing these urban industrials in the 1920's.' My paintings are original, fresh, other reviewers say, but too late. Raymond push forward Mariah Compton, paintings of big faces with round eyes. Mariah not construction crony, she sleeping crony. Raymond hole ass."

"What an interesting configuration," Ginny said, then added, "Is there anyone here who is grieving for Raymond?"

Heads slowly shake.

"I can only add to the pile," Leo said. "Divorce case. Raymond represented the husband on a contingency fee. My daughter Steffi's a CPA, and she worked for the wife's attorney. Millions at risk. The judge gave it all to the wife. Every cent. Raymond made nothing. My daughter spent months on the case–financial records, tax returns, meeting with officials in remote locations, waves of obfuscation by Raymond, assets cleverly concealed via shell corporations on several Caribbean islands. Steffi uncovered the lot. After the settlement hearing, he threatened her when they wound up alone on the same elevator, some nonsense about rituals in the Caribbean where females are sacrificed, dying under mysterious circumstances for defying males and upsetting the natural harmony of the universe. Steffi said 'Oh, well,' but she also made notes and called me afterwards."

"Did you read that as a serious threat?" Ginny asked.

"I actually did," Leo said. "Weird as it sounds."

"Because Raymond killed his wife," Ginny said in a steady voice.

"You've talked to the sister, too?" Leo said.

"I have, and I've confirmed everything Helen told me," Ginny said, leaning forward. "Rosella had cancer, breast cancer metastasized to the bone, and she was terminal. But she was also fully alive, still active and involved, definitely not on her deathbed. Didn't need hospice care. That story about his reading mysteries while spending months as a caregiver is just bullshit. He did administer painkillers, especially in the night, when she was miserable. And she died in the night, of an overdose. But Raymond claimed he administered a standard dose by injection, and in her confused state, Rosella took a massive dose orally, on her own. Helen tried, but nothing was ever proven or even seriously questioned."

"What did he have to gain since she was dying anyway?" Fiona asked.

"According to Helen," Ginny said, "The estate was being seriously eroded by nursing and other health care costs they were paying out-of-pocket because Raymond didn't want to be there 24/7."

"Some wake this is," Charlotte said.

"Means, motive, and opportunity. We all have them," Ginny said. "Every one of us had access to that sleeping porch, as well as the strength and dexterity to close up that bed. And now it's evident that we all had a reason. Who would've thought? Raymond in our midst, pontificating for months about mysteries, and all the while he was behaving quite badly."

So who? Which one of us committed the murder? Isn't that the question we came here to answer?" Leo said.

"It could be any one of us." Ginny stated the obvious as she looked around the group. "Living up to our name, scurrilous."

"Aren't we leaving someone out?" Leo said. "Another major player?"

"Ah," Ginny said, light dawning. "You're right. *And then there were seven*. At the lots-drawing."

"Emma Rae? She just came to help us," Fiona said. "Knew the area, figured out where to have the killer and victim meet. She set up the envelopes, administered the draw, and then she left. That's it."

"The two of you *are* the company," Charlotte said. "You needed that park project to survive — you admitted it. Financially, but also for long-term prestige. Parks throughout Vermont. It would make your reputation. And with Raymond out of the way, you can re-bid."

"If only," Fiona said, dismissively.

"*You* suggested we play this game," Rina said. "Ooster barked."

"To celebrate and parallel our reading interests," Fiona said. "Come on, we all agreed to play *the game* as you call it."

"When we took our envelope, Emma Rae held the basket up, high, so we all had to reach for our lot," Charlotte said, demonstrating. "She made us line up, like school children. Before we drew, she pretended to mix up the envelopes, but I think she was putting them in the order that you wanted. So you and Raymond would get the dots."

"That's preposterous," Fiona said.

"You came out here beforehand with Emma Rae to look at the set up," Leo said. "I arranged for you to have the key. When we chose our rooms, you said, 'one guy up and one guy down,' and Raymond couldn't do stairs because of his knees. You knew he'd be on the porch."

"And you know all about poisonous plants. I'm guessing you had more than blueberries in your poison kit," Ginny sad. "That was your plan. Pretend to kill him with the blueberries, really kill him with something else, slow acting. Probably in that flask of whisky I saw by his bed along with the cranberry juice. You'd put it in during the retreat, he would drink it sometime, maybe not all of it here. Dies next week or after. The Ambien and the sofa bed were serendipitous." Ginny said. "Or maybe not. Maybe the sofa bed was Plan A all along."

"Aren't you clever?" Fiona said, with a hint of sneer. "What an assembly of detection. And fiction. Not to mention that every one of us will have our DNA on that sofa bed. We all went in there when we were choosing rooms. Charlotte and Rina made up the sofa bed, Ginny opened it with Raymond inside, Leo helped her cover it up with the bedspreads."

"You'll never prove a thing," Fiona said.

Sounds of sirens and approaching vehicles interrupted the conversation.

"I am up last night," Rina said. "Much snow falling. I take photographs. Special camera I have, for my work. Take pictures in dark. I use for my paintings, later. Many pictures I have. All over cabin, looking outside, from different angles. I give to police. They like."

The Best of Times

Michael Wiley

On a February morning, icy snow clicked against Sam Kelson's office window.

The Chicago sky was gray.

The light inside the office was gray.

The woman sitting in Kelson's client chair wore an emerald green bikini, dotted with blue feathers and silver spangles. A sheer cape fell from her shoulders over the back of the chair. A long feather poked from her hair. She wore a Mardi Gras mask.

"My name is Abra," she said.

"Let the good times roll," Kelson said.

"Yeah, whatever."

"Aren't you cold?" he said.

"I'm freezing my tits off."

"I promise you they're fine." Kelson tried to hold his tongue and failed. "More than fine. Wonderful."

"Do you always say what you're thinking?"

"Yes, ma'am. Will you take off the mask?"

"No. You'd treat me differently."

"I'm already treating you differently."

"That makes no sense."

"You'll get used to that. What do you want me to do for you?"

"I woke up this morning like this. Shoes on. Mask on. Bikini. Everything. The last thing I remember, I was a thousand miles from here, in a hot crowd in the French Quarter. I want you to figure out what happened."

"Where did you wake up?"

"The Drake Hotel."

"Fancy. I've done jobs there. Wallets and jewelry stolen from rooms. The management doesn't like the press that comes with police reports. Do you think you were roofied?"

"I think I drank too many Zombies. I have the worst headache ever."

"It's hard to talk to you this way," Kelson said. "Will you please take off the mask?"

"You seem to be doing fine."

"You should hear me when I really let go. How did you find me?"

"I asked the concierge for a recommendation."

"Petey?"

"He said you're the most honest guy in town."

"I don't mean to be. I took a shot to the head a couple years ago. Now I can't help myself—I talk and talk, and I tell the truth as I understand it every time."

"You sound like the kind of man I need."

"I love when women say that."

"Before I fly home, I need to know what happened."

"Then take off your mask," he said.

She frowned but peeled it off. She had a tattoo under each eye. The one on her right cheek said *Abra*. The one on her left said *Cadabra*.

"Wow," Kelson said.

"I was drunk. I was in love."

"What's love got to do with it?"

"I was dating a magician. He did tricks for tips in Jackson Square."

"You fell in love with a street performer? Were the mimes all taken?"

"You wouldn't believe what Ian can do with his hands."

"You'll make me blush."

"He took me on as an assistant. I was a grad student at Tulane, studying Roman history. When I met Ian, he called me his wild child, so I went to Electric Ladyland thinking I'd get a tattoo on each shoulder. *Remus* and *Romulus*—you know, raised by a wolf. I came out with *Abra* and *Cadabra* on my face. Never get tattooed when you're wasted on Hurricanes."

"I'll remember that."

"The good news is our tips doubled."

"The bad news?"

"Jennifer."

"Uh-oh," Kelson said.

"Ian's girlfriend. They'd been together for four years. He didn't love her."

"Misdirection."

"I'm sorry?"

"Magic trick, right? Misdirection. He tells you he doesn't love her, but he's getting it at home with her and getting it on with you behind the curtains. You think he has you in his arms, and then he pulls her out of his hat."

"It wasn't like that. Jennifer was a lawyer with the Orleans Public Defenders—always at work, always busy."

"So she paid the rent while Merlin did tricks for tourists."

"She had no time for him. I did. But then he disappeared."

"I suppose that's what magicians do."

"In the middle of our Zig Zag Lady bit, a drunk hit him in the head with a Michelob bottle. When the ambulance came, I stayed to pack the equipment. I never saw him again."

"Poof."

"I checked the hospitals. No record of him. He was just gone."

"A vanishing act. Could the drunk with the bottle have been a set-up?"

"Ian's blood looked real."

"When did this happen?"

"Last summer—at the end of July."

"How about Jennifer?"

"Gone too. A few days after he got hit in the head, I went by their apartment. No one was there."

"Does Ian have a last name?"

"McGregor. He performs as Ian the Illusionist. I've Googled him a thousand times."

"Any reason he'd want to disappear?"

"I might've threatened to tell Jennifer about us. I don't like her."

"She probably has mixed feelings about you too. Did you Google her?"

"Sure. Jennifer Lozada. A couple months ago, I even called her office. They said she'd quit."

"At the same time Ian disappeared?"

"I didn't ask," she said.

"That was dumb."

The woman shivered, the feathers on her bikini quivering.

"Sorry," Kelson said. "If she quit at the same time, they could've planned the disappearance together."

"I get that. Or she could've been as upset as I was. I dropped out of grad school."

"People don't just disappear."

"Ian did. Last night *I* did."

"But then you reappeared. I want to know more about the girlfriend."

"Ian didn't like to talk about her. I only know she earned her law degree at LSU, and she was from Indianapolis."

"Not quite next door to us, but...." On a hunch, Kelson turned to his laptop and Googled the Cook County Public Defender's office. Then he dialed the number and asked to talk to Jennifer Lozada.

The receptionist said the office had no one by that name.

"Started working there last summer?" he said. "Moved from New Orleans? Maybe has a boyfriend who wears a top hat?"

"Nope," the receptionist said.

Kelson hung up. He Googled *Ian McGregor Illusionist*. Photos and videos popped up on the social media pages of tourists who'd watched him perform in Jackson Square. He was tall—easily six three or four—skinny as a rock star, with long red hair. "Hard to miss," Kelson said. "Hard to make disappear." In three of the photos, Abra appeared alongside the magician, holding a tip box, a multi-colored scarf, and a wand. In the photos, she looked warm with excitement.

Sitting across from Kelson now, she shivered, her feathers trembling.

"You couldn't have stopped to buy a coat before coming here?"

"As I said, I woke up like this. With nothing else. No money."

"How did you get here from The Drake?"

"When I stepped outside, five taxis almost crashed trying to get to me. I said I had no money for the fare, but one of the drivers offered to bring me for free."

"How do you plan to pay *me*?"

"Can I write an IOU?"

"Do you work?"

"I'm sort of *between*."

"Huh. What was your last job?"

"Magician's assistant."

"In July?"

"There's not a lot of demand for my skillset."

"Mine either," Kelson said.

"We seem to be made for each other," she said. "I'm planning to start my own act. I've been practicing." She shivered.

"Hold on." Kelson stepped from his office into the corridor. He shared his floor with a computer training firm. He went into the coatroom, between the two main classrooms, and grabbed the biggest, warmest parka from the rack.

When he returned, he dropped the coat in the woman's lap. She held it like a giant quilt. "I could put three of me in this. Where'd you get it?"

"I stole it from André the Giant."

She wrapped herself in it, sighing as the warmth spread. "Do you have any boundaries?"

"Sure, I live behind a wall of truth. If the guy I stole it from knocks, I'll tell him I took it. Then you'll be looking for a new detective."

She seemed to disappear inside the coat. "I must look like a walrus."

"In Chicago, this counts as sexy from October to April. C'mon, let's go back to The Drake."

*****

Twenty minutes later, Kelson and Abra pushed through a brass revolving door into the hotel lobby, shaking snow from their hair.

At the concierge desk, a little man in wire-rimmed glasses brightened as they approached. "She found you."

"I wasn't hiding," Kelson said. "How's shakes?"

The concierge grinned, exposing little teeth. "Ah, you know...."

Kelson smiled back. "No, I don't. Any chance I could see some registration records? And video of the check-in desk?"

"You know I don't have access to all that."

"But Sylvia does," Kelson said. "Sylvia is Petey's sister," he told Abra. "She runs security." When Petey still grinned up at them, Kelson said, "You think you could call her?"

After a few minutes, a slight woman who looked like a female Petey came through the lobby. When Kelson told her what he wanted, she led them to an elevator and down to a utility floor where she shared a gray workroom with her security staff. She sat at a computer, typed in the room number Abra gave her, and said, "Nope."

"Nope?" Abra said.

"You aren't here."

"I *think* I am," Abra said, though she looked unsure.

"No one booked the room last night—or the night before."

Abra reached inside the parka and pulled a room card from her bikini top.

Sylvia ran it through a machine, then jerked it out when it matched the room number Abra gave her. "Where did you get this?"

"It was on the night table when I woke up."

Sylvia typed at the computer again. "No one paid for that room."

"Poof," Kelson said.

"I'm starting to feel sick," Abra said.

Kelson did the math. "You say you were partying until midnight in the French Quarter and then blacked out. Let's guess a direct flight from New Orleans takes a couple hours. Add an hour or so on either end for travel to and from the airport. That puts us at four a.m., probably later. What time did you wake up?"

"Nine?" she said.

Kelson asked Sylvia, "Can we see the reception video between four and nine?"

They fast-forwarded through the recording. In the early morning hours, few people came to the desk, and the lone clerk sat for long periods staring at her phone. Starting at six, a line formed as guests checked out. Aside from a pair of United Airlines pilots and a couple other early arrivals, no one approached to check in.

"Nope," Sylvia said, "you aren't here."

"Can we see the lobby cameras?" Kelson said.

"I don't know what you expect to see." She typed some more, and a split screen showed three views of the lobby. She fast-forwarded from four a.m. Assorted late-night partiers stumbled from the revolving doors to the elevators. A sleepless guest came down in a bathrobe and sat on a lobby armchair.

"*Stop*," Kelson said. He tapped the middle recording. "Back that one up."

"What?" Sylvia reversed the recording, adjusted it so it filled the whole monitor, and played it forward at regular speed.

"There." Kelson tapped the side of the image, where two people appeared at the top of the broad stairway leading into the lobby. The pair paused, then went back down.

"Where did they come from?" Sylvia said.

"Is that me?" Abra said.

Sylvia magnified the image and played the recording slow motion.

"That's Ian," Abra shouted. "And that's me."

"Holy cow," Sylvia said.

"He took you up the elevator from downstairs," Kelson said. "You remember none of this?"

Abra looked dazed. "I remember partying hard at Saints and Sinners and then waking up with snow falling outside the window."

"Why would he do this to you?" Kelson said.

"*How* did he do it?" Sylvia said.

"He's good with his hands," Abra told the woman. "He can escape from chains and padlocks."

"Unless he can work a keycard machine ten feet behind the counter, he couldn't do this."

"He can slip the watch off one man's wrist and slip it onto another's without either of them knowing it. You think he'd have trouble with a keycard?"

"Why did he bring you here?" Kelson said.

Abra looked nervously at Sylvia. "Can I have my key?"

The security chief stared at her wide-eyed. "*No*. It's not your room."

"Where am I supposed to stay?"

"Why would he bring you?" Kelson said.

"I don't know." Her eyes moistened. A single tear rolled over the *Cadabra* tattoo. "What am I supposed to do?"

"Whatever it is, you can't do it here," Sylvia said.

Abra stared at Kelson.

"What?" he said.

"Where am I supposed to go without money?"

He looked to Sylvia, and the security chief narrowed her eyes—Abra was no business of hers.

Kelson sighed. "C'mon then," he said.

They rode the elevator up from the utility floor and drove back to Kelson's office. As they stomped the ice from their shoes in the corridor outside his door, a huge man stepped from the coatroom empty-handed, looking bewildered. "Oops," Kelson said. He shoved the key into his lock and pushed Abra into the office.

"You're more trouble than you're worth," he said.

"Since I'm broke, that's not much." She sat down on Kelson's client chair.

"At least you're interesting."

"Can't pay the rent with interesting." She shuddered.

"Stop that—I'm not stealing you another coat."

She shuddered again.

"What aren't you telling me?" Kelson said.

"I've told you all I know."

"Why would a guy who jilted you fly you here and stick you in a hotel? If this turns out to be one of those sleight-of-hand things, I'm going to be mad."

"If we find him, maybe he'll explain. And maybe he'll buy me a plane ticket home—if I don't kill him first."

"If he won't, I'll bet his girlfriend will."

"I don't like Jennifer."

"Right." He sat down at his laptop and Googled *Jennifer Lozada New Orleans defense attorney.*

A black-and-white from an old version of the Orleans Public Defenders website showed a round-faced woman with short blond hair. "Hello, friend," Kelson said.

Then he Googled Chicago-area defendant advocate organizations, leaving out the words *public defender.*

When he dialed the Lawyers Committee for Civil Rights and asked the same questions he'd asked the Public Defender's office, the man on the other end said, "No Jennifer Lozada, no New Orleans."

At the Legal Assistance Foundation, the receptionist raised his hopes by transferring him to the office manager, who dashed them again. "No" and "No."

A Legal Aid Chicago woman said, "Sorry, no Jennifer Lozada."

Kelson almost didn't bother to ask, "Moved here last summer from New Orleans?"

"Oh," the woman said, "you must mean Jennie McGregor?"

"In fact, I do," Kelson said.

*****

Legal Aid Chicago was on the ninth floor of a white-pillared bank building on South LaSalle. When Kelson and Abra stepped up, the woman behind the front desk said, "I'm not judging, honey, but those are messed-up tattoos."

"Is Jennie McGregor around?" Kelson said.

The clerk still eyed Abra. "And what's with the coat? You friends with an elephant?"

So Abra unbuttoned the parka, exposing the bikini.

"Hell, no," the clerk said.

"Ma'am," Kelson said, "we'd like to talk to Jennie McGregor."

With her eyes on the bikini—"Bet you don't have an appointment."

Abra said, "*I'll* bet they hired you because of your knack for customer relations."

"I'm a volunteer," she said, as if that put her in the office next to the CEO. "I keep out the riffraff."

"I thought Legal Aid served the needy," Abra said.

"We help the poor. You just look like you've got poor taste."

"*Ma'am?*" Kelson said. "Will you see if Jennie McGregor is available?"

"Who's asking?"

"Tell her Abra, from New Orleans," he said.

The clerk snorted. "Abra?" She tapped the touchpad on her phone.

*****

Jennie McGregor sat behind a desk stacked high with case files, folders, court briefs, and assorted scraps of paper. As Kelson and Abra entered her office, she took off a pair of glasses, caressed the bridge of her nose, and blinked.

Kelson admired the messy desk. "Ah, you're one of the good ones."

She eyed Abra. "What are *you* doing here?"

"That's what I'm trying to figure out," Abra said.

"When was the last time you saw a clean desktop?" Kelson asked. "All work, no play, right? Fighting for those who can't fight for themselves?"

The lawyer turned to him. "*Who* are you?"

He offered a hand and a smile. "Sam Kelson."

"He's helping me," Abra said.

"I try to be one of the good ones too," he said. "Not that it always works out."

The lawyer turned back to Abra. "You shouldn't even know we're here."

"*We're*—as in *you and Ian*?" Kelson said. "You'd better check with Houdini about that."

"What are you talking about?" the lawyer said.

"Where's Mr. Magic now?" he said.

"Ian? At work—at Happy Bean Coffee."

"He's a barista? Oh, that's got to hurt," Kelson said. "Where was he last night?"

She pursed her lips. "With me."

"Liar."

She blinked again.

Abra said, "I blacked out last night while partying in New Orleans. At a quarter to five this morning, Ian snuck me into The Drake Hotel. He must've brought me here."

The lawyer allowed herself a dubious smile. "Last night you were...in New Orleans?"

Abra yanked open the big parka again.

"Oh my," the lawyer said.

Kelson said, "We have Ian on video at the hotel."

"But he promised," the lawyer said. "He said he'd give up performing. He said he'd give up—" she stared at Abra "—you."

Kelson said, "You couldn't have found something better for him than Happy Bean?"

"He doesn't have a lot of skills."

"Me either," Abra said. "Ian really loves magic."

"He really loves *me*," the lawyer said. "When I found out about the two of you, I gave him a choice. He chose me."

"You staged the drunk with the Michelob trick?" Kelson asked.

"Ian really got hit in the head. The drunk was a man named Charlie— I defended him on a vagrancy charge in New Orleans. Ian wanted a grand exit—a great vanishing act. Charlie was supposed to use a breakaway bottle—a stage prop—but he lost it and used his own. Ian still gets headaches."

"Maybe he's having second thoughts," Kelson said.

"We made a new start," she told Abra. "We're happy. *Ian* is. Why would he do this now? He said he would forget about you. He left all his things behind."

"If he changed his mind, he could find me easily enough," Abra said. "I've been advertising my new act."

Kelson said, "Ian finds you online and sees what used to be, except he's missing from the picture. So he reverses his last trick. Instead of vanishing, he makes you appear. Pretty creepy."

Abra nodded. "But from the magic side of things, pretty cool."

"Not cool at all," the lawyer said. She reached under a pile of papers, produced a phone, and dialed. When Ian answered, she said, "Okay, David Copperfield, come to my office—*now*."

✦✦✦✦✦

Cartoonlike coffee beans danced across Ian's uniform shirt. More beans danced on his Happy Bean hat. His red hair—which flamed over his shoulders in the online pictures Kelson had seen—was cut close over his ears.

"Oh, Ian," Abra said.

He looked about to cry. "Hey, baby."

"Don't 'Hey, baby' her," the lawyer said.

"I'm sorry," he said to the lawyer. "I'm sorry," he said to Abra. "I'm…" he decided Kelson didn't need an apology.

"Why?" Abra asked.

"I missed the crowds," Ian said. "The excitement. The costumes— great bikini, by the way."

"Cut that out," the lawyer said.

"Our landlord won't let me keep rabbits," he told Abra.

"The pet deposit would cost a hundred a month," the lawyer said. "We *agreed*."

Abra said, "But why did you leave me alone at the hotel?"

"The flight landed late," he said. "I needed to open Happy Bean at six."

Kelson said, "You couldn't leave her a message?"

"I thought that would be weird."

"A *message* would be weird?"

"And it would ruin the trick," Ian said. "The first rule of magic is *never explain*. I planned to go back after my shift." He looked at Abra. "Where would you go in a bikini?"

"I relied on the kindness of strangers," she said.

"I want to do magic with you again," he said.

"*No*," said the lawyer.

"Chicago's a wide-open market," he told Abra. "If you're willing, we could try."

"I don't need you anymore," she said. "I've learned your tricks."

"But they're *my* tricks," Ian said.

"Do you really want to push that?" Kelson said.

"You left me," Abra said. "You hurt me." She curled her lips at him. "Did you drug me?"

"Never," Ian said. "I just kept feeding you Zombies. Anyway, *I'm* the one who got hit in the head."

"Bad move," Kelson said.

Ian glared at him. "What are you, a referee?"

"Yeah," Abra said. "Shut up."

"Really?" Kelson said.

She turned to Ian. "I won't be your assistant anymore."

"You won't be *anything*," the lawyer said. "You'll pack your bikini-butt onto an airplane and go home."

Abra and Ian turned on her together. "Shut up."

An indignant noise came from the lawyer's throat.

"Partners?" Ian said. "*The Ian and Abra Show*?"

Abra shook her head. "*Abra and Ian.*"

"*Abra and Ian the Illusionist*?" he said.

"You're pushing again," Kelson said.

They glared at him, but Abra said, "*Abra and Ian, Extraordinaires.*"

"The French is good," Kelson said. "A touch of New Orleans in the Windy City."

"What about the other parts of us?" Ian said.

"I'm over you—as you," Abra said.

"Probably for the best," he said. "Jennie and I got married." He turned to the lawyer. "What do you think, honey? Magic only? No fooling around?"

"Do I have a choice?" she said.

"If it was me, I'd kick him out on his ass," Kelson said.

"Shut up," she said. Then, to Ian—"Do you keep your job at Happy Bean?"

"Until the act brings in more than my paycheck," he said.

"And if it never does?"

He tipped his hat to her. *"Would you like room for milk?"*

She frowned. "Okay...."

"Yeah?" he said.

"Yeah."

He turned to Abra. "Yeah?"

"Yeah." She shivered.

Kelson clapped. "Let the good times roll."

A Time to Mourn

Eve Fisher

The funeral was at nine in the morning on that June day of 1885, and by the time everyone got back to the house, the hot prairie air had a smell like baking bread. Nell was stifling in her black bombazine, her bodice drenched with sweat. She looked over at her two boys, Bill and John, stiff in their black suits, their blond hair so wet it looked as dark as their father's. Bill was seven, but John, Patrick's spitting image, was only three, and something twisted in her, knowing how soon he would forget.

She got up and went into the kitchen, where Martha, her mother-in-law, and Pearl, her sister-in-law, were busy getting the dinner dished up.

"Sure, and you should go rest yourself," Pearl urged.

Martha nodded. "Yah sure. We got everything going good here."

"I feel better if I keep busy," Nell replied. And it was true, or it would be if she could just get out of this black: but the shock if she changed on the very day of her husband's burial would be too much for the neighbors.

Martha shrugged. "You want to take up the biscuits?" Nell pulled out the big black baking tin. "We put them on that platter. The one with the wheat on it."

Nell dished up the biscuits. When your husband died, and you were left with two boys, and you yourself were an orphan, with no relatives, it was Providential to have in-laws willing to take you in. She had to show her gratitude. She had to be willing and helpful. She had to begin as she meant to go on. "What else can I do?"

"Them pies need slicing."

Nell took a knife to the apple pies. Better here than in that crowd of people, all whispering things that made her cheeks sting with shame. Patrick Stark, healthy and strong as an ox, dying so sudden? Heart failure? Never. An overdose of laudanum. For why? What was the real story behind that? The real story, she told herself determinedly, as she'd told herself over and over again since last Tuesday, is that he'd strained himself hoisting bales of hay. He'd come in tired and sore, too tired to eat, too sore to sleep, and he had dosed himself with laudanum, despite her worries and protests. Once, twice, three times… and then he had lain himself down and never got up again. Leaving her with the children. Leaving her without a home save that of her father-in-law. Leaving her alone.

She stood up straight. "Is there anything else I can do?"

"Nah. Now we go in and eat."

*****

James Stark owned one of the two general stores in Laskin, South Dakota, and three quarter-sections of land out in the county. The land he'd divided among his oldest sons, William, Harold, and Patrick, who lived on and worked the land. Now Patrick's land was to be farmed by William and Harold, the profits split and a good share held in trust for Patrick's children. The youngest of James' sons, Graham, Pearl's husband, ran the shop under James' supervision. James Stark was in his fifties, still fit and strong, despite his white hair and beard. Martha, a Norwegian immigrant, was his third wife: he never spoke of either of his first two, and rarely of her.

It was a very quiet house. Martha, old before her time, worked like a carthorse and never spoke of anything but work, and that usually not beyond the kitchen and lean-to. Graham slid through life like a shadow, speaking only when forced to in a burdened voice. James, silent in the morning over breakfast and dinner, walled himself behind the newspaper between the two. After dinner he went out, returning late to release Pearl to help with housework. After supper, James took over the shop entirely. As the evening progressed, loud shouts of laughter from below rang upwards like echoes from a foreign land.

Nell quickly became friends with Pearl. You couldn't help but love Pearl, for her lively Irish spirits, her loving heart, her lovely face. Pearl and Graham had one son, Arthur, the dead spit of his father. The boy was barely three, and named for Tennyson's poems. Nell took charge of Arthur while Pearl worked in the shop, for it was she who really kept it going, offering advice and help and promises, while her husband stood in the back and looked dully over the goods.

"Well, and it's not really a job for a man, is it?" Pearl made apology over her mending. "Selling things. And all those calicos and threads. He does get that bored with the ladies running in for a bit of ribbon or a choice bit of trim. Small blame to him, says I. And it's no trouble to me at all, not at all." Her wonderful smile flashed. "I've always been too fond of dress, that's what my mother would say. And now here I am, having the run of a shop. What is the world coming to when wickedness is its own reward, that's what she'd say."

She giggled like a schoolgirl, and Nell thought once more that if it weren't for Pearl, she would go distracted in this silent house. But where could she go? What else could she do? Laskin already had two dressmakers, and the only other job of work open to a woman with two small children was washing: heavy, backbreaking, disreputable.

The boys seemed happy enough, though Bill missed the farm terribly. His great joy was to be taken out to the land and allowed to follow Uncle William or Uncle Harold as he had once followed his father. But it was rare that they came to town, and never did they bring their wives. They were all busy on the land, and Nell could well understand that. She had been once. And while then there had been days when she had hated it, the endless work, the loneliness, the isolation, now she missed it terribly. When she had felt closed in, she had only to step outside. How she had loved the sweep of it, up to the greater sweep of the sky! The space of it. The air and the color of it. Sometimes the sheer interiority of her life now — walls upon walls, in the house and in the town — seemed suffocating.

But it was not only the silence and the town life that bothered her. There was a growing unease about her father-in-law. He moved as little as a rock, and that rock seemed to be always the breaker against which she must crash. When she served food, his body made no room for her laden arm, but required it to reach across him. When she cleaned, he always needed something that required him to stretch himself above and across her bent back. And in church, one Sunday, he had slumped in their pew until his arm rested hotly against hers. And his eyes…

She could barely think it to herself, much less whisper it to anyone: all she could do was avoid him. She waited to work, or sit, or go outside, until she was quite clear where James Stark would be. One day, as she performed her little minuet, she glanced up and saw Graham looking at her, and the slight movement of his knife-colored eyes made her heart thud. He knew. But the next moment, it was gone.

*****

The daily round continued. Autumn brought the rush of gathering, preserving, pickling and salting what came from the garden and the pig. It was a shame, with a feast first of spare-ribs, then of fresh meat, that Pearl – who had to be called in from the shop to help - had entirely lost her appetite for any of it. Nell suspected it wasn't the headcheese so much as that Pearl might be again what she'd confessed she'd longed to be, with child, and Nell cheerfully took over the rest of the distasteful work. After two hard weeks of harvest labor, cellar and attic were stored to bursting and the kitchen scoured clean. The three women could get on with the usual Saturday baking.

Nell put a second batch of bread to rise in greased pans as Pearl picked up bits of raw dough from the table and nibbled them.

"Yah, you get worms from that!" Martha called from the cook stove. She was frying doughnuts in a seething vat of the recently tried lard, and her face was crimson from the heat.

"That's but an old wives tale," Pearl said. "And it tastes so good."

Martha shrugged. Nell covered her bread and said, in a low voice, "It's a sure sign. When are you going to tell Graham?"

Pearl's blue eyes looked sidelong through their long golden lashes. "When it quickens, when else? It's just foxfire before then."

Martha turned, a platter of doughnuts in her right hand. "When what –" Her left hand flashed her wedding ring to her heart.

"Martha?" Nell leaped forward.

Martha thrust the platter at Nell and tried to step forward. "Ach!

What–" Her face crimsoned more as she fell to her knees. Her corsets held her straight the rest of the way to the floor.

It was as cold a funeral as Patrick's had been hot. The ground was iron-hard. Snow fell over the black hats and veils as the minister read the service. The wind scudded little drifts of snow across the road as they walked back, pricked out tears of cold, if not of sorrow, from every face.

Indoors, Nell headed straight to the kitchen, her black bombazine comfortingly warm. Pearl, blotchy from crying (the one thing she could not do gracefully, Nell noted), came in to help her. It was the same menu as before. Funeral food: scalloped potatoes and ham, biscuits, pie, and coffee. Afterwards, they cleaned up, with help from other townswomen, while the men smoked cigars in the parlor and rumbled about the news.

"What a mercy it was quick!" Mrs. Mortensen said only what everyone had said for the last three days, and all the women nodded. "And at least Mr. Stark isn't left with any young children." Someone tittered, not Mrs. Mortensen.

"What do you think Mr. Stark will do now?" Mrs. Torvaldson, the banker's wife, asked Nell.

"I… I don't know," Nell replied, startled at being asked her opinion. Mourning a husband meant a year without society, and she did not yet know the townsfolk very well.

Graham's dull voice came from the door. "Maybe he'll get married again."

"Graham!" Pearl cried. "And Martha not yet cold."

Graham shrugged and walked away.

*****

Late that night, Nell lay in her cold bed, listening to the wind howling outside. What she had barely been able to think to herself had suddenly made itself plain. If James Stark desired her, what was now to stop him? What if he wanted to marry her? Her whole body shuddered. It could not be. She would rather die. Surely there were laws against something as horrible, as unnatural as that. A man would… No, it was impossible. She had to have mistaken his behavior. And if she had not, she vowed, she would move to a shanty on the edge of town and take in washing before she would become involved with her husband's father. Patrick! Patrick! She whipped herself over into a ball under the covers, and cried her heart out.

*****

Winter days were short. The shop shut early now, and James Stark showed a surprising talent for reading aloud in the evenings: newspaper articles, novels, poetry. Graham seemed indifferent as he whittled in his corner, but all the rest, even Nell, were rapt by that fine voice rising and falling in the gathering dark. And then, by eight o'clock, nine at the latest, everyone was in bed. Coal and kerosene were too precious, even for a shopkeeper, when everything had to be imported from the East.

Rising at four-thirty, Nell worked doggedly to light the kitchen fire, heat water, and get breakfast served by six-thirty, usually by herself, for Pearl's condition was one of almost constant sickness. Often all Pearl could do was sit by the lean-to door in case she needed to rush out quickly. Nell did not mind: anything she could do to help Pearl was a satisfaction. But James Stark was a very early riser, and instead of heading straight to the barn to tend the cow, he now lingered in the kitchen, starting the fire, fetching water, leaning against her as she tried — it was so cold! — to get warm over the kindling flame. He said nothing but common words of work, of courtesy, to them both. But he had never done so for poor Martha, and Nell – "Nellie," he called her now – felt embarrassed, ashamed, fearful, and… flattered?

And then, one morning, Graham was there, before the women. Nell and Pearl lingered on the steps, hearing the two male voices, James' low like thunder, Graham's surprisingly sharp. They stepped into the kitchen. James glanced once at her and Pearl, who shakily sat down by the door, and went out to the barn. The fire was kindled.

"I'll fetch water," Graham told Nell. "And then I'll go help Father."

He was protecting her, Nell realized. And wondered why.

*****

Pearl's light, active body was now heavy with child, and while she was no longer sick, she sat most days, all day. Nell wished they could both have fresh air, but they were shut up in the rooms of this house, battened and ceiled as it was against the wind, with the odor of cooking and coal, sweat and manure thick in their nostrils no matter how much Nell scrubbed and washed. And the diet, bread, fried potatoes, beans, meat, with a dollop of preserves or canned fruit, was heavy as lead. Nell knew that fresh greens were what Pearl needed, and fresh milk, but the cow was almost dry, and there was no hope for anything but what they had until spring. Winter stretched out forever in a whirl of wind and snow and dark long nights.

The two women spent the scant afternoon light sewing and mending, looking after the three boys, although Bill spent most of his time in the shop. James Stark had given him a pennywhistle, a map, and a promise to take him to the Huron State Fair come summer. Every night, James and Bill, John, and Arthur lingered at table, the boys mesmerized by James Stark's stories of Dakota Territory as it had been when he arrived thirty years ago. As Nell washed the dishes and scrubbed the pots, she heard him talk of buffalo herds that had stretched like a dark cloud across a sea of grass, a cloud that made its own thunder. Of the great hunts that left piles of buffalo rotting under the sun, and had provided them with the buffalo hides that kept them warm this long, cold winter. Of the sod house he had built, when he decided to stay and not follow the buffalo across the Jim. It was the warmest house he'd ever known, he claimed. But no mention of the dirt of it, Nell noted, nor of the first wife who'd lived in it but a year and died giving birth to the twins, William and Harold. Or the second, who'd given him his other two sons.

But the stories were thrilling. She would glance over at her boys, open-mouthed, and find his eyes upon her.

"See?" they said. "See how I've won *their* hearts?"

*****

In church, Nell stood between James and Graham, her boys beside James. They loved him. Nell shared a hymnal with him. He sang well, just as he read well. He was devout in manner, sober in conduct and habits, clean in person. His courtesy, exquisite, polished, courtly, to her and to her sons drew the attention of their fellow parishioners. She knew what they were thinking. In June, her mourning would be over, and

James Stark was vigorous enough for a fourth wife. She blushed, but did not shudder.

✶✶✶✶✶

On a cold, snowy morning at the end of March, Pearl's time came. Nell threw her shawl over her head and went racing to the doctor's, so quickly that she was back before the breakfast potatoes had time to burn. Nell ran up and downstairs with hot water, towels, and whatever else Dr. Peterson required. Soon the cries were loud enough to distress the boys in the kitchen, who dropped their forks. James Stark, who had sat like a ramrod through it all, now got up and herded the boys – with their plates – into the shop, where they joined Graham for the rest of the day.

Pearl's little girl was born by suppertime.

"I want to call her Violet." Pearl's white face smiled tremulously down upon her baby. A dark-haired crown was all that could be seen above the swaddling.

"Where in God's name did you get that idea?" Graham asked from the door, his tone surprisingly hostile.

"It's a lovely name," Nell said, trying desperately to scrub away the smell of childbirth that filled the air.

"From a book by Charlotte Yonge," Pearl replied. "Mrs. Mortenson lent it me."

"Oh." He shrugged. "I'll sleep in the store tonight." And he went downstairs.

Later, as Nell, with an aching back, cleaned the last of the pots and pans in the kitchen, James Stark stood in the doorway and asked about the baby.

"She's a beautiful little girl," Nell said, without looking up from her pots. "Dark hair and violet eyes." She turned, to find his eyes fixed on her. "Pearl is going to name her Violet."

He nodded, and went into the parlor. He returned with the family Bible. Carefully he sat down, thawed the ink at the stove, and wrote down the name and date of this new member of the family.

"'Children's children are the crown of old men,'" he quoted, "'and the glory of children are their fathers.'"

As he rose and took the Bible back to the parlor, Nell thought that he was not yet an old man.

*****

Graham slept in the store for the next two weeks, and fell ill with a bad cold that quickly turned ragged. The coughs nearly tore him in two. James Stark had his son moved into the parlor, and kept the stove alight, water steaming away on it, no matter the cost in coal. Pearl and the baby were not allowed near her husband, nor were the boys, for fear of infection. Nell nursed him diligently for Pearl, bedding herself down in the sitting room where she could hear him in the night. But Graham got worse, despite rubbing with kerosene and dosing with camphor. Dr. Peterson feared pleurisy. He bled Graham lightly, and left a small brown bottle of laudanum to ease his cough and help him sleep.

"You'll need to be careful of the dose," Dr. Peterson said.

Nell flushed. James Stark, standing by the bedside, came to her rescue, assuring the doctor that "Nellie" would be very careful of her, sorry, his son and Pearl's husband. Nellie flushed even more.

Every four hours, Nell went into the parlor to give Graham his medicine. He would wake, briefly, swallow, and return to sleep, until awakened by another wracking cough. At suppertime she went in to feed him broth and found him trying to get up.

She pushed him back down: he was weak as a child. "Lie back down, Graham. Do you need the honey pot?"

"Pain," he gasped. "Medicine… I need to sleep… Forever."

Her heart cramped. "No, no, no. You need but a little more to sleep."

He clutched her wrist. "I need… enough to sleep… forever," he repeated.

"No, you don't. Why, in less than a month it will be May, and the sun will bake the sickness out of you. All will be well."

"Will it?" Graham asked without eagerness. "And how… will it be… for you? May… June… No more mourning… A short time."

"It's seemed very long to me."

"I won't know you… if you're not… in black."

"I don't like black."

"My father… He… He…"

"Hush," Nell interrupted. She did not want to discuss James Stark with Graham. "Here. Take this now, and you'll sleep like a lamb."

Graham supped his half teaspoon eagerly. "Leave it by me."

"No!" she cried. She put the bottle in her apron pocket, then put more coal on the parlor fire. "Now rest yourself. Sleep."

*****

Afterwards, she took her apron off, setting the bottle high in the kitchen cupboard, and sat with Pearl and Bill at the kitchen table. Arthur and John were already in bed, and Violet was in Pearl's lap.

"Oh, Nell. You look so tired," Pearl said, concerned.

"It's nothing that a good night's sleep won't cure. Did I hear someone come in earlier?"

"Mrs. Mortenson called. 'Twas very kind of her, I'm sure, but she is a talker. All sorts of nonsense out of her today. Mr. Stark shooed her out at last, saying I needed my rest."

Bill looked up, with his clear blue eyes. "She said that you were to be married, Mam, come summer. Is that true?"

Nell flushed, and Pearl gave the child a sidelong glance through those golden lashes. "You see what I mean?"

"But she said everyone —"

Pearl interrupted the boy. "Bill, it's time to take Mr. Stark his evening coffee in the shop."

Bill leaped up. His greatest treat was to spend the last hour of the evening with his grandfather.

Once the boy was gone, Pearl asked, anxiously, "How is Graham? Truly?"

"He will be fine, I promise you," Nell assured her. Pearl was still so white from childbirth, and her wide blue eyes were apprehensive. "I have told you before, Pearl, I would never let your husband die. I love you too well. I will do all I can to save him for you."

Pearl nodded, her mouth fixed.

*****

Nell lay in her pallet on the sitting room floor. Above her was the master bedroom. She heard the floorboards creaking as James Stark put himself to bed. She tried not to pay attention. Everyone expected it. Graham, Mrs. Mortenson, even little Bill. She had come to expect it herself. She had come to… She shook herself. Were those footsteps she heard? She lifted herself up and listened. Light… No, not his footsteps. Likely not footsteps at all. She was imagining things. She closed her weary eyes and fell into a well of darkness.

*****

Sounds from the kitchen. The stove lid, ashes being raked, paper crumpled, wood, coal, lid back, ice breaking on the bucket… Nell sat up in a rush. It was morning. She did her hair and other essentials before going into the kitchen. James Stark stood by the stove, warming his hands over the fire. The boys came thundering down the stairs, followed by Pearl, holding Violet.

"I must see to Graham," Nell said. "He's not coughing yet, that may be a good sign."

"Let me," Pearl said. "Sure and I haven't seen my own husband for a fortnight. Surely it will be safe enough just for the look."

Nell took the baby, and Pearl went running into the parlor. A moment later, Pearl gave a demon's shriek, and they all ran in. Graham was lying on his sofa bed, head thrown back, his lint-blond hair and bony face looking the sickly mirror of his father.

"He's dead!" Pearl screamed. "He's dead!"

Arthur and John began to howl, but Bill simply stared.

"The children," Nell began, but Pearl interrupted.

"And this!" Pearl snatched the little brown bottle from Graham's bedside and held it up. She turned on Nell like an avenging angel. "How could you have left this with him?"

"I… I didn't!" Nell cried. "I took it with me… You saw me put it up in the kitchen cupboard…"

"Never did I! And how much did you give him?" Pearl hissed. "As much as you gave Patrick?"

Nell felt as if only her corsets were holding her up. The attack horrified her. "I never —"

"Everyone speaks of it. They all say that you quarreled. That he –"

"Pearl." James Stark said the one word, and she was quiet. "Bill, run and fetch Doc Peterson. Right away."

"Yes, sir." Bill was off like a shot.

"We will go into the kitchen."

James Stark marched the boys out of the room. Pearl's eyes blazed on Nell as she swept past. Nell stood where she was. What had happened? How had the bottle gotten from the kitchen to the parlor? Had Graham gotten up and managed to get past her, lying on the sitting room floor? Had she been so exhausted she did not awaken?

"Nell." James Stark's voice called her. "Come and have coffee."

She walked woodenly into the kitchen. "Where are the boys?"

"Upstairs, with Pearl." James Stark looked hard as iron, and Nell's legs gave way as she sat down. He poured her coffee. Dr. Peterson came in. "If you will follow me, Doctor."

The silent house seemed to engulf Nell. She tried to drink her coffee, but her hand shook, her stomach revolted. They would all believe that she had given him an overdose. That she had killed him. They believed she had killed Patrick, and if they had not before, they would now. Patrick, whom she'd loved. Oh, they had had terrible quarrels. But she had loved him. That was why they fought, because she loved him, and he was turning himself into a beast with drink… And then he had tried to stop. He threw himself into his work, but his hands shook, and his body ached, and his mind… And it only got worse. Just a small dose, that was all. Just a small dose she had given him and then another, for he was shaking all over by then, and crying with pain. And another, when the shrieking came, scaring the life out of the boys. And another, when the shaking rocked the whole bed. And another… And… And he had stopped shaking. And he had never moved again…

She looked up as the two men returned.

"Heart failure," Dr. Peterson said. "From fluid on the lungs." He shook his head. "I'm sorry for your loss, James. I'll stop in at Walworth's, if you'd like."

"I would appreciate that," James Stark replied, and escorted him out.

When he returned, Nell looked up at him, beseechingly. "It was heart failure?"

"No. But that is what he'll say, to spare us. It was laudanum." He leaned against the counter and stared down at it. "I am bitterly ashamed."

"No! I did not do it!"

"I know that." He looked out the window, at the brown street. "Oh, Nellie. You have found in this house a sorry refuge. A house of deceit and lust and lies. My grandchild is my child, Nell. Graham knew. He… colluded to spare Martha, and then to spare you. Or perhaps to spare himself?" He shook his head. "But whether he killed himself, in despair, or she killed him, I will never know."

"Pearl!"

"She got up in the middle of the night." Nell gasped, remembering that light footstep, and suddenly seeing Pearl's little white foot slipping out of James Stark's bed… Something twisted deep inside of her. It was all true, and she had never known… "'A pearl of great price.' Too great. It has cost me everything: my self-respect, my honor, my son…" He turned from the counter, his eyes wet. "I must go up and speak with her. I have placed a notice on the door of the shop. Would you shutter the windows, and then look after the boys?"

All that day, in the dark of shuttered windows and the silence bought by the notice "Death in the family." Nell watched the children, prepared food, received condolences, and thought furiously. What was she to do now? She could never marry James Stark now, and who was to say that he still wanted to marry her? Or ever had wanted to marry her? Her face was grim as she considered that he had tried to deflect attention from the truth of his liaison with one daughter-in-law by creating the illusion of desire for another daughter-in-law. And both of them murderesses, in desire, in act, in will, in result. Something he would never know, not for certain. Until, perhaps, sweet Pearl would find a need to be rid of him…

William and Patrick, with their wives, came by nightfall. Sitting at supper, everyone played their roles of grief: widow, father, brothers, sisters-in-law. Nell could barely eat. After supper, Nell retreated to her room, pleading exhaustion, but truly because if she stayed, she might scream the truth out: and no one would believe her. Instead, she packed her trunk, and the day after the funeral she and the boys went to the city, to Sioux Falls. She took in washing, she saved her pennies, she declined all help from James Stark. When she read in the newspaper that Pearl had died of blood poisoning two years later, she trembled for fear that James Stark would come for her. But he did not. She never heard from him again. She never went near Laskin again. Years later, when her sons came into their inheritance and farmed up there, she learned that James Stark had found a fourth wife, a young German woman who bore him three daughters: the first he had named Nell.

Wanted
John M. Floyd

"I know what happened, Bud," Eddie said. "I know she poisoned you."

As he spoke, thirteen-year-old Eddie Webber sat with his knees drawn up to his chest and his arms hugging his ankles, looking out at the rolling hills and muddy river north of the farm. Then he turned to look at the wooden marker sticking out of the still-fresh mound of dirt beside him. On the marker were the roughly carved words BUDDY — 1876 — BEST DOG EVER.

It was almost two days ago that he'd found his little dog's body, had literally tripped over it in the dark on his way to the outhouse after supper. Heartbroken, he had sprinted back to the house in tears to tell his pa, and the two of them had buried Buddy together, digging by the light of a lantern on top of the little rise behind the barn. The next morning Eddie had carved the words onto a board and sharpened one end and stuck it into the brown earth beside the grave.

The only one who hadn't cried was Thelma. She had hated Buddy, and besides, in the six months since Pa had married her, Eddie had never seen Thelma shed a tear over anything. He had also never seen her smile. Thelma's face, and her heart too, were as hard as the anvil the town blacksmith used for hammering horseshoes. Eddie honestly couldn't imagine what his pa saw in her, and sometimes he wondered if Pa knew either. She'd just shown up one day at the farm not long after Eddie's ma died of snakebite, and never left. Big Joe Webber was what everybody called "agreeable"; he didn't like quarreling with anybody about anything, including—apparently—who and whether he should remarry after the sudden death of his one true love.

"If I knew Pa would be okay," Eddie said to Buddy's grave, "I'd leave now, just pack some clothes and the money Aunt Edna gave me that time she visited, and head for the Dakota Territory. Charlie Stewart's uncle said they're hiring men and even teenagers up there, in a place called Deadwood, to help look for gold, and you know I'm not scared of hard work. But I'd hate to leave Pa with Thelma."

Eddie sniffled a little, partly because he missed his dog so much and partly because of his own miserable situation, and wiped his eyes with a shirtsleeve. "I'll talk to you again tomorrow, Bud," he said. "Maybe we can figure out what to do."

As he rose to his feet and dusted off the seat of his overalls, Eddie heard a bark, and for a second he thought Buddy had tried to answer him. Then he realized it was the yapping of Luke Johnson's big sheepdog, on the neighboring farm half a mile west. The wind usually blew from that direction.

When he'd trudged back to the house Eddie heard his stepmother's voice before he even got to the door. It was the same old complaint: there was never enough money, Thelma had to work too hard, Joe didn't work hard enough, the boy wasn't earning his keep, etc., etc. It looked like they might not even grow enough corn this year to keep the horses fed. At one point Eddie heard her say that what she really needed was for that outlaw Dorsey O'Neal to come riding through here one day. "I know what he looks like from them wanted posters nailed to every wall and tree in town," she ranted, "and if I saw him coming I'd grab that rifle right there and shoot him dead, and get the reward."

"That'd be fine with me," Eddie's pa's weary voice said. "We could use a new milk cow, and a new roof too, for that matter."

Eddie crept to one of the porch windows, peeked in, and saw Thelma glaring at his pa. "I said *I'd* get the reward," she reminded him. "And the first thing I'd do is leave you and that worthless kid a yours."

Eddie heard his father groan, saw him shift in his chair. "Don't talk like that, Thelma. Eddie's a good boy. And we'll get the farm back on its feet, I promise, as soon as—"

"Soon as what, Joe? Soon as you stop drinking?"

She had a point there, Eddie knew, and from the sudden silence he understood that his pa knew it too. Big Joe had acquired a fondness for liquor the week after Eddie's ma had opened the kitchen cupboard to get some flour and found a rattlesnake there instead, and he still drank way too much, after work hours. Never in the daytime, never out in the open, but he drank at night after Eddie was asleep, and it was usually obvious the following day. It was getting worse, too, and all of them knew you couldn't run a farm if you couldn't get out of bed till midmorning. But the very worst thing about the situation was that even though Eddie's ma's death was what had steered his pa toward the bottle, it was Thelma who kept him there. Eddie suspected she was a witch, or a devil's angel who'd somehow made good her escape from hell and landed here in west Texas.

One day the following week Eddie was working with his pa, patching a fence in the back pasture, when Eddie noticed a raw place on his father's right wrist. Eddie asked about it, and Pa said it was something Thelma had talked him into. She'd heard somewhere that if a night drinker is kept handcuffed to the bed while he's sleeping and can't wake up and get to a bottle, he'll eventually lose the urge. Since Joe's urge was strongest and his resolve was weakest during the wee hours, and since there'd been a pair of cuffs in a back closet because of his long-ago and short-lived stint as a lawman, Thelma had been handcuffing his right wrist to the bedpost beside his pillow every night and keeping the key in a dresser drawer on the other side of the room.

"But that's crazy," Eddie replied. "Dangerous, too. What if this outlaw everybody's talking about happens to come around, while you're chained up?"

"O'Neal? I doubt Dorsey O'Neal'd waste his time with poor farmers. Besides, the newspaper says he's up north."

"It's still a bad idea." Eddie knew this subject was embarrassing to both him and his pa, but he couldn't seem to keep quiet. "Why doesn't she just find and throw away the bottles you have in the house?"

"She says I'd just go into town and buy another one during the night." Suddenly Joe Webber looked infinitely sad. "And the thing is, I probably would."

Eddie said no more, but still thought the handcuff thing was stupid. It also reminded him of his own situation, trapped in his own way, seemingly unloved and unwanted in a place that was becoming more and more scary to him all the time. With his own eyes Eddie had seen Thelma bending over Buddy's food dish the day before his beloved dog had died—something he'd never seen her do before and something he hadn't told his father about—and afterward it was only logical to figure that some of the rat poison they kept in the shed had found its way into Buddy's supper scraps. And considering the look she always had in her eye anytime Eddie was around, he found himself wondering whether the same thing that happened to his pet might one day happen to its owner. Or to his pa. In Eddie's view, Thelma was capable of anything.

This thought was actually on Eddie's mind a few nights later, when he woke up after midnight with a stomachache—even though the reason was most probably the creek water he'd drunk the previous afternoon, during one of his rabbit hunts. Whatever the cause, a quick trip to the outhouse was in order, a trip made less appealing by the fact that a storm was coming. Eddie could hear the rumbles of thunder. He climbed out of bed, painfully aware of similar rumbles in his gut, snuck out the back door, hurried to the small privy, and turned his attention to gaining some relief.

While he was inside, he heard an especially loud clap of thunder—it almost deafened him — followed by strange crackling and popping noises. He tried to peek out at the house through the cracks in the privy wall, but the boards on that side were too tightly fitted. By the time he'd finished his business and thrown open the door, the main house was blanketed in smoke and belching flames from every door and window.

Eddie's first thought — a horrible thought — was of his father, handcuffed to his bedpost. Terrified, Eddie ran toward the inferno, but couldn't even get close. The heat was so intense it singed his eyebrows. It crossed his mind that the storm might help put out the fire — but there was no rain, at least not yet. Just wind and lightning and thunder.

And then he saw his stepmother. She was standing off to one side, her face painted yellow-orange by the roaring flames, her nightdress billowing and snapping in the wind.

"You!" she screamed, when she spotted him. "Did you do this? Did you set my house on fire?"

Eddie didn't even know how to respond — how do you reason with a crazy person? He just stared at her. Then he recovered, and shouted, "Where's my pa? Did you get him out?"

"I barely got myself out," she said, glaring at him. "You lit it, didn't you!"

Eddie looked again at the house. In a small voice he said, "I have to save him." And he was about to try, too, heat or not, when he saw Thelma's eyes look past him and grow even wider. And then both boy and woman were staring at a short, dirty, barrel-chested man in a tall hat who was standing there in the yard, watching the fire. The man turned slowly, backlit by flashes of lightning, and looked back at them.

"You shut your mouth, woman," he said calmly. "It was lightnin' started the fire — I saw it strike." To Eddie he said, "As for your pa, if he's in there, he's a cooked goose."

"Dorsey O'Neal," Thelma said, gawking. "It's you, isn't it. What are you doing here?"

O'Neal shrugged and spat a stream of tobacco. "I was planning to rob you, and I still will, if there's anything in that barn or shed worth stealing." He smiled. "I think I'll take you, too, though you sure ain't much to look at."

"What?!" she said.

O'Neal pointed to the corral. "Get out there and find you a horse. You're going with me."

Even in the flickering light of the flames Eddie could see the terror in her eyes. "No," she shouted, "no, look — take *him*. Take the boy."

O'Neal looked at Eddie, then back at her.

"He's strong," she was saying, babbling now. "You could sell him, across the border—"

Dorsey O'Neal stood there for a long moment, staring at her as if in deep thought. Fifty feet away, the house was burning to high heaven.

"Take him," she screamed. "Take him — no one here wants him."

"I swear," O'Neal said, "I thought I was mean and evil, but I don't believe I ever met nobody as evil as you." Having made that announcement, he took out his gun and shot her between the eyes. As Eddie gaped at him, he holstered the smoking pistol and said, "She was right, though, kid, you do need to come with me. You look fit enough. You might bring a good price, from certain folks I know down in—"

And then something strange happened: above the howling of the storm Eddie heard a THUNK like a heavy load dropped from a wagon, and O'Neal's tall hat seemed to collapse on top of his head, his mouth went slack, his eyes rolled, and he fell facefirst into the dirt.

Eddie's pa stood there, breathing hard and looking down at O'Neal. Big Joe Webber's long underwear was torn and blackened and his one wrist was still cuffed to a long, broken bedpost that he held in both hands like an axehandle. Then he looked up at Eddie and his face cleared and the two rushed into each other's arms. It was only after they disengaged that his pa saw Thelma lying there with her eyes and mouth open and a bullet hole in her forehead. Eddie expected him to cry out, but he just stared at her. Then they stumbled together to the shed, where he helped his pa saw through the handcuffs, find a length of rope, and bind the unconscious O'Neal's wrists behind him. The rain finally started up, too late to save the house, and within seconds all of them were soaked to the skin. Eddie saw his pa look down at O'Neil awhile, then use his bare foot to turn the outlaw face-up so he wouldn't drown in a puddle.

"What'll we do, Pa?" Eddie shouted, over the roaring of the storm.

Joe Webber, his blistered face calm now and streaming water, said, "Well, son, we'll bury your stepmother, and then, if I decide not to kill this fella myself, I guess we'll haul him into town in the wagon and claim the reward."

Eddie blinked. The reward?

"Thelma was right about that much," his pa said. "It'll be enough to build a new house and get us started again. And don't worry, ain't none of it going for liquor. What happened tonight's cured me a that." He looked down at his chafed wrist. "Who knows, maybe she was right about that part, too."

*****

Eddie never told his pa about planning to run off to the gold fields, and he never told him about Thelma's last words to Dorsey O'Neal, begging him to take Eddie with him instead of her. Some things were best left unsaid.

Eddie did go out every day to the little hill behind the barn, though, and talk to Buddy. He continued that for months, long after he and his pa had finished building their new house, and even though he knew in his heart that he was now way too old to be doing that kind of thing.

One late afternoon, almost a year after the deaths of his dog and his stepmother and nine months after the hanging of Dorsey O'Neal, Eddie sat there in the dry grass and told Buddy he was thinking of becoming a doctor. Somebody who could help sick folks, even those who are sick in the mind like his pa was for a while, and like he suspected Thelma had been too, in a different way, and after he told Buddy that and had risen to his feet, he again thought he heard a little bark in reply. He looked up and squinted in the direction of the Johnsons' farm. No wind today, not a breath of it. Even so, it must have been one of their dogs.

Eddie stuffed his hands into the pockets of his overalls and headed back to help his pa feed the horses.

It looked like even the corn crop would be good this year.

Killer Advice

Michael Cahlin

To say my dad didn't have much luck with wives is like saying the Minnesota Vikings didn't have much luck in Super Bowls. Each had been to the altar four times and each left a loser. Okay, my dad's four brides were the real losers being dead and all. I didn't realize he had murdered each one until much later.

Now maybe you can imagine your old man a murderer but I can't. And a serial killer? Please. Especially *my* dad. If you had asked me to describe him before the murders — though one he swears was an accident — I'd have said he was nothing special in every category save one. Otherwise he was Mr. Magoo in height, bald as a cantaloupe, with a Buddha-belly torturing tailored suits and a penchant for Italian silk neckties he wore even when he didn't have to.

His one preternatural claim to fame? My paterfamilias was an Olympian talker. Dad could strike up a conversation with a stranger in the next stall or spend twenty minutes giving pointers to a telephone pitch-person interrupting dinner because he didn't want to hurt the landsman's feelings.

Yeah, yeah, sounds like I don't like my old man. I do, kinda. Embarrassed by him, sure, but who isn't by their parents? But I respected him, the way you did Willie Loman and felt sorry for him at the same time because he couldn't help being a down on his luck loser who, if he made a five-dollar sale would boast it was fifty, spend a hundred celebrating, then unerringly lose the sale.

So discovering dear old daddy was a murdering mastermind, a genocidal genius, a cold-blooded serial killer was not like discovering Clark Kent was Superman. I mean, yank off Kent's cheaters and *ba-bing!* there's the Metropolis Marvel. It's more like discovering the homeless grifter at McDonald's was really Michael Jordan. Or that Elmer Fudd was the true prince of darkness. Or that weird guy in the next apartment was Hannibal Lector's mentor.

But don't let me sway you. You need to make your own decision because I can't for the life of me figure out why my old man has flown cross-country at this particular moment in time. He certainly didn't come just to see me and the grief counseling my brother believed he needed was baloney.

Let me bring you up to speed.

This is day four of my dad's West Coast trip. We're doing an Otis Redding — sittin' in the mornin' sun, watching the ships roll in — on Santa Monica Pier. Pops had just dropped the bombshell about his first wife, the one who overdosed on sleeping pills, and was waiting for me to say something. But my throat is dry. I have forgotten how to breathe and form words.

Why? Because until this very Kodak moment, when my father confessed to murdering his first wife, *my mother,* and anteing up a canceled airline ticket and a phony driver's license as proof, I believed I had killed her. Gotta say it's not every day a family member truly surprises you.

*****

"Danny, there's been a terrible tragedy."

The drama-drenched voicemail belonged to my brother's wife, a self-obsessed social media influencer, and, when she remembered, the mother of two, who — after her *Me, Two!* blog accidentally went viral with the movement — only cared about two things: what she thought about her newfound fame, and what you thought about it. I called her "Me-Two," just not to her face.

Me-Two's story — which you can read on her blog — purports wife number four, Mary, woke depressed and racked with pain from a nasty Lupus incursion. Dad and Mary had chatted briefly about how they planned to escape the blazing Boca sun, then Mary excused herself and left the room. Dad heard the toilet flush, the sound of water filling the bath, then nothing, followed by a sudden *bang.*

"It didn't sound like a gunshot," Me-Two quotes my father. "I thought she'd lost her balance. Sometimes she gets dizzy."

He knuckled the door and called her name. Entering, he found her slumped in the tub, blood pumping from a jagged hole turning the bathwater biblical though nary a drop stained the expensive Agrob Buchtal tile. Even in death, Me-Two observed, Mary was the consummate housekeeper.

I got the "inside scoop," the one Me-Two would have killed for, the day after I picked him up at LAX. Me-Two and Stevie had said things were really bad when they begged me not to attend the funeral so I could take Dad off their hands the moment it was over. But even forewarned, I was unprepared for the fragile, stooped-over, shriveled, defeated echo of my *old* man that deplaned aided by two stewardesses.

Knowing how much Dad loved to hobnob with the famous and monied, I planned daily adventures to Beverly Hills, Malibu, and Hollywood Hills. I figured we'd drive around, bond, and I'd convince him to take the grief recovery class my brother had paid for. At the very least, I'd hoped, spending time with him would take my mind off my own problems. Stupid, huh?

"She'd been in horrible pain for months, Danny," Dad said while tossing bread crumbs to pigeons the size of feral cats on the Santa Monica Pier. "Couldn't eat, couldn't sleep. Wouldn't let me out of her sight." Mimicking, "Mar-*tee*, I need you. Mar-*tee*, please don't go."

"Was it difficult to be with someone so needy?"

"Oh no, Danny! I know you boys didn't approve of her but I loved how much she needed me. Loved that I'd be able to help during whatever time she had left."

"Then why?"

"Because she loved me, too. She knew what I had gone through with Delores." (Wife two. Keep up.) "She didn't want me to go through that again."

"She killed herself because she didn't want *her* debilitating illness to inconvenience you?"

"Not exactly."

"She *is* dead, Dad."

He tilted his George Hamilton-bronzed face toward a glorious mid-morning sun. "I know. I was with her while she did it."

"Like a coach?"

"Like a friend, her best friend."

He leaned back on a bench dotted with a Rorschach of pigeon blots, knotted manicured fingers, and studied a man and a small boy in raggedy cutoffs fishing further down the pier.

"Do you remember our boat?" Dad said peering into the past. I nodded. His left arm held me close. I couldn't remember the last time that had happened. "Delores loved our boat. It was her father's you know." I knew. "He died before you and Stevie came to us." I knew that, too.

The little boy netted something and his joyous cries scattered the birds.

"You have no idea what it's like to watch someone you love and cherish, someone you carry in your heart, someone you'd kill for, suffer. In pain, every day. Bedridden, losing their memories, their body betraying them. And no matter what you do, in the end, it will not be enough. They're going to get sicker and die anyway."

I didn't know if he was still talking about Mary (wife four) or moved onto Delores (wife two). We'd been bouncing between them for the past few days so it was hard to tell. I delicately answered "No," selfishly thinking of my own failing marriage. I admit all this death talk had me entertaining dark fantasies about my soon to be ex. But turning those thoughts into action? No way could I do anything like that.

My father continued, "Who expected me to outlive Delores? I was older, in and out of hospitals so often I should have had a punch card for a freebie. Delores meanwhile, was never sick a day in her life. And good? She never questioned taking you boys in."

His voice drifted. His sadness, a presence between us. I waited, content to watch the boats until he wiped the tears from his face.

"Not many women would have stuck by me Danny, especially at the beginning. Your mother hounding me, calling my employers. Got me fired more times than I can count. I couldn't make a living, couldn't see you…" His harshly cologned hand gently bussed my cheek.

"Leaving you and little Stevie, knowing how unstable your mother was, nearly killed me." I knew that story, too. "I hired lawyers and wrote letters, but your mother was intractable. The courts were different back then." He said this contemptuously. He set his Starbucks on the bench, fished inside a rumbled paper bag he insisted on bringing, and withdrew a banded stack of yellowed envelopes thicker than a Stephen King novel. The postmarks dated back twenty-six years.

"I wrote every week. Missed you both so much. If it wasn't for Delores…"

"Mom said you wanted nothing to do with us."

"That's a goddamn lie!" So loud everyone in earshot swiveled our way.

"I know how she twisted things."

"Danny, your mother wasn't"—he was going for diplomacy—"well."

I wanted to scream. Who did he think lived with her between his departure and her death? Endured the beatings, the dramas, the drunkenness, the police, the men, the blackened looks from neighborhood kids forbidden to play with us? I knew perfectly well my mother wasn't Carol Brady.

"Towards the end," I started, careful to suppress my anger and not disturb his arm loosely nestled 'round my shoulders, "she was obsessed with how much money she'd inherit from your insurance policy if you died."

Even though he appeared ready to weep again, my father managed a merciless laugh. "She wouldn't have seen a dime! I told her as much in her lawyer's office."

"You saw her?" That was new.

"About a month before you boys came down."

Translation: a month before she died.

Subtext: a month before he murdered her.

"I had finally arranged a sitdown. But before either shyster could start their money meters, our eyes locked and, in a voice honey-dipped in contempt and disgust she said, 'Martin, the only way you'll ever see your sons is over my dead body.' Then she stormed out. I'll tell you, Danny, I've never seen chiselers speechless before but it wouldn't have mattered if they'd been shouting because I wasn't listening. I knew she was right. I'd never have my boys *ever*," his watery voice rose, then evaporated, "as long as she was alive."

"That's when you decided to kill her?"

He unwrapped the Dodgers warm-up jacket I'd made him tie around his waist and took his time shucking it on.

"Yes. Though I didn't start planning it until I received your letters."

"You know we didn't write those."

"Of course I did, son," he said comforting me. He withdrew a smaller stack of faded dog-eared letters. I recognized the looping script of my youth and even though I tried to stop it, I felt like a little boy again, trapped in the past.

As part of that legal settlement, we still weren't allowed to see our father, but we began getting his letters. Mom's version was that he refused to see us and it was her lawyers that forced him to write. That even though he was a lying, conniving, evil SOB more interested in money than the children he had abandoned—*she* felt it was important that we communicated. "He is, after all, your blood father," she spat like a gypsy curse.

Dad wrote the letters, mom intercepted them, wrote hateful responses, then Stevie and I recopied them. When they were up to scratch, she'd seal 'em, stamp 'em, treat herself to a drinky-poo, and, I'm sure, slap a hex on them before she mailed 'em.

I read a couple before their venom, undiminished by time, forced me to stop. "How could you keep these?" Flipping them back in the sack as if they had thorns.

"Because I knew one day, I'd tell you the truth. Though by now I thought you'd be a father."

Ignoring the dig, I just came out with it.

"So, how did you do it? How did you murder my mother?"

"Danny," he sparked, "it was easy."

Wife 1: My Mother

As I listened to my father, I couldn't help but admire him. Crazy, huh? But my life got so much better after my mother died, I've always felt guilty. My brother and I were jettisoned to a real home, with two real parents, neither of which drank, drugged or drubbed us. Sure, I was… challenging, but I know my life is catastrophically better today because of her death.

So, why did I think I had killed her?

My mother was in serious trouble months before her suicide, but I didn't know where to go or who to call. We didn't have Dr. Phil or Oprah in those days. We didn't know we were latchkey kids, or abused kids, or living in a dysfunctional family. Looking back, it's a wonder we survived though I suppose there's the rub—only two of us did.

Her drinking escalated. She shoveled in the pills. Afraid she might overdose, I began emptying chalky powder from each blue and yellow capsule. I thought I was saving her. Hah! I knew something was up the moment I pedaled my Schwinn onto our block and the porch light wasn't on. That my brother might have forgotten to switch on the light never crossed my mind.

I knew.

The police car in the driveway foretold her death. Inside, an officer, uncomfortable in a plastic-covered chair, confirmed my prediction. He tried to proffer an explanation, but I saved him the trouble.

"The pills." It wasn't a question.

That night, Stevie and I slept at a neighbor's. The next day, another cop and a seen-it-all clock-punching woman from social services radiating *eau de* Virginia Slims pulled me aside and explained that a nice couple wanted to adopt cute six-year-old Stevie but, barring a miracle, I would become a ward of the state. Between that, the funeral, and the guilt, I don't remember more than a sense of shock. But I clearly remember the day after the service, when the same social worker giddily confessed that in all her years, she'd never seen anything like this: my father's lawyers had called out of the blue, and upon hearing the news, Dad immediately agreed to take me and Stevie.

Except there was nothing miraculous about it. It was all part of my dad's murderous plan. I couldn't help but notice how easily he told me what had really happened. He was enjoying the conversation.

On the Thursday before my mother's "suicide," my father faked a heart attack. With two real ones to draw from, his performance was flawless. "Luckily," he and Delores were blocks from a hospital when it happened. A hospital not only airport-close *and* undergoing renovations, but one Dad had spent weeks reconning shift changes.

Clutching his bum ticker, Dad was admitted posthaste, strapped to an IV and, prescribed sedatives which he tongued. He waited for the overnight nurse to conduct a bed check, then he yanked out his IV, deliberately dotting the sheets and floor with blood. After changing into street clothes, he snuck out of the building, sprinted several blocks, flagged a Checker to the airport, and forty minutes later was munching pretzels on the red-eye to Kennedy under an assumed name. Pre 9/11, nobody bothered asking for his only premeditated prop: a fictitious driver's license.

He landed well before five, paid cash for the rental—the clerk barely glanced at my father's fake ID—and was across the street from where my mother, brother, and I were sleeping about seventy-five minutes later. His original and not very well thought-out plan was to follow my mother to work then either run her down or mug her.

But the best laid plans of mice and murderers often go awry. Dad watched as Stevie and I left for school. Then laid in wait for his ex. And waited. And waited. After an hour he freaked. On a strict timetable, he *had* to be on the 8:55 a.m. return flight or all was lost.

"I'll tell you, Danny," he said, polishing Versace sunglasses with his Armani necktie, "I didn't know what to do. I thought about cutting her brake cables but what if you or Stevie were with her? Smash a window? I was already afraid a neighbor clocked me prowling around. I was just about to call it off and hightail it back to the airport when the universe showed me how to kill her." His green eyes glowed.

"A drugstore delivery car drove up. Coffin black. Young kid took his sweet time getting to the door. Knocked, waited, then dropped a small bag inside the screen and left. Like he'd done it before. Like it was no big deal. Confident, I crossed the street and was about to knock when your mother scared the daylights outta me and opened the door! For a second, I thought she had recognized me. But the bitch was so out of it, she could barely stand."

He leaned closer. "She looked ghastly in a ratty turquoise teddy, her breasts falling out, stumbling, and weaving. I prayed anyone looking would think I was helping her. Wearing gloves I had palmed from the hospital, I stepped inside, dropped the package in her trembling hands, and closed the door. She didn't even look up. I could have been anybody."

He polished off his remaining Starbucks, but it wasn't enough to extinguish his disgust.

"She was slurring, 'I need my medicine.' Jesus, I hated her! I carried her to the bedroom but she wouldn't get back into bed until I brought water. When I did, she gobbled the pills. I waited until she passed out, then woke her. I told her she needed her medicine and watched her swallow another handful, and then another, and another. I found more bottles in her nightstand and helped her take those, too. I counted sixty and prayed that would be enough." His face flushed.

"While I waited, I peeked into your room. It was a pigsty, like the rest of the house. But I remember thinking, you'd be with me soon." He squeezed my shoulder.

"I checked her pulse as best I could, then darted out the back, hopped the fence, and tried not to skip to my rental." Looking at me, he added, "Your coffee's getting cold."

The next time your father confesses to killing your mother let me know what you say. I dumbly sipped and braced for the grand finale.

"The rest was cake. Drove back to the airport, dropped the Hertz in the lot, made my flight, had a celebratory drink, and landed in Miami fifteen minutes early. I cabbed near the hospital, made my way through the construction entrance, grabbed a used hospital gown from an unattended cart, stripped to my jockeys in a men's room, and buried my clothes in the bin. All I needed was one more break."

The restroom was near the area under construction. Dad's original plan was to pretend he had woken up confused in the middle of the night, didn't know where he was, and, in a dissociative fugue, meandered onto the construction site and passed out. Maybe that would have worked had Dad made it into the site unnoticed. But he didn't.

"I crashed into my doctor making rounds with a throng of students just as I exited." I could see he was reliving the thrill. "I panicked and dove into my dazed and confused act and they tranqued me on the spot. I woke up in my hospital bed. Some nurses were bawled out, but all in all, everything worked out just fine."

As did the rest of his plan.

That night, Dad practically had a real coronary fretting over the holes in his Master Plan. He was so stressed, he had to be sedated, which only solidified his story.

"By Saturday, I was sure I was going to jail," he said looking through me. "I waited all day for someone to say something, but nobody ever did. *Ever.*"

By Tuesday, Dad was feeling better. On Wednesday, "on a whim," he had Delores call their lawyer with instructions to contact my mother's lawyer and once again demand visitation rights.

Dad squeezed my arm. "You were on a flight to me three days later. I never regretted my decision or my actions."

Not knowing what to say, we moseyed up the Santa Monica Pier stopping at the Pacific Wheel you see on television, Dad telling me what Coney Island was like when he was a kid. A film crew was shooting a commercial. I couldn't tell if it was for sneakers, jeans, or a soft drink. Dad naturally struck up a conversation with the director and I half expected Marty to get a walk-on.

Back in my car, we motored up the coast to Malibu where I pointed out mudslide damage, the beach where *Gidget* movies were filmed, lied about where famous movie stars lived, then took an unmarked, mostly dirt road up a canyon. Dad marveled at the sprawling houses with massive decks carved into the mountains and said how he'd have to contact the owners and "do business." That he couldn't afford the light bulbs in these palaces, let alone the electric bill, didn't deter either of us—him from lying, me from nodding like I believed it.

We bantered about Los Angeles gridlock, Florida humidity, whether Pat Riley had another team rebuild in him, if the Marlins had a shot at a pennant, and how loud Stevie's cat, Milo, snored. Dumb stuff sons and fathers talk about when they don't want to talk about whatever it is they should be talking about.

I remember nothing about him from when I was a baby. He swears he sang *Clementine* and other songs to me every night. That he was the kind of father he never had. I was five when he left. Fifteen the next time I spied him at the bottom of an airport escalator. Little Stevie babbling about "meeting daddy and my new mommy." And though I was scared and angry and didn't know how to react or what to say to my estranged and heretofore vilified father–let alone our "new mommy" –I pointed them out, let go of his tiny hand, and watched my baby brother fly into their arms.

When we pulled around a very treacherous curve, Dad spotted our destination and stopped mid-sentence. The view was breathtaking. Mountains stretching out forever, monstrous homes, some with ranches, two with *ski lifts* to shuttle guests from the garage to the main house to the tennis courts to the pools. Plural. Whatever your concept of money, trust me, it's dwarfed in Los Angeles, the city of excess. We parked, rolled down our windows, and looked out into the distance. When the silence grew too much, Dad told me how he murdered the love of his life.

Wife 2: Delores

"It's very... peaceful here," he began, captivated by a woman stuffed into khaki jodhpurs putting a color coordinated mare through its routine across the way. "You know, when I was a kid I never believed in much. I enlisted the day I turned eighteen and I saw things, did things, that convinced me there was no God. Religion was just another lie like whiter whites or a perfect marriage. But after your mother died, when I was lying in my hospital bed waiting for someone to question me, waiting for the cops to bust in and take me to jail, just *waiting...* I finally had the sense there might be something out there, something bigger, I should believe in.

"The next few years were difficult. I lost the business—" I had no idea which one he was referring to. "You left for college, the car accident, another heart attack, but I never regretted my decision. Never regretted my actions. Hell, your mother would have killed herself sooner or later, maybe even taken one of you with her. I couldn't have stood that."

I swallowed saying she might have gotten better, found AA, religion, something. It seemed important that Dad keep on talking.

"My dream was always that the two of us would grow close. But you were so angry, so distant, I didn't know how to reach you. Delores said you'd come around, but you never did. I figured this was my punishment, my penance for what I had done. And I was fine with it, Danny, I honestly was. Please believe me. I never in a million years thought I'd be forced to do it again. And this one—" his body sagged, "—was much harder."

Whatever you could say about the parenting skills of Marty and Delores—and you could say a lot—there was no denying their love and devotion to each other. Now that I'm married or rather, now that I'm watching my marriage disintegrate, I see that. How she put up with his Mr. Big Shot-ism I'll never understand. But she was his anchor, his conscience, and secretly, I wished Julie and I were able to be more like them.

By then, I had escaped to the left coast. A struggling waiter desperate to change the "a" to an "r." My brother Stevie, meanwhile, became a wildly successful optometrist opening a high-end practice that made him wealthy even before he franchised. Delores handled the books for a small hardware chain, Dad was hawking something or other. They bought a better boat, moved into a trendier condo on a nicer golf course, dined out, traveled overseas.

"It was like a second honeymoon," he gushed, dipping a spare rib into hot sauce at a dive restaurant that initially didn't pass muster until he discovered the venerable downtown eatery had been frequented by the likes of Raymond Chandler and the Kardashians. "You kids were gone, we had money, I hadn't been sick in years." He signaled for another craft beer.

"Then, Delores complained of stomach cramps. They said it was menopause at first, then the flu, then a virus she picked up overseas. They ran test after test, nothing."

His face clouded. "By the time those asshole docs X-rayed her, the cancer was everywhere. She was already dead, only we didn't know it. They told us exploratory surgery might prolong her life a year, maybe three. And it was possible the cancer could go into remission, but it never did."

With Stevie footing the bills, they tried everything. Experimental drugs and treatments, including trips to Austria, Hamburg, Switzerland, New Mexico. Wherever there was an experimental cure, Dad was on it, Don Quixoting with cancer caretakers and survivors all over the globe, searching for hope.

"At the end, during her final lucid moments, she told me, 'I'll save you a place in heaven, Marty. It'll be okay.' Do you understand, Danny? She was dying, but she was comforting *me*." His voice broke.

"I begged the doctors to let her die. It's what she wanted. What we had discussed for me—because we both knew I was supposed to go first. When she lapsed into a coma," he checked over his shoulder, "I prayed the Lord would take her. But she refused to let go. After six days, I stopped petitioning God and instead, became His instrument. I put on the same latex gloves I'd used on your mother and turned up the morphine drip. I held her hand and stroked her forehead and talked to her until she was gone."

I don't know what my body language was saying but Dad exploded, "Don't you dare look at me like that! Don't judge me! Do you think the rich and privileged suffer like she did?"

My father appeared to shrink even further into himself.

"I don't know how long I waited. If someone had walked in, I was prepared to accept the consequences. But nobody did. I made sure there was no heartbeat, no pulse before I readjusted the drip. Then, I closed my eyes and slept the sleep of the righteous. When the morning nurse found her and woke me, I didn't need to pretend. The tears I cried were ones of joy."

He leaned into me. I put my arm around him, maybe for the first time. He sobbed like a baby and I let him. But something about his story troubled me. I didn't catch it until later. Did you?

Back in the car, I pointed out the county prison, the skyscraper used in the opening credits of *The Adventures of Superman*, and Phillippe's— home of the original French dip sandwich. We parked and meandered through Union Station which Dad instantly recognized from his favorite Hitchcock thriller, *Strangers on a Train*.

The next night, we ate at the Cheesecake Factory in Beverly Hills. He asked the usual questions about my life—was I happy, how was my marriage, had I heard from Julie, did I regret dropping out of law school, did I need any money. I lied as best as I could and, to his credit, he didn't push.

Somewhere around the second piece of cheesecake, a slab of chocolate death as dark as a dictator's heart, Dad waxed poetic about the beach, then Maui, traveling, camping, and finally, inexorably, he arrived at the accidental murder. I was all ears.

Wife 3: Shannon

Contrary to popular opinion, my father did not fall apart after Delores's death. Whereas the smart money (mine included) pegged him as one of those guys who loses his will to live and dies soon after his life's partner—Dad tricked us. Not only did he live, he thrived! Returned to work—killing it selling reverse mortgages—hung with his grandkids, even took a photography class, where he met Shannon, a wealthy widower of seven months.

Casting against type, Shannon loved camping, boating, fishing, whitewater rafting, gardening, and anything outdoors. Barely five feet in heels she didn't own, she had pixie no muss/no fuss sunflower hair, and an ingenuous Hollywood smile. Their attraction was mutual, instant, and according to my uncensored father, very sexual. Whether it was true love or pheromones steering both parties through transitional waters, I don't know and it doesn't matter.

Within weeks, they were inseparable. Soon after, they sailed on Dad's first fishing safari, then on to Martha's Vineyard, and drove to the Catskills, where they camped under the stars and went on day hikes.

Stevie said pops looked so healthy, they started calling him Man Mountain Marty. I had to agree. He seemed like a different person when we Skyped, far from the husk sitting across from me.

"I can't say I loved her, not like I loved Delores or even your mother at the beginning," he said between mouthfuls. "Shannon was more like a pal, more like someone who was always fun and said, 'Hey, let's just go, Marty.' So we did."

Snaring the last piece of death cake, he said, "I use to think you only had one shot at love but I was wrong. Turns out you get plenty of chances. And depending on what you're willing to do, you can make a life with a variety of different people. Is it the same life? No. Better in some cases, worse in others. What I'm saying is, if it doesn't work out with Julie, there'll be somebody else. You're what," he paused doing the math, "thirty-seven? Hell, I'd already killed my first wife at your age, you have plenty of time to find someone new—even start a family."

I just about tossed up dinner.

"Hey, that's a joke, son."

Maybe.

But what if it wasn't? What if my kindly old man wasn't a victim of circumstances but instead tailored circumstances to his victims?

"I fully expected to spend the rest of my days with Shannon," he continued after draining his decaf.

Shannon didn't make it through the honeymoon.

"We were sitting around deciding what worlds to conquer, when she turned and said, 'Marty, you wanna marry me?' I said yes, and we packed our camping gear and flew first-class to Tusayan, a tiny town in Arizona so quaint I might retire there. Chief Something or other married us in a beautiful ceremony though I didn't understand a word. That night, we slept under the stars where I made love better than my idol, John Wayne, ever did."

He winked. "Shannon had never been to the Grand Canyon and was so excited, we didn't check into our hotel. Just dropped off our bags and dashed."

The rest was so tragic, it's almost funny.

"You ever been to the Canyon?" I shook my head. "It's humbling. When you stop and think it's been around since the dawn of time and it'll be around long after we're gone…" He huffed a cleansing breath. "Man is so small."

A vacant look wiggled across his wrinkled face as the events replayed inside his head.

"She wanted this certain pose. Her arms spread wide, like the most spectacular gorge in the world was all hers. I had to lie on the ground and angle my iPhone to get the right perspective. Made me queasy watching through the viewfinder. 'Careful,' I said. 'No worries,' she replied, waving and laughing while I snapped shots. Then we exchanged places. After a few seconds I'd had enough but Shannon skipped to me like a little girl. 'One more, Marty,' she sang and handed me her glasses. Looking back, I realize how stupid that was—but we were on our honeymoon, having fun. You just don't think—" He paused long enough to sign the credit card slip.

"It happened in slow motion. I remember kids yelling. People talking. Someone smoking though you're not supposed to. While I was refocusing, Shannon had moved back a couple of steps. A woman behind me said, 'Harvela, look how close she is to the edge. I could never do that.' As soon as she came into focus, I shouted, 'Shanny, move in!' and waved my arm for her to come closer," his arm doing it now, "but nobody remembers that. She must've thought I wanted her to step back because she did and tripped. The same woman screamed. I raced to the lip of the cliff, threw myself on the ground because I was afraid to stand. She was still falling but I couldn't hear her scream."

Dad crunched the remaining ice in his glass.

"They had to airlift her body by helicopter. Made the local news but not national. The park police told me this happened all the time. So many, there's a book: *Over the Edge: Death in the Grand Canyon.* Plenty of witnesses saw what happened. There was never any question of foul play, Danny, because there wasn't any. It was just one of those things."

Maybe, but I had my doubts. Don't you?

What if Shannon wasn't an accident? What if, like murders one and two, number three was premeditated down to finding that book *before* his trip and waiting for witnesses at the canyon's edge *before* they posed for pictures? My head hurt. One scenario, he's a kindly, old, potbellied geezer. The other, a *very* scary force to be reckoned with. Which Dad was he? I didn't know but I was determined to find out.

*****

The following day, we cruised Hollywood Boulevard. I pointed out Musso & Frank, a timeless bistro featured in *Swingers*, *Ocean's Eleven*, and *Mad Men*. I hadn't planned on stopping at Grauman's Chinese Theater until an SUV cut me off smack-dab in front of the cement footprints.

Unlike my father, I didn't get heavenly signs from the Big Shooter, but even I understood this one. When Dad saw it too, he rocketed out of the car. When I caught up with him, the consummate salesman had taken hold and was holding court, chattering and snapping selfies with tourists from Boise and Wichita. I lost him again when a bus of Asian tourists unloaded. When I saw him next, salesman Dad had vanished, replaced by small, sad Dad staring at the five-pointed terrazzo-and-brass stars embedded in the sidewalk and weeping.

"Shannon would have loved this," spreading his arms like the snapshot that cost wife three her life, "the shops, the people. We talked about visiting, but…"

That night, we stayed in, ordered pizza, ate popcorn, and sometime during SportsCenter, my father began his final and most recent tale.

Wife 4: Mary

They met at a bereavement class. Mary had just buried her husband of forty-seven years. "The last thing I expected was to meet someone and fall in love, Danny."

I didn't believe him. Do you?

Over several weeks, the group met with a shrink, dealt with survivor's guilt, and shared meals. As I was discovering, oldsters loved eating. The attraction started slowly—she more into my father than he was into her. At least, that's how he tells it.

"I knew she was needy and grieving, I was too, but she was also experiencing the excitement of having sex with another man, Danny," batting a knowing man-to-man look my way. "She was a virgin when she married and remained a faithful wife. It's hard to explain until it happens to you but when you lose a mate, you're so hurt yet so happy it wasn't you, you want to celebrate life. Sex is a great way to do that. I knew what she was doing and I let her do it."

If Shannon had been the antithesis of a Marty-mate, Mary was the poster girl. Professionally-styled hair, polished nails and toes (matching, of course), and an impeccable dresser despite a lifelong quest to lose the ten pounds she never could. Before you knew it, they were jetting to Atlantic City, then Paris and Madrid.

Unlike Shannon, Dad waited a whole five months before getting hitched and moving into her elegant condo overlooking a members-only gated golf course in Boca Raton. While Dad played the market, Mary's money came from jewelry. She and her two daughters owned a ritzy brick-and-mortar catering to—if you can believe it—ostentatious Instagrammers and YouTubers.

Stevie and I were ecstatic for Dad. Figured our old man had a few more ticks on the clock and after all he'd been through, he deserved to be happy. You'd think by now we'd be tired of being wrong.

You know the rest. But I wanted—no, I *needed*—more. So after he retired to his bedroom, I called my brother hoping for answers and tried to hide my disappointment when Me-Two answered.

"You can't send him back. Danny! It's barely been a week."

"That's not why I'm calling. Is Stevie there?"

"If you read my blog, you'd know *Stephen* is in Maui for his annual franchise convention. I'm joining him in the morning, so you'll need to keep Marty until we return."

"You're taking the kids?"

"Are you crazy? It's the middle of their school year. My mother's here."

"Tell Jackie Dad and I said hello."

I could hear gears grinding in Me-Two's head. "Did you know Marty asked her out?"

I admit it didn't surprise me.

"Right around when he met Shannon. Jesus, that would have been all I needed! Jackie really dodged a bullet."

I changed the subject.

"Did you or the cops think…"

"Marty killed Shannon? Sure. The husband is always a person of interest in these matters," she replied matter-of-factly. "You'd know that *if* you read my blog."

"But Dad was cleared, right?" Unable to weed the plea in my voice.

"Mostly."

"I don't understand. And don't direct me to your damned blog."

Me-Two hid her hurt between a huffed breath and an excessive pause. "The eldest daughter…"

"The pretty one?"

"Nancy. The one obsessed with true-life murder shows. She's convinced her mother would never take her own life."

Instead of *Isn't that what every child thinks*, I asked, "And the other daughter, whatshername?"

"Ellen said her mom was depressed and talked about how tired she was."

"Does Nancy have any concrete reason to believe… what she does?"

"My blog, Danny, but yes. Nancy says her mother hated taking baths. Didn't enjoy sitting in dirty water. And on the rare occasion she was forced to sit in a tub, she would never ever sit with her back to the faucet. Her mom hated that."

The toilet flushed behind my bedroom door. When Dad didn't come out, I said, "In your blog, you reported the blood from the gunshot smeared the wall and drained into the tub, missing the tiled floor."

"So you do read it!"

"If Mary was a lefty, that lines up."

"And, if she's not?"

I didn't answer. Instead, I asked for the investigating detective's contact info.

Me-Two cleared her throat. "That's also strange."

"How so?"

"After clearing the case, he vanished. And before you ask, I checked with his captain. The detective was retiring. This was his last case. Sold his house, cleaned out his bank accounts, and moved away."

Feeling my stomach drop, I said, "That's more than strange."

"Not to the captain. Says it happens more than you'd think."

Like accidentally falling to your death in the Grand Canyon. But I kept that to myself.

"Have you spoken to the detective since he left?" But I knew the answer.

"Just email. The captain, too."

"Can you text me his email and phone if you have it? I'd like to talk to him."

I heard the clicking sounds of a text and then a ding on my phone.

"Anything else, Danny? I need to pack."

"Kiss my brother and the kids. *Oh!* Do you know where the investigating detective moved?"

"Small town out west. Had a funny name. Tucson. Tuscany…"

"Tusayan."

"How did you know?"

I hung up without answering. My father was staring right at me. Not the bumbling caricature version but the murderous carnivore.

"Just my luck, the goddamn detective was retiring and *had* to close his last case," he started.

"Mary wasn't a lefty, was she, Dad?"

"I told her from the beginning, I didn't sign up for sickness."

"So you killed her?"

He snorted. "I wasn't going to waste her money on medical bills. What was the point? Her daughters were already getting the lion's share of her inheritance. I was just protecting what was mine. You can understand that, can't you, son?"

I shook my head. "And Shannon?" I whispered.

Rage twisted his face. "She *lied* to me! Said she had money. Not to worry, we'd be fine." He raised both hands like an executioner. "She had less than me! Serves me right for not doing my due diligence."

His next words chilled me to the bone.

"I won't make that goddamn mistake again."

I waited until he calmed down and asked another question I feared I knew the answer.

"Where's the detective, Dad? How did you steal his money, his pension?"

From his Italian wallet, the man whose blood runs in my veins produced a driver's license with the flourish of a Vegas magician. An Arizona driver's license. All I saw was "Detective" before my eyes started swimming.

"People are idiots," my faux-detective father said. "Nobody pays attention, especially to seniors. They barely see us. Can't wait to dismiss us." He rose to his full height and before my eyes, he *Keyser Sözed* into the hunched-over, doddering figure I saw deplane at LAX.

"What happened to Shannon?" he said in a hollow, confused voice. "Is she all right?"

"I just moved here and lost my d-d-driver's license? Can you help me?"

"What? My Delores d-d-died in her sleep?"

"Of course, I-I-I want m-m-my sons."

With Oscar aplomb, his confused mien and crocodile tears ended as abruptly as snapping off a switch. Seemingly in no rush for my response, Dad examined the framed photos on my wall, stopping at a print of Ali punishing Frazier. It took me another few seconds to figure out what he was waiting for.

"Dad, why are you here?"

"Finally."

"You're obviously not grieving."

"True."

"Then why?" I said, truly perplexed. What about you? Did you figure it out?

In his hands was a picture of my wife.

"I thought it was obvious," he said, turning the frame facedown. "To help you, son."

Visions of Reality
Kevin R. Tipple

"Look, John, I just want you to shelve the product." Mr. Phillpots, the store manager, pointed with his black pen, jabbing the air for emphasis as he added, "A book is a book. Nothing more. No deep meanings. Just get them out there. Got it?"

"Books aren't a product like a sack of potatoes, Mr. Phillpots. They mean much more. All books aren't equal. Some of that stuff is just trash."

This was a losing proposition because the man had no soul. How do you explain such a concept to a non-book lover? It was hopeless, and instead of being a good and loyal yes man, I had tilted at the windmill again.

In annoyance, Phillpots tossed the pen down on the desk and rocked back in his expensive orthopedic chair. A chair that he wouldn't need if he actually did something useful and worked the sales floor like the rest of us. The money saved could have been used to fix the aging air conditioning system that was losing the ongoing war with the brutal Texas summer heat. After staring at me for what seemed forever, he started shaking his head like I was a bad dog that had made a mess on the carpet.

"Listen, I know you've been having," his pudgy fingers made the obligatory quotation marks, "some emotional problems lately." He paused for a moment, his beady little eyes gauging my reaction. My face burned in embarrassment and I shifted slightly in the chair. Phillpots lowered his voice in an attempt to be comforting and supportive; reminding me of how my calls to the employee hotline had been handled. "It's okay, really. I've thought for a long time you needed help. I'm very glad you're getting it. So, let's make this simple." He paused and then did that stupid little nod he always did right before he issued one of his edicts. "While you're here at work, I just want you to do what you're told. Just put the product on the shelf. Don't think about it. The books aren't alive or anything. They are just product. They can't hurt you at all. All you have to do is put the books on the shelf. Just do it."

The room spun and then steadied shakily as I realized he knew about me seeing the doctor. He probably knew all about the dreams and everything else. My life was not my own or private.

When the dreams started I tried to ignore them. That just made everything worse. They got more and more vivid, so real that it was as if I was living them. Then something happened and I started seeing things when I was awake—or, at least, when I thought I was awake. I wasn't sure anymore when I was awake and when I was asleep. Everyone else swore they didn't see what I did.

Finally, my primary doctor had insurance approval and sent me to a therapist. I didn't get better. I just quit talking to people about what I saw. They all thought I was crazy. Why give them proof?

Everything was supposed to be covered by patient/doctor confidentiality. If Phillpots knew, who else did? It would have been cheaper to advertise my mental state in the paper.

"Well?" he asked.

Oh, great. Not only was I classified as a nut job in his mind and no doubt by now in the employee records, but now he also knew I hadn't been listening. Playing for time, I shrugged.

"Well, okay then."

Phillpots shifted through his papers, picked up his pen, and went back to work. After about half a minute or so, he stopped and stared at me. He blinked twice as if he thought his beady little eyes were lying to him. He pulled off his glasses and leaned forward, being sure to make eye contact just like the employee manual said on page nine. His voice was angry calm but one could hear the traces of New England in it which always came through when he was stressed.

Moving to Texas had been a culture shock in more ways than one for him. I wasn't sure if it was because Texas wasn't as it was portrayed in the media, or that those of us who were native Texans saw the world differently than a transplanted Yankee. Sometimes I felt a little sorry for him. Those moments were fleeting and far between, as I had been called into his office way too often since he took over seven weeks ago. The man certainly did like to hear himself talk.

"So, John, go out there and shelve Romance and Horror. Alphabetize them while you're at it. You're one of the few people I've got who can read and knows the alphabet. Such a rarity here. Remember to police and face out any title that has four copies or more. Not three. Four." He tried for a half-smile that once again reminded me of a constipated rat with a load of cheese. "Make it look good out there."

I stiffened in my seat and swallowed hard. He knew how I felt about those books. There was something wrong with them. They had a power over me. I gulped for air and tried to speak, but he wasn't going to give me the chance.

"Do it or quit," boomed Phillpots. "Get out of here and decide while you work."

Quitting wasn't an option. I nodded and got myself together enough to rise from the chair and stumble out of his office, pulling the door shut behind me. Kathy was waiting outside in the short hallway. She smirked at me while I moved by her. I wondered how much she had overheard and then realized it really didn't matter because she did all the records for him.

Horror and Romance—the twin seducers—and I had to shelve them. It was as if those books spoke to me, pulling me in. The therapist said there was a simple explanation. I was disassociating from the real world or some such nonsense. The answer was, of course, medication. Take the little happy pill and all would be fine. I hadn't noticed any difference. Maybe I needed the large-sized happy pill.

I saw the knowing smiles and smirks as I entered the stockroom. Jennifer beckoned me over while she placed the final few books on a fully loaded handcart. This was the bubble-headed idiot who wanted to be store manager.

She was extremely proud, and had so often said that since she had her business management degree, she didn't have to read anymore. As assistant manager, Jennifer had big plans for our little store, which she had made really clear in the few weeks since Phillpots had hired her a month ago. Rumor was that we were going to start acting the same as the slowly dying mega chain. Plans were being made for the obligatory coffee bar. The weekly singles' night had started. Jennifer had made sure to create, as she put it, "an encompassing and enriching web presence" and had done so on one of the social networking sites because "it was hip, it was cool." The books didn't matter to her, either, though they were somewhat more important than the staff.

"Let's get these out first, John." Then, with a wink and a smile she added, "See, it's loaded up with all the ones you enjoy."

My palms were already sweating before I even touched the handle and felt the charge. I yanked my hands back, wiping them off on my pants before finally gripping the burning cold handle. Time slowed to nothing while I stood there staring at the cover of the top book. It depicted a naked white skull that floated above a pulsing sea of flame. A big spider perched in the empty socket of the right eye. It waved a large hairy leg in greeting.

I shook my head and the leg stopped in mid-wave. The feeling slowly passed and I realized Jennifer was talking to me.

"Don't just stand there, John. Get going. Shelve those and come back for more."

It was like I was wading through molasses as I moved by her, heading for the sales floor, leaving her to snicker some more behind my back. It seemed to take forever before the backroom doors flapped and I was spit out into the store.

Weak in the knees, I pushed the little metal handcart ahead of me like a boulder I had to roll uphill. Fiction, and all its evil connotations, sat buried in the dark back corner of the store, which somehow seemed appropriate. I much preferred my brightly lighted Self-Help/Psychology section up front by the large windows and adjacent to Gardening and Outdoors. I stole a backward glance at the light as I passed the always musty World History section and headed deeper into the gloom.

I tried to figure out exactly where I was to shelve. Jennifer had recently rearranged the sections all across the store for no discernable reason. The only outcome seemed to be frustrated customers and employees. In her wisdom, she still hadn't moved the signs, saying customers "liked adventure." Most of our customers were unemployed guys and frazzled and exhausted moms with loud out of control kids. Both groups often looked as if they had been out in the wilderness for months. I figured they were adventured out.

I made a turn and found myself in the Romance section. Lurid covers with the typical shirtless male saving the scantily clad beautiful damsel in distress abounded on every shelf. I tried to avert my eyes when a book jumped off a shelf and soundlessly landed on the carpeted floor in front of me. Face down, it waited for me. I felt a puff of wind and could smell flowers, then the sensations were gone. The book quivered and lay still again, setting the trap for me.

I didn't have a choice. I swallowed hard and picked it up. I turned it over in my hands and the cover came alive. A stunningly beautiful red-haired woman in a clingy, low-cut white dress held the reins of a black stallion. Her emerald eyes sparkled while the horse pawed the ground. Spanish moss swung heavy and thick in the trees behind her. The figure shifted a little as a breeze fluttered her gown alluringly. She held the reins out to me while a horn sounded in the distance. "Come, my love," she said from beneath a cloudless sky, "they travel without us." I knew it would be so easy to give in.

It felt so real. I knew logically it wasn't, but I felt that I was right there with her. The temptation was there and it was all I could do to place the book gently back on the shelf.

She blew a kiss as I turned away. Two of the overhead lights blinked out and it grew even darker with every step I took down the aisle. I headed for the back corner of the store, knowing that Jennifer had to have put Horror there. When I turned another shelving corner, I finally came face to face with the Horror section.

Directly in front of me a large hardback book dominated a shelf. The cover featured a huge black castle that reeked of menace. A green light blazed upward through the windows and through the cracked stonework turrets. One red eye, from some sort of large winged creature in the air above the castle, stared out at me.

Suddenly, the last two of the overhead lights flickered and went out. The rear of the store plunged into darkness and the sound of the air conditioning died away. The red eye brightened and became a blinding beam in my face as something screamed.

*****

At the front of the store, registers whirred to a stop. Sales disappeared from screens and customers and staff milled about in confusion.

After several minutes, the overhead lights came back on. Screens flashed, and the registers chirped and then came back to life. There were a few snickers from relieved customers who moved back into some semblance of orderly checkout lines.

The restored calm was shattered by the scream. It rose in pitch and climbed swiftly into an earsplitting shriek. It cracked and wavered to a stop as if to gather breath. It quickly began anew with fury. Even Mr. Phillpots, safely tucked away in his office to avoid dealing with actual customers, came running out onto the sales floor.

This was a situation he was actually going to have to handle, and he knew it. The daily power outages were playing havoc with everything in the store, but this sounded like a real problem. His shoes squeaked with every step he took. It soon became clear that something had happened back in Fiction.

"That damn John," he muttered to himself. "What did he do now?"

For once, all the lights were working, and for Mr. Phillpots it was the worst possible time. John lay on his back with his arms outflung. His hair stood straight out from his head and smoked a little in the slight breeze from the air conditioning vent. His eyes had rolled back in his head with only the whites showing, while his mouth hung open slack-jawed.

A whiff of something dank rose from John's open mouth as Mr. Phillpots knelt next to his former employee. It was obvious that John was dead, but Mr. Phillpots checked for a pulse anyway. He jerked his hand back. He looked at his hand and his fingertips were slightly pink. John was colder than an ice cube, a burning cold that he had never felt before even back home in New England, and it felt like the cold had seared into him. There wasn't a pulse at all, and Mr. Phillpots was acutely aware that not only did his fingertips hurt, he could also feel the blood in his body moving with the very beat of his agitated heart. Slowly he stood up. For a second or two, he thought he heard someone snicker low and deep, but nobody around him was smiling.

"Someone get a blanket and call an ambulance." Mr. Phillpots turned away from the body toward the customers and moved smoothly into damage control mode. "Folks, we're sorry for the inconvenience. Nothing to see here, so please move along."

He gestured and then waved his arms a little harder trying to shoo the small crowd of customers back. Several had pulled out cell phones and were taking pictures, and probably video, and doing nothing at all to help. Like the vultures they were, they weren't about to move for anything unless he could come up with an incentive. At least with this nonsense happening in the middle of the week, a cash incentive wouldn't cost that much.

"Folks, as a thank-you for shopping with us today, we'll take an extra ten percent off of our already low prices. Our little way of saying thank you and we apologize for the inconvenience." With a practiced smile of sincerity he added, "So, please go ahead and shop all you want, and we'll have this matter cleared up shortly."

There were appreciative nods and smiles, and some of the people began to move away. Others crowded closer, and Mr. Phillpots moved aside as one man stepped over an outflung arm to get a book off the shelf. Another squatted next to a leg and pulled the book he wanted off a low shelf. They went about their business while Mr. Phillpots stood there and wondered where Jennifer was and why the ambulance still hadn't shown up. Like everyone else, he was oblivious to the fact that the cover of the hardback, which rested just an inch or so from John's outstretched fingers, had changed slightly.

Everything was the same except for the small figure clutched in the talons of the winged creature. Depending on how you looked at it, it seemed as if the familiar figure fought in vain to get free.

Wave To Me

Martin Zeigler

Vernon pulls out his cell, thumbs the speed dial, listens through the rings. He knows she's there, knows she's looking at her own cell right now, at the caller id, trying to decide: should she take it, should she take it?

Vernon, of course, wants her to. The sweet taste of victory depends on it. Same time, he finds himself thinking: *I were her, I'd let it ring.*

And for a second or two it seems Melanie's leaning that way. But on the seventh ring she picks up.

"Vern," she says. "Honey."

A slight hesitation on the *honey*, Vernon notices, but he gives her extra points anyway, for including the word when she doesn't have to.

"Hey, babe," he says. "How's it going?"

"Going *okay*."

He likes her inflection on the *okay*, as if things really are okay. Come to think of it, from her side of things they probably are, but not in the way she's pretending to get across.

"Where you at?" he asks, as if he doesn't know.

"Didn't you get my text?"

"Text?"

"About going shopping?"

"Oh, yeah. Yeah, I did," Vernon says, sounding as breezy as possible. "What I mean is, what *store* are you at?"

"Oh. Well, uh, right now I'm just walking through the mall. Looking for sales."

Vernon follows Melanie with his binoculars as she slides open the glass door of the fifth floor apartment and steps out onto the balcony.

"You know me and sales," she adds.

Vernon chuckles knowingly. "Yes, I sure do. Find anything nice yet?"

"Sure. A couple things."

"Like what?" Vernon asks in a tone he hopes sounds bright and inquisitive.

Cell phone to her ear, Melanie begins pacing the small wedge of balcony not taken up by the glass deck table and the mission-control-sized barbecue grill. "Oh, you know," she says, "the usual things — dresses, tops, shoes...*you* know."

"What kind of shoes?" he asks, playing the part of the supportive husband who champions his wife's interests.

From out of the shadow of the overhead balcony she emerges into the late afternoon sunlight. She's put her hair up, Vernon notices, the way she used to put it up when they went to someplace fancy. And she's wearing a dress he's never seen before, a white number with pastel stripes that reminds him of a dress she wore ages ago when they first started going together. And for an instant she smiles the kind of smile that drove him crazy enough to propose to her — a smile that, along with the do and the dress, is now clearly not meant for him.

As for the shoes he's asking about, he couldn't care less.

"Vern, since when have you taken an interest in my shoes?"

"Hey, I love your shoes. But what I'm really interested in is your tops."

It just comes out. Vernon certainly didn't plan on saying this. But now that he thinks about it, it's a nice touch, the playfully suggestive remark on the part of the amorous spouse.

Too bad *his* amorous spouse doesn't think likewise. Even through his binoculars he can see her roll her eyes as she attempts her idea of a gentle reproach. "Oh, Vern."

"Hey, babe, you know me. I can't help it. So what kind of tops *did* you buy?"

"Actually, I'm...uh...still looking."

"Uh huh."

"Haven't bought anything yet," she says from the porch railing.

Vernon nods to himself. *Hey, at least that part's honest. That's a step up.*

✶✶✶✶✶

The sticky note. How long ago was it when Vernon found that yellow slip of paper on the dining room table? Two years? Five? A decade?

Honey,

Thought I'd go out and pick up some nice

things for our new home.

Back in a couple hours.

Love,

Mel

It was early in their marriage, put it that way, though he can no longer even place *that* date. It's buried deep in his brain somewhere along with all those dates thrown at him in high school history. His wedding date versus the firing on Fort Sumter? All the same to him now.

But he still remembers that note, and how reading the words "new home" had brought to mind an image of a solid foundation, a rock, the two of them growing old together in the wonderful bungalow they'd just closed on. And he remembers hoping that in writing those words, Melanie must have felt the same way.

But then there were the other words on that sticky note — the "couple hours", the "nice things" — and unfortunately Vernon remembers those, too — the "couple hours" that stretched until way past two in the morning and the "nice things" that turned out to be nothing when Melanie finally stepped through the front door.

✶✶✶✶✶

Now, tracking Melanie's every move from a parking garage, Vernon says, "Hey, it's still early, babe. What say I drive out there to the mall and meet you somewhere for dinner? Wouldn't that be a kick? You name the place."

"Dinner?" Melanie says — a bit nervously it seems to him, but maybe he's just imagining it.

"Nothing fancy. Something quick. And afterward you can go on with your shopping."

"Vernon, you shouldn't...uh...I mean, you don't have to drive all this way."

Yep, she's nervous, all right.

"Vernon, honey, why — why don't you go somewhere closer? You always wanted to try out that new burger place."

"Mmm...that does sound good."

"There you go," she says.

She's smiling again, and he can almost detect a glint of relief in her eyes.

He can't see the guy's face, though. His back is to him as he works the grill. And even when the guy turns to face Melanie it's difficult to gauge his expression, but Vernon imagines he's smiling right back at her. And who wouldn't?

Vernon allows her a second or two of comfort and security before announcing, "Hey, babe, you know what? To hell with the burger joint. I can always do that. As you say, it's close by. A food court at a mall sounds so much better right now."

"But—"

"Yeah, I know. A bit of a drive, but I'll be careful."

He takes advantage of her loss for words by adding, with a teasing lilt, "Who knows? Maybe I'll do a little shopping myself while I'm there. I've been known to do that once or twice."

He sees her smile invert itself, watches her as she shrugs helplessly to her beau at the grill, who shrugs in the same way right back. He sympathizes, apparently.

"You know what, honey?" she says at last. "I'm — I'm really not all that hungry."

The guy sets a plate of barbecued ribs down on the deck table alongside a bowl of what looks like potato salad. Melanie slides a chair back and takes a seat. Mr. Ribs does likewise. Vernon can both see the sliding and hear it.

"What was that?" he asks.

"What was what?"

"Thought I heard something. Chairs scraping or something."

"Oh? Oh, well, because I'm right here next to a café. An outdoor café. I...uh...just stepped outside to get some fresh air. In fact, now that I'm here I think I'll just drop in and grab a quick bite — an apple or small salad or whatever. I'm not that hungry, like I said, but you know, just to tide me over. So why don't I call you—"

"Don't move a muscle, babe. Don't touch a single lettuce leaf. I'm coming to join you. I'm heading out the door as we speak."

"Vernon! No!"

Though he's been expecting, maybe even hoping for this kind of outburst at some point, it still startles him. It even seems to take *her* by surprise as she utters a corrective cough and tries again. "I mean...."

She casts a desperate glance in Sir Ribs's direction, and Vernon shifts his binoculars to see what kind of guidance he has to offer. Taking in his full profile now, Vernon can definitely understand what she sees in him. Sturdy build, smart dresser. Not a jeans and t-shirt kind of guy, but more slacks and rolled-up shirt-sleeves. Graying at the temples but not flabbing out anywhere. Solid nose and chin.

And the strong silent type, because as far as Vernon can tell, he isn't saying a word, not even now in her hour of need. But that silence seems to be enough as far as Melanie is concerned. Just looking at him must have settled her down, because now, in a more composed tone, she says over the phone, "Please, honey, you know how sometimes you like to go out and do things on your own? Well, that's all I want to do. Just spend an evening by myself shopping at my leisure. You understand, don't you?"

"Uh, sure," Vernon says.

"Good. So how about us doing the restaurant scene some other time? Next week — or actually the week after would work better for me. Make it the end of the week. Friday or Saturday. Or Sunday. How's Sunday sound? Honey?"

"Yeah, sure. Fine," Vernon says with a pinch of disappointment and a dash of understanding. "I'd like that."

"Good. I'd like that, too. So I'll see you when I get home. Okay?"

"Okay."

"Bye now."

"I love you," Vernon says.

"I love you, too," Melanie says, as if reading the line.

"No, I mean I really, really, really love you."

Melanie holds her phone at arm's length and shakes her head in frustration at the man across the table as he dishes out a generous portion of ribs onto her plate.

"I love you too," she says, bringing the phone up to her mouth like a walkie-talkie. "Now I really have to—"

"You mean that, babe?" Vernon asks, trying to sound as if he cares one way or the other.

He knows how anxious she must be to eat dinner alone with her latest man, how impatient she must be for the dessert afterward. Her appetite takes on many forms, after all. What would this be since that Night of the Disappearing Nice Things For The Home? Number Eighteen? Number Thirty-seven? Number Three thousand four hundred and ninety-six? He's lost count.

"Yes, Vernon," she says. "I mean it. And I'll see you in a couple hours. Bye-bye now."

"A couple hours? Two hours?"

"Yes. Yes. Maybe three. Now I need to go, all right? Now goodbye, honey."

Even Vernon is getting a bit tired of this. "See ya, babe."

She clicks off. He watches her set the cell down on the table, brushing her forehead with the back of her hand in pronounced relief. The man reaches under his chair and produces a bottle of wine. Melanie nods her approval as he extracts the cork.

*****

Vernon remembers the first time he followed her.

Once again she'd informed him of some seemingly reasonable activity that would keep her out and about at all hours, but this time Vernon was right behind her. Or at least two or three cars behind.

She'd led him, without her knowing, to a farm on the outskirts of town. He couldn't very well eat her dust as she turned up the private dirt road, so he pulled off onto the shoulder of the rural highway and sneaked a look through the trees, wishing he'd brought a pair of binoculars. But even with his naked eye, he could detect naked lust. It was a wonder Melanie and Farmer John didn't instantly rip off their clothes and literally roll in the hay right there in the maw of the steaming barn.

Still, back at home and hours later, Vernon kept quiet on the matter. Strife and conflict would only make things worse, he felt.

That's just the way he was.

At work, for instance, whenever pay raises were considered, he never once fought for an increase. Still doesn't. No sense in casting himself in a negative light with management by seeming to grovel or complain. If he's deserving, he'll get a raise. If not, oh well. Better luck next year.

And even after following Melanie in the ensuing months to *other men* at *other places,* to the point of standing outside their motel rooms with his ear to the door, he chose to stay mum, hoping these *dalliances,* to put them mildly, were nothing more than a series of emergency flares that would burn themselves out.

When it became apparent these flares would be lining a never-ending road, he began to think of a better way to handle this. A way that didn't involve sitting down and talking to her or following her around every waking moment.

*****

Focusing his binoculars, Vernon allows Melanie plenty of time to indulge in those scrumptious-looking ribs and in the white-shirted eye candy across the table. After all, no need to deny her this special meal.

He then phones her once again.

"Vernon," she says, again on the seventh ring. No *honey* this time, though. In its place, an abrupt, "What is it?"

"Took you a while to answer," he says.

"Yes, well, the mall's a bit crowded. I didn't hear the phone."

"Yeah, I know what you mean. Noisy here, isn't it?"

Hesitation. "You — you're at the mall?"

"In the flesh, my darling," Vernon says cheerfully. "I couldn't wait to see you. Thought I'd surprise you after all."

"Oh. Well. You're right. This is a surprise."

"In fact, I believe I see you. Yes, there you are. I think. Wave your hand."

"Wave my hand?" She gapes wide-eyed at her eating partner, pleading with various desperate gestures for his assistance.

"Yes, Mel, so I can be sure it's you. You're a ways away."

"It — it can't be. I mean I'm inside a store right now."

"Which one?"

"Just a store. I didn't look at the name."

"What kind of store? Clothing? Cosmetics?"

"A *store*, Vern. I'm in a store. Okay?"

"Well, you must have walked right back out again without knowing it, because I see you!"

"I told you, I—"

"I'm waving at you. Don't you see me?"

"Uh...no."

"I'm positive it's you," he says. "Wave to me."

Visibly exasperated, Melanie swirls her free hand in the air a few times before slapping it back on the table. "There. I'm waving. Now please—"

"It *is* you, sweetheart! It *is* you!"

"No it isn't, Vernon. You obviously see someone else."

"Mel, first of all, why would they be waving at my request? But more to the point, I ought to know my own wife, especially when she's waving to me."

"But I'm not—"

"I mean you *were* waving," Vernon says, "until you put your hand down on the table just now. By the way, that *is* potato salad, isn't it? I love potato salad."

Silence. Golden silence.

Melanie's reaction is pure textbook. The staring at the back of her hand to see if she really did put it down. The perceptible grinding of the gears. The wary turn of her head toward the view from the balcony. The slow rising off her chair and stepping toward the railing. The cautious surveying of the surrounding neighborhood.

It's as if Vernon had handed her a list of instructions and she'd followed them to the letter.

"I'm pretty hard to spot," Vernon says. "But if you look a little to your right you might see me at the top of a parking garage."

She turns in that direction, shielding her eyes from the sun. At one point she looks directly at him — right into his binoculars, it seems — but it's clear she doesn't realize it.

"You need a pair of binocs like mine," Vernon says. "Maybe you should go shopping sometime."

Could be the brightness of the sun, but it seems her face has suddenly drained of color. "You — you're really here?" she says, the fact finally sinking in.

"Who's the hunk?"

"You're spying on me?"

"I wouldn't call it spying if the two of you are out there in the open, practically on stage. But he sure looks like a dreamboat, whoever he is. Whatever happened to that pig farmer from way back?"

"What are you talking about?"

"Forget it. That was a long time ago. Let's talk about the present, the chef with the pecs. Maybe you should buy him one of those aprons with the funny sayings."

"Oh, God. Oh, God."

"Now where have I heard that before? Don't tell me. Don't tell me. Now I remember. Pine Tree Motel, just outside of town."

She staggers backward as if a blast of wind had swept through the railing. The gallant Mr. Ribs rushes over and eases her into her chair. She reaches back to pat his hand. He nods, gives her shoulder a quick rub, then returns to his seat.

Phone back to her ear, she glares in Vernon's general direction. "Just go back home, okay? We'll talk about this later."

"No, now's a good time. Where'd you pick this loser up? What is he — number one million, three hundred thousand, five hundred and seventy-four?"

"All right," she says. "You want to talk about this now? He picked *me* up. At the gym, earlier today. That's right, Vern. He asked me to give him a tour of the city, and I was more than happy to. Afterward, he took me back here to his place. You still there, Vernon? You still want to talk?"

He catches her defiant smirk as she arms herself with a deep breath and continues. "He's got something you don't seem to have. What are they called? Oh, yes, balls."

Whoa. Now that hurt. "What the heck do you mean by that?"

"You can't even get up the nerve to ask your boss for a raise. How's that for an example?" She turns to her man and flashes him a wink. A promise of things to come, perhaps?

"I make enough," he says.

"Enough," Melanie snorts. "I see. Enough is always good enough for you, isn't it?"

"Sometimes it's more than enough."

"Is that so?"

"Yep. Because I still have enough left over after the damage."

"What's that supposed to mean?"

"I'm out of bars, Mel. So long."

"Wait a minute! Vernon! Vernon!"

He clicks off but keeps looking through the binoculars. Melanie stares straight at him, anxiety in her eyes, a silent *Vernon! Vernon!* on her lips. He remembers those lips, vaguely, but mostly what he tastes is victory.

But then, above the steady whoosh of traffic over on the interstate and above the sounds inhabiting the smaller streets beneath him, he hears her voice, ever so faintly, and he suddenly recalls a day on their honeymoon when, in a fluttering, striped summer dress, she beckoned him from a distant rock, calling his name.

A fleeting memory, but just like that, all thoughts of victory vanish. In their place, a single question: "What have I done?"

He presses the speed dial again, wishing it were faster.

Through his binoculars he sees her glancing at the display. "Yes, it's me," he pleads. "Answer it, Melanie. Please answer!"

In a corner of Vernon's circular field of vision, the man at the table glances at his watch, then slides his chair back, stands up, and slowly approaches her.

She puts the phone to her ear but says nothing.

"Melanie? Listen to me. I need you to put him on the line. Right now. Melanie?"

"Vernon? Why would you want to talk—"

Maybe it's the raising of her eyebrows, or the slight dropping of her jaw, or the way she turns to the man as he gently plucks the phone from her fingers and drops it in his shirt pocket, but somehow Vernon can tell that she now understands.

"No! No, listen!" Vernon shouts. "Pick it up! We need to talk. Do you hear me?"

Gripping her shoulder with what looks like more force than necessary, the man guides Melanie back into the apartment. As he turns to shut the sliding door, he glances up in Vernon's direction and flashes a thumbs up.

Lost in London

Lev Raphael

It wasn't long after moving into my flat in Central London that I realized it might be trying to kill me.

I came there to teach creative writing and a course of classic horror novels for summer abroad students from Southern Michigan University (everyone on campus called it SMU). The literature students would be reading what I was calling New Gothic: *The Haunting of Hill House*, *Misery*, and *Rosemary's Baby*—favorite books of mine I felt sure they would devour, given how many of my students raved about TV series like *The Walking Dead* and *The Game of Thrones*.

I'd have plenty of time to myself during the month abroad when I wasn't in class or reading student papers, and I looked forward to all the great museums in London and the theater. I had been given a sizable per diem, so I had plans to see Canterbury, Stonehenge, Oxford, Cambridge, Durham Cathedral, and if scheduling worked out, maybe even train up to Edinburgh for a weekend.

Since I was only an assistant professor of English at SMU, way down the pecking order, I was actually surprised to have been invited to the summer program. I expected a plum like that would stay within the sacred circle of tenured faculty.

"You haven't been here long, Paul, but you seem to be very popular with the students," the chair had explained, squinting disdainfully at me as if she couldn't quite understand why and doubted the student evaluations. Was I wrong to personalize it? Maybe. Lara Abbondanda's face was typically a mask of rejection while she stalked the halls of our department as gloomily as the Phantom of the Opera nursing his grievances, despite being a clone of the young Julia Roberts. Maybe it was her looks that made the chair mean: she likely assumed colleagues thought nothing of her extensive scholarship on Virginia Woolf, that she'd advanced so far so fast only because of her movie star resemblance.

"And you *did* have to take some time off last semester." She eyed me suspiciously.

"I had a gallbladder attack and was in so much pain in the ER they had to give me morphine. I never had it before and, uh, it made me ill. I couldn't teach until I was completely recovered."

She knew all that, of course, but she sneered as if I'd suddenly revealed a pitiable weakness.

It was a good thing that she didn't know I'd hallucinated at the hospital.

But her contempt stung me anyway because I had an ugly secret: my family's history of … well, let's call it "instability." My grandfather had killed himself by drinking Clorox after his wife of fifty years died of a stroke. A teenage cousin had jumped off a bridge when his girlfriend ghosted him. My twin sister Ruth had suffered from depression and been hospitalized after her second divorce.

That's why I hadn't told anyone about the nature of my hallucinations, not family, not friends. I didn't want to raise any alarms especially since I sometimes hallucinated when I was slammed by a migraine. At those times, I would imagine I was a cracked glass about to split wide open and spill whatever was inside. The sensation of being on the verge of bursting was so real it scared me shitless until the migraine medication finally knocked me out.

What had happened in the ER overnight was very different, though. After being treated for stabbing pain so bad I couldn't stand up straight and could barely breathe, I'd had a long conversation with my late father, a chat with a lovely lady who brought me a picnic basket, and I safely landed a plane that was on fire. I didn't have to ask the nurse in the morning who those people were, because I knew they were phantoms—and I sure as hell had never even dreamed of taking flying lessons.

"We're done here," the chair said in her typical, brutal style of ending a meeting.

And so we were.

But not really, because I knew that the courses in London had to be a wild success or it would hurt me when I went up for tenure in two years. Now and then while planning for the summer, I wondered if the chair was actually setting me up for failure, if she was one of those people who could sense a vulnerability and exploit it without even knowing its exact nature. I had never handled anything as ambitious as teaching abroad—what if the stress was too much and I fell apart? Trepidation plagued me now, ever since those dark hours at the hospital, and even though I'd never felt afraid of flying before, just before boarding the plane for London, I imagined the horror of crashing into the North Atlantic and drowning amid hysterical passengers. I couldn't sleep on that flight and barely ate anything we were served.

*****

I arrived a week before classes were to begin at upscale Regents College, situated in picturesque Regents Park. Their regular students were children of oligarchs and sheiks—or so I'd heard. I arrived early not just to give myself time to recover from jet lag but to get comfortable and oriented. I quickly found a terrific gastro pub, The Queen's Arms, a few streets away from my Pimlico flat on Warwick Square. Based on the way that customers bantered with the servers, it seemed more like a neighborhood hangout than a tourist spot. To me, it was like something out of a movie with its indigo paneling outside—and that evocative name.

The Gin & Tonics were sumptuous and the menu one I would be happy to work through from top to bottom, starting with the pan-fried sea bream and the chicken, ham and leek pie.

There were also two inviting Italian restaurants, one casual and one upscale, not far from the flat, which meant that I would have great alternatives to microwaving my dinners. Or cooking for myself if I felt that inspired. And across the street from my flat was a Victorian-era church advertising classical music recitals through the summer which sounded very tempting. If I were a painter I would have been eager to capture its heavily rusticated façade on canvas, though simply passing by made me smile. There was nothing as beautiful or historic in my suburban Michigan town, and even though I wasn't much of a church-goer, I looked forward to trying a Sunday Mass there.

When I entered the flat that very first time, I discovered what Americans call a duplex and the British a "maisonette." The word looks like something charming the French might have invented. I don't think they did. Of course it appeared completely innocent on the outside, situated as it was on the top floor of a building in one of those pristine white 19th Century rows facing a gated little park or garden, each building's entrance graced by a little two-columned portico. It was something right out of Jane Austen or maybe Trollope, certainly not Stephen King.

On the surface, I had a truly lovely temporary home filled with the scent of lavender from various bowls of potpourri. Antique architectural prints in ornate frames hung in almost every room, marble-topped half-moon console tables were matched by gilt wall sconces, and pairs of marble obelisks like the kind you'd see on a fireplace stood guard on each of those tables. Chinese-themed wallpaper in different patterns and colors covered most of the walls and fringed Persian rugs lay atop the shiny, slippery herringbone parquet floors. I wondered if the flooring was original and well-preserved, or something more recent.

Expensive-looking vases of all sorts were almost as numerous as the deluxe art books filling shelves in the high-ceilinged living room. The furniture was eclectic: graceful gleaming antiques mixed with expensive-looking modern pieces, and while it wasn't Downton Abbey, it was definitely posh. But everything seemed slightly out of size, as if rescued from a more spacious home.

And it had an indefinable atmosphere of a kind of private small museum filled with history, remembrances, and something else I couldn't quite identify. Something unsettling, odd, forlorn.

Overall, I was initially impressed by SMU's choice of Warwick Square for faculty teaching in London. SMU professors always stayed here, I had been told, but as I toured my new home, I had the strange tingling sensation of being an intruder, the wrong piece for the right puzzle. Unless that feeling was simply jet lag.

The layout didn't seem to make a lot of sense and I wondered if it hadn't been remodeled to fit someone's idiosyncrasies. There were three bedrooms of various sizes and a foyer and half bath hung with hunting prints on the main floor. The large combination living room/dining room and kitchen were one floor above (the opposite would have made more sense to me), along with a master bathroom that looked recently refurbished in marble tiles, both countertop and floor. There was one of those "rainfall" shower heads in the large walk-in shower. Everything in that room glowed with newness.

Ditto the small galley kitchen which was a bit of a shock, eye-opening with bright-red cabinets and matching red quartz countertops. I suppose it would clear your head after a night of heavy drinking or pep you up if you were morose. Or possibly make you feel worse if your mood was intractable, since there was something a bit ghoulish about that much red in a comparatively small room. Even the tea kettle on the electric range was red.

The fireplace with a white and black marble surround and matching mantel evidently didn't work since it was filled with a Delft-looking vase of pink silk peonies. Above it hung what was a valuable painting—if it wasn't a fake. I recognized the signature of the Edwardian portrait painter Boldoni because I'd seen his portraits at various museums before and his gauzy brushstrokes were familiar. But there was something a little off about it. Boldoni's women were typically young, charming, sexy, dressed as if for a ball and ready to sweep down a staircase to greet an admirer or two.

The portrait's gold frame was wildly baroque in sharp contrast with the portrait itself which was surprisingly stark. Against a background the color of dried blood, an elderly woman with some sort of elaborately feathered and beribboned hat with a wispy veil sat on an over-stuffed chair of almost the same color behind her. The prim black gown didn't match the hat and her pale, oval face with thin nose and lips was fixed in a ferocious scowl.

But what really gave me the creeps were her eyes: very dark and cold even behind the veil. She seemed to be demanding an explanation: What was I doing intruding on her domain? As if that wasn't enough, there was some sort of dyspeptic little terrier in her lap who looked like the nasty kind of dog that would let you pet him before snapping off a finger.

"Great," I thought, "We're going to be roommates. Fun times!"

A balcony filled with majolica pots of bright red, orange, and yellow begonias overlooked the quaint gated garden below, and their sweet spicy fragrance alone was like a vacation. There were towering, wide-spread lime trees with their lovely heart-shaped leaves inside the gates, cozy-looking benches, graveled paths, and a profusion of flowers my garden-loving mother would have appreciated: lush peonies, foxglove, phlox, clematis, lavender, larkspur, delphinium—and her favorite, big fat roses. She had taught me their names as if imparting our family history, but I'd never had success growing anything more than a beard, and even that was just a chin strap.

The view of all that verdant space dotted with color was spoiled for me, though, because a dumpster loomed at the corner of the park gate closest to me and no matter the time of day, it was always overflowing with black plastic trash bags—as if the dumpster refused to be emptied no matter how often trash was collected by the city. And not just overflowing—bags were piled at its sides. At times that image put me in mind of a raft people were clinging to so as to keep afloat after a shipwreck—there were that many gross bags huddled all around it. If I looked at it too long, I could almost feel the dizzying, choppy waves and taste the panic of my fellow survivors…

Luckily I couldn't smell the trash from my balcony, though I thought I might, given the weather. London was having a crushing heat wave and to my dismay, the flat not only lacked AC, it was on the top floor. By afternoon, the temperature was over 90 degrees in there. That's what one of my apps told me.

*****

I was barefoot, having stripped down to shorts and a t-shirt trying to stay cool my second day there, when my iPhone rang. It was the London rental agent our university worked with, Jocasta Folkston-Jones. We'd had a few emails about arrangements, like how to contact her in emergencies, but we hadn't met in person and I doubted we would have to.

"And are you madly enjoying your new digs?" she asked as cheerfully as if they were a birthday present. "I imagine they're quite a change from Michigan." She pronounced it "Mitch-i-gun." I didn't correct her.

"I'm still tired from the flight and I wasn't prepared for the heat."

"Ah, one never is in London, but it builds character don't you think? You're an English professor, surely you must know what George Bernard Shaw once said, 'An Englishman thinks he is moral when he is only uncomfortable'". Before I could respond or figure out how exactly she meant that, Jocasta rushed on, "Isn't the décor brilliant?"

I agreed that it was impressive, except for the portrait, which seemed grossly out of place.

The agent laughed what romance novelists call "a silvery laugh" and said, "Oh, yes, she's rather a baleful cow, isn't she? That's Granny and there's quite a story. The family lived in some great big Georgian pile in Sussex, I believe, and the husband gambled away everything they had except for the flat you're in, and some of the bibelots and furnishings. Plus the painting. The husband died soon afterwards and it was widely believed his wife was involved—though nothing was ever proven of course. She must have been a misery and everyone hates that painting which I'm sure is a *perfect* likeness. Do you want my advice?"

"Uh … yes, okay."

"Ignore the old trout! It's what I tell all of you Michigan professors staying there in the summer. Now, do call if you need anything. Ciao!"

Putting down my phone, I found myself once again locking eyes with "Granny."

Who would want a portrait of herself looking so stern, forbidding? And why did the owners of the flat hang it so prominently? Didn't they see what I did? Wouldn't it spook guests?

Maybe it was hung there as some kind of joke, maybe her family enjoyed mocking her for some reason. Me, I was not amused.

Well, I did my best to ignore the sinister painting, but whenever our eyes met I started to feel that its subject was the presiding spirit of the flat and she truly wanted me gone. I tried not to look into her eyes too often, but the painting had a kind of dark magnetism and sometimes I couldn't help but stare at whoever she was. I felt judged in some way, inferior, an obnoxious American, when I spent too much time in front of the painting. Though I'm six feet tall and stocky, those eyes made me feel small.

The heat, meanwhile, didn't let up. Even the traffic noise and the sound of people's conversations as they passed along the street below seemed smothered, and at least during the day there was a spectral kind of calm in the flat. I heard no noise from adjoining flats—maybe their owners were gone for the summer?

The black and red in the portrait made me think of Poe's "Mask of the Red Death" and once the story entered my mind, I couldn't entirely shake it loose.

*****

Tormented by hotter weather than I was prepared for, that second day, I opened all the windows for cross ventilation and the flat rebelled. It summoned fierce winds that blasted right through the place, front to back, sweeping all my papers off the heavy round table I was using as a desk, ripping a shade half off the kitchen window downstairs and almost completely unraveling the paper towels from their rack.

Friends back home didn't believe my texts about that last bit, so I sent them photos of the towels pooled onto the floor as if yanked down by malicious hands. *Her* hands.

All those pretty rugs weren't tacked down in any way, so the longed-for cross ventilation turned them into woolen landmines. Each one was tossed about and twisted onto itself or rumpled in ways guaranteed to make me fall on the highly waxed floors if I wasn't hyper vigilant about straightening them perfectly. And their fringes grabbed at my feet as I scuttled around the flat trying to restore a minimum of order.

Closing the windows, though, was a non-starter given the afternoon heat that lasted well into the evening, so restoring some kind of order was vital. If I tried weighing them down, I was afraid I might be making things worse. But I went ahead and moved some of the enormous art books onto corners of rugs most likely to attack me, hoping I wouldn't trip over the books themselves.

And I felt sure that wandering around partly undressed was not something the portrait approved of. I would have been happy to throw some sheet over it, but then I was worried I might somehow damage the painting in the process and incur the wrath of the owners and my department chair. After all, I was representing the university—and all of Michigan, too, I suppose.

I had slept well my first evening in the bedroom I guessed might be the coolest, though why I chose it, I can't say now. Maybe because the tasseled curtains edged in gold braid, the wallpaper and duvet were all a soothing sky blue and it had the feel of some 18th century boudoir. Cool or not, I slept deeply after my flight, waking up almost dazed.

The second evening, though, after that phone call, I was troubled by the heat and by street noise which seemed to come in from the windows like distorted, muffled voices you hear in a swimming pool as people walk along its edge. The sheets were silk and the bed as firm as mine at home, but sleep kept slipping away like something you chase in a dream, even though the room had light-blocking shades. I'd had a few shots before bed of Aberfeldy scotch I'd bought at a nearby Sainsbury food market, hoping it would knock me out, but despite the familiar bright, cherry cola taste, I was wide awake and felt as warm in bed as I had during the afternoon when the street below smelled of over-heated stone and asphalt.

For some reason, I found myself remembering a puzzle posed by a philosophy professor in the required freshman course I took at the University of Dayton: "If you turn away from a table, does it still exist when you can't see it?" The question had infuriated me and the ensuing discussion had left me dizzy.

Rolling over and over, I found that the hypothetical table merged in my head with Granny's portrait upstairs. I felt drawn by morbid curiosity to see if the painting was really there, really so ominous even while a voice inside me murmured, "Nonsense, stay where you are."

This wasn't a suggestion. This was a *command*. And I felt as if someone was squeezing my head between vicious, implacable hands. Just what I needed, a migraine, now, and I was pretty sure I'd left my medication in the bathroom upstairs.

Somebody hooted with laughter outside as a chattering group passed by and the derisive sound echoed in my room which seemed oddly darker than when I'd gone to bed. I could barely make out the bedside clock in the obscurity of the room, but that didn't make sense. Was something wrong with my eyes? I tried grabbing it to bring it closer.

That's when I heard a low, threatening growl.

Was I dreaming?

No. I heard it again. Percussive, the same low note repeated without a rise or fall. Like a warning. And it was somewhere in the dark bedroom, somewhere very close. Under the bed? But how was that possible?

It stopped and the pain in my head mysteriously vanished, but before I could take a breath, the growling came again and my hands suddenly felt so cold I hugged myself and buried each hand in an armpit, wondering if I could be feverish. Then I felt embarrassed to be so afraid and forced my arms to my side.

I tried to think rationally: Nobody could have slipped a dog into the flat, a dog that had been hiding itself until now. I had to be hallucinating, or maybe there was a weird echo effect on the street below and the dog was outside somewhere? Could the morphine I'd been given months ago have lingered in my system somehow, or messed with my brain chemistry? Or was this some new twist on my migraines?

When I sat up and tried to slip out of bed to check the window, the growling was so intense it seemed to push me onto my back and pinion my arms and legs. And now it somehow emanated from the doorway and the sound was deeper, more vicious and I pictured a much larger dog than the one in the painting.

Surely this was no migraine, this was a nightmare, the classic kind where you're trapped by some invisible force. I struggled but couldn't free myself and the pressure I felt on my shoulders was so heavy I submitted, afraid of injury if I tried any harder to fight off whatever had taken hold of me. My skin felt as cold as if the room had magically become air conditioned or summer had turned to winter.

In movies people who are terrified often puke, but I couldn't have brought anything up. My guts weren't in turmoil, they were frozen. Something ugly washed over me like a dank, low-lying fog and tears welled up in my eyes. I heard what might have been the noisy hum of the fridge upstairs but it felt like the buzz of hornets swarming to sting me over and over again.

Trapped, desperate, I started to pray: "Hail Mary, full of grace, the Lord—" and the growling faded. I waited, waited some more, and it seemed gone.

Thank God, I thought, starting to stretch and flex my aching hands.

Then I heard a malicious low chuckle.

That's when I passed out.

*****

When I awoke the morning of my third day, I was reminded of a line from Fielding's *Tom Jones*. The prior night's "nocturnal riots" seemed so fantastical I couldn't possibly have dreamt them given how dull my dream life usually was—and I don't think morphine-induced hallucinations counted either.

Was I a victim, then, of the scotch I drank before bed mixed with some lingering effects of jet lag? Or was I beginning to fall apart already like I dreaded?

I tried to shake off my anxiety as best I could. So I did not look under the bed, I just grabbed my phone and padded upstairs to the kitchen, sleepily tripping on the stairs but managing not to fall or drop my phone. Then I inspected the spot where I almost fell and found there was nothing uneven in the stairs and the carpeting covering them looked brand new—but I made a mental note to be careful at that spot.

The owners had left a canister of coffee beans with a note on creamy stationary headed **WELCOME** and filled with typed advice about where to shop for groceries and how to use the small washer and dryer tucked into a corner of the kitchen. There were also instructions for using the expensive-looking coffee bean grinder and the ordinary French press. Now I truly began to enjoy their hospitality, given the previous night.

I was once again sipping a strong brew at the tiny round wrought-iron table wedged under the window with its grim view of endless roofs, a table that would have looked more appropriate on a patio or terrace. The matching chairs were not very comfortable, but the dishes and glassware I found were all very ordinary, and not colored red, so I wasn't assaulted by that color again.

As I ate a piece of buttered toast, I also chewed over the previous night as slowly as I could, trying to remember each and every detail in order, as if I were an eyewitness to a crime and being interviewed by the police.

So what *had* happened to me last night?

Could I really have imagined it all? Or was it a dream masquerading as reality? Because in the morning, the flat seemed to be bursting with normalcy. The sun was shining in and the air in the flat was redolent of that faint, ubiquitous fragrance of lavender that couldn't be anything less ominous or weird. And even though some windows were opened (or "cracked" as we say back home in Michigan) I wasn't caught in a wind tunnel.

All was well, but I still felt that nagging sense of being an intruder, almost like the itch you get at the back of your neck when you suspect someone is staring at you—and you turn and find that someone is.

Then my phone rang and I was surprised to see Jocasta's name appear on the screen again.

"How are you, my dear?" she trilled.

"Fine, I guess. Is something wrong?"

"Not a thing, not a thing. I just thought I'd check in on you and see if all was well. You know, new city, England's so different, culture shock and all that...."

"Well, nobody's set me on fire yet, so that's a plus."

"What? What on earth are you talking about? *Fire?*"

I haltingly told her what had happened to me on my previous stay in London, an experience I'd shared with very few people because it was so bizarre and humiliating.

Back in 2006 when smoking indoors was still legal, I'd been listening to a smooth jazz combo in a crowded Soho club where I'd tied my light-blue Polo summer jacket around my waist because it was so warm. All the tables were taken and I was standing in a crowd near the bar, having just finished a Sidecar. Everyone around me seemed to be smoking in a style that looked very European: When they weren't taking a drag, they held their cigarettes down by their thighs.

Someone must have moved too close to me in the crowd because it suddenly got warmer and I looked down to see one trailing sleeve of my jacket flickering red and orange in the gloom of the club.

And getting redder *fast.*

I shouted "Holy crap!" and tore the jacket off, stomping on the wild flames.

Ah, British reserve. Not a single person around me asked if I was okay or even flinched, though they did make a bit of room for my tarantella. And the band kept playing.

"What is *wrong* with you fucking people?" I shouted as I stormed out of the club, my ruined, blackened jacket in hand, swearing to no one in particular that I'd never return to England.

"*Jazz,*" Jocasta sneered when I was done with my sorry tale, and somehow I heard in that one word the admonition "You should have known better." It was clearly my fault.

I asked her, "Do you call every professor staying here so often? At the beginning, I mean?"

Her pause was just long enough to be suspicious.

"Of course! One does like to be polite. By the way, you do know that Princess Diana once visited the owners of that flat? She was apparently some sort of very distant cousin. Of course she wasn't a princess yet when it happened, but still, it's a rather exciting place to stay. One might even call it historic."

I wasn't sure what to say and finally came up with, "I did not know that."

"Hmm ... you don't sound very keen. I thought all you Americans were *mad* about the royals, and her most of all. Well, silly me. Sorry! By the way, *do* mind the Hepplewhite."

"The what?"

"The *furniture*. You can't miss it. Anything in the flat that's rosewood, sycamore, or satinwood and is decorated with marquetry and has inlays that depict seashells? It's unmistakable. Those chairs with delicate legs and open backs in the shape of shields? That lovely bow-fronted sideboard? The flat is simply *bursting* with the stuff."

"I promise not to break anything," I said. "I'm not a rock star who trashes hotel rooms."

"*Most* amusing!" And that's how Jocasta ended the call.

Had I insulted her by not raving about Princess Diana? Or was she being quietly sarcastic and I'd missed the joke?

Armed with another cup of coffee, I stepped into the living room to study the portrait. Despite whatever had happened last night—or might have happened—the portrait didn't scare me now, which seemed strange. As I viewed it from different angles, I didn't get that sensation people often describe of portraits, of uncanny eyes following you—and the dog seemed like a harmless little beast in daylight, a lapdog, not remotely ghost material.

But there was something a bit uncanny about the building itself. Despite all the cars and pedestrians passing by outside, I had not seen anyone either entering or leaving it, hadn't met other tenants in the tiny elevator, and heard no sounds from any of the other flats on my floor.

Could everyone be gone for the summer? Or had Granny somehow subdued them all? Now that *was* ridiculous.

I mused about this in the shower, all the while struggling with the vague sense that I was being watched—as if Granny's eyes could see through walls. Of course that was nonsense.

When I was done and turned off the water, I couldn't get the shower door to open.

I pushed and pushed the handle, worried I might break the glass if I was too forceful, but I became more and more desperate to escape. *Why wasn't it opening?* It was as immovable as if someone was on the other side of the door determined to keep me from getting out.

And what would happen if I couldn't break the glass, which seemed pretty thick? Who would hear me shouting for help?

I took a deep breath in and out, I let go, stepped back a little, closed my eyes and told myself to relax, that the problem must be something about the fit of the door or the humidity from the powerful shower head or maybe my hand was too wet—but how was I supposed to dry it off if the towels were on the towel rack just outside? Then I realized I hadn't washed my hair, so I rubbed both hands in my dry hair and—bam!—the door opened just fine.

Something even more bizarre than feeling spied on popped into my head: Granny had wanted to trap me inside.

Well, that wasn't going to happen.

Breathless now, I decided for the future I'd sling a towel over the top of the door just in case the problem was only wet hands. Because if I couldn't get it open next time I showered, I would have to break the glass and who knows how badly injured that would leave me.

As if to undermine my resolve, I heard that chuckle again and this time it was nastier, almost malevolent—and the room suddenly felt weirdly cold. I dried myself off hurriedly and pulled on my bathrobe, but that chill in the room had all the power of a tremendous storm moving through with high winds that tormented people, trees, cars and anything that wasn't tied down. I'd lived through more than one in Michigan.

Now I was too agitated to eat lunch.

I worked on my class notes for the rest of the day, trying to stay cool, and rewarded myself with another dinner at The Queen's Arms which already felt like a haven from the flat. I was there early, found a corner table for two and decided to take my time and order a drink while perusing the menu. The 30ish bartender who looked professorial minus the tweed jacket waved and so did some of the servers. I guess they all knew I was going to be in London for a while.

It was a square, cozy room with a mirrored wall behind the bar framed by olive green and white-streaked subway tiles that matched the olive of the paneling inside on the lower two panels of the walls. Plenty of the bottles glistening behind the bar had names I didn't recognize like Sipsmith, The Kraken and Monkey Shoulder and so did the handles for what was on tap. One of those had a round blue and white logo with what looked like a three-masted galleon. It read: Ghost Ship.

Was that a message of some kind?

I asked the lean tanned server who looked like a runner what it was like.

"Quite citrusy, I'd say." And she gave me a toothy brisk smile that seemed even brighter given her deep black curly hair, black slacks and blouse. "How are you finding the city so far?"

"I'm settling in."

"Lovely!"

The beer was as good as it sounded, and just the right note to counter the stifling heat outside and the torrent of texts on my phone that I waded through before ordering dinner.

Some of the twenty students I'd be teaching and taking on excursions wanted to know things they could easily have checked on Google like what the drinking age was, of course. And what currency the English used. Others asked if they needed to bring the assigned books, to which I said "Absolutely." There were questions about tipping, whether it was safe to ride the Tube, could they wear American flag apparel on July 4th, should they avoid drinking the water like in Mexico, how were you supposed to cross streets if everyone drove on the "wrong" side, should you avoid smiling at people when you passed them on the street, would they be able to understand the English spoken in England—and so much more.

I started on a second beer before I was through and the pub was beginning to fill up by then. Most people looked like they had come from work and the chatter was uniformly convivial and high-spirited. I was fascinated watching one person after another manage to carry several glasses of beer back to a full table without spilling a drop. I guess that took practice.

When my honey-roasted cold ham with fried eggs and chips came, I surprised myself by asking the server if she believed in ghosts.

"Of course! London is full of ghosts. Stands to reason, yeah? A city this old wouldn't be the same without them."

* * * * *

That evening my sister called me to see how I was doing. We had been talking more now that she'd become an ER nurse after going back to school at thirty, had a new boyfriend, and was always in a quietly pleasant mood. My mother had once darkly confided in me, "I've always thought there was something missing in her, even when she was a toddler." She hadn't explained what she meant, and I was sorry she hadn't lived to see Ruth dig herself out of debt, stop drinking, and establish a more stable life for herself. Maybe what my mother saw without being able to name it was that my sister was a seeker, someone who had to fail and fail again before she could find her way home.

That was a positive spin.

And after my mother's sad judgment about Ruth, I was afraid to ask if she thought there was something missing in *me* even though I'd always been the high-achieving good boy compared to my sister.

When I told Ruth about what I thought had happened in the flat, she said, "I'm sorry, but I'm not surprised you had a weird night. It's those awful books you brought with you. They're creepy."

"I picked them because students complain about having too much to read—even English majors—and I can't see anyone not finishing them. Those novels are *terrific*. But what do the books have to do with anything?"

"Paul, I see two possibilities," she said in her new crisp, no-nonsense voice that I still wasn't quite used to. "Either they've stirred up your unconscious or they've stirred up something else, something in that apartment."

"It's called a flat." I don't know why I felt I had to make such an unimportant point.

"Whatever. You're stressed out—this is your first time teaching

159

abroad, and let's be honest, London's not your favorite city, right? It was brave of you to go back after what happened in that club."

"Thanks. But I'm really prepared for this, I'm psyched about the classes, the money's good—and I don't feel stressed." That last bit was only partly true.

"Okay, then it's the flat and what you've brought into it." I was surprised how totally reasonable she sounded.

Despite that, my hand started shaking and I put the phone down and switched to speaker. "Are you saying there's something wrong with me?"

"Come on — of course not!"

"Then what? You think that books can, like, summon spirits?"

"Well, aren't you the one who always raves about the Power of Literature?"

"But not supernatural power!" I regretted being angry, I knew my tone was defensive. Deep down I suspected she might be right.

Ruth sighed. "It's too late, sweetie. You're there, the books are there, and it sounds like you have company. How's your head, by the way?"

She meant the migraines. I tried not to make a big deal of them, but sometimes they left me so dizzy and weak, so sensitive to light that I had to lie down with an eye mask for hours on end, even after taking medication, because the world around me whirled and blinded me.

It was not something I enjoyed discussing, even with my doctor or my therapist, so I changed the subject and asked her about the new hospital where she was working, and we got into a long conversation about staffing problems that soothed me a little because it was so mundane. And we talked about the pub I had so quickly grown fond of because Ruth was a real foodie and even when she'd been deeply depressed, a lovely bottle of wine and a delicious meal could move the needle.

*****

My jet lag was fading and I hoped I'd get a good night's sleep despite the continuing heat wave, but I had a nightmare of being trapped in a desert and being blown to my knees by a sandstorm and then buried alive. I woke up sweaty, scared, and trembling and headed a bit unsteadily to the bathroom next door to my bedroom for a Xanax which I'd moved there from upstairs. I knew it could work as quickly as fifteen minutes to knock me out and it was guaranteed then to keep me asleep for hours.

The bathroom was all blue and white with elegant chrome fixtures and wallpaper sporting gigantic, writhing vines and roses which were pretty enough by day, I guess, but felt overpowering at night, oppressive. They made the room feel smaller, and fogged in like I was, they were almost alive.

Me, I looked gaunt in the mirror, my face splotchy, my curly black hair as wild as the flowers surrounding me. As I drank a second cup of water after downing my pill and turned off the light to go back to bed I heard a feathery whisper: "You don't belong here."

It stopped me cold—and infuriated me. What the hell was going on? Was this some weird English practical joke?

I stormed through the flat, angrily flicking on every single light switch and turning on every lamp on each floor, tripping on some loose carpeting on the stairs, and almost knocking over an urn-shaped malachite table lamp with gold trim that I had somehow not even noticed before. Each room that I bathed in unexpected light seemed startled and resentful, but I didn't care. I was looking for—

Well, what, exactly?

I was surely alone. But I checked anyway, both upstairs and downstairs, and then back again, a second time. There was a dark, sullen feel to each room as if I had disturbed someone's deep sleep or stopped a criminal about to do something nefarious. As I tore around on my wild little search, I kept thinking "You're crazy" followed by "Fuck that!"

There was nobody hiding in a closet or under any of the beds or even behind any of the lush velvet curtains—and I couldn't believe someone had installed hidden microphones. As the Xanax started to take effect and all the blazing lights struck me as ridiculous, I felt exhaustion weighing me down. Stepping heavily around the flat, careful to keep my balance to avoid tripping over any of the fringed carpets and the art books holding them down, I slowly turned everything off and weaved my way back to bed.

I had not even glanced at the portrait because I was afraid it might somehow have changed for the worse during the night and I was ashamed of my fear. And I felt as if it had somehow orchestrated my hostile reception as I again turned lights on and off, on and off, momentarily obsessed.

*****

Late in the morning of my fourth day in London, as soon as I'd had a cup of coffee I logged on to our department's faculty-only website and found the phone number of Susan Liberato, the expert in 19th century American Literature who'd last summer taught a Henry James seminar along with "London Lovers," novels set in the city but written by foreigners.

"I wondered if you'd call," she said when she heard my name. Her tone was warm but perhaps somewhat guarded.

"You did? Why?"

"Well, everyone from the department over the years who's taught in London has had some trouble … settling in."

"Did you?"

She laughed and it sounded a bit fake, which surprised me because in our casual chats in the mail room and before or after department meetings, she had always seemed pretty straightforward. A broad-shouldered, athletic-looking woman in her fifties, she was the opposite of the academic stereotype—there was nothing cloistered, arrogant, or phony about her. Many of my colleagues at SMU smiled and acted as if they felt collegial towards me, but their eyes were as cold as if I posed some kind of threat. When Susan smiled, it was real.

"Well, yes and no," she said. "It's not, shall we say, the most appealing apartment I've ever stayed in. Despite all the antiques. Maybe because of them. The place has too much atmosphere, I guess."

"Did you sleep okay when you were here?"

"Not at all, but then you have to remember that I was teaching Henry James's ghost stories and I was certainly immersed in all that very delicious dread."

This time her laugh sounded real, but before I could decide how to probe any further and ask why she hadn't wanted to teach in London this summer too, she said, "Listen, Paul, I have a call coming through—keep me posted on how things go with your classes. It's a lot of work but the students tend to be very eager, when they're not hung over, of course!"

Staring at the iPhone after she ended the call, I cursed myself for not having gotten right to the point with Susan, asking her if anything weird had happened while she was living in the flat. But then I wondered if she would have told me the truth, all of it. And then there was a worse possibility: she might have shared my question with hostile members of the department who would talk about me as some kind of nut job. I couldn't risk that with academic jobs disappearing faster than glaciers in Tibet and Switzerland.

To clear my head, I went grocery shopping at Sainsbury's which was a pleasant ten-minute walk away through what felt like a village to me, given that most of the buildings were only a few stories tall and the streets and uneven sidewalks were so narrow. Thanks to high-powered AC, the store was ice-cold inside and so I lingered in front of items I had no intention of buying, things like prawn-flavored crisps and sticky toffee pudding—both of which sounded and looked a bit nasty. I bought more bottled water, some egg salad and watercress sandwiches for lunches, and a variety of microwavable frozen dinners for when I might feel too lazy to go out. The single malt whiskeys were the most inviting items, though much cheaper than back home, and so I bought some more from distilleries I hadn't heard of before—Aberlour, Tamnavulin Speyside, and Old Pultney—because I liked the names and the look of the bottles. And it didn't hurt to stock up for my nighttime reveries.

The grandmotherly cashier was patient as I fumbled with change since the coins were hard to tell apart after only a few days in England. Luckily nobody was behind me on line that early since I was also a bit clumsy at bagging my own items in the bright orange Sainsbury bags I'd purchased the first time I shopped there.

"Having a party?" she quipped, nodding at my booze and I said, "I'll let you know."

She laughed, and I sauntered out after an hour of browsing the aisles as if nothing strange had been happening to me back at the flat.

The balcony was shaded at that time of day and I decided on an early lunch out there. I was enjoying a sandwich and a glass of Perrier until a large black bird landed on the railing and started croaking at me. It was a raven or a crow, looked mean, and I grabbed my sandwich and ducked back inside, sliding the glass door shut. The damned thing wasn't at all startled. It hopped onto the café table where I'd left my water, dipped its beak into my glass as if taunting me, and then flew off.

I could feel my pulse pounding in my ears as if I'd just stepped off a wild carnival ride, so I sat down on the blocky couch jammed into a recess of the wall right near the balcony doors. It was covered in a weirdly hairy purple material and I'd avoided it after one try my first day, but I didn't care right now. I set the sandwich down on a small dark marble square in front of it that did duty as a table and when I looked up, I felt the baleful eyes of that awful portrait piercing me. I had a wild desire to rip it from its wall and stomp on it. My pulse beat faster as I imagined how satisfying that would be, but I closed my eyes and leaned back, the scratchy fabric of the couch restoring me to some sense of proportion.

It was just a fucking bird. What was wrong with me?

To truly clear my head, I called for an Uber to take me to the Tate Britain to see the Dante Gabriel Rossetti paintings and the Henry Moore sculptures. I grew up in Manhattan and museums had always soothed me when I was upset about anything at all, whether they were crowded or not, as comforting as a long silent rest in a steam room. And as sacred in their own way as churches, people there also often hushed and reverential, perhaps aware that they had crossed into a different space, a different reality. Museums so often gave me room to breathe.

The Uber ride to the Tate was quick through the growing heat, but I hoped the city would eventually cool off enough for me to stroll there since it was chockablock with art I wanted to encounter. Google maps said walking would take just fifteen minutes.

Though I'd seen photos in various guide books and online, the façade of the Tate's late Victorian building blew me away with its bold columns and statues, its wide grand stairs. Entrance was free and I was soon inside and the air conditioning more than adequate to combat the muggy day outside.

I breezed through the gorgeous, light-filled rotunda with its black-and-white marble floor, heading off to contemplate Rossetti's "The Beloved" in a gallery blazing with Pre-Raphaelites. Inspired by the *Song of Songs*, it had verses from that poem inscribed on the gilt frame: "My beloved is mine and I am his" and "Let him kiss me with the kisses of his mouth: for thy love is better than wine." This was my sister's favorite painting because she believed she looked like the main figure and I dutifully took a photo on my phone to send to her.

The woman at the center of the lush, crowded canvas is wearing an ornate rich green robe that contrasts sharply with her lush red hair and pale complexion. She has the sweetest, dreamiest green eyes. Reproductions I'd seen before hadn't captured the quiet compassion that wells up in them and I felt transfixed, as if staying there long enough could heal the anxiety and worse that seemed to afflict me at the flat.

There were very few people in that long, airy, high-ceilinged gallery and I lingered for a full fifteen minutes or more, gazing at and communing with this remarkable painting. Eventually, I broke the spell of those eyes because I was starting to tear up—it was so beautiful! I would have plenty of time to come back and see the whole collection of Pre-Raphaelites in the sprawling gallery trimmed with green and gray marble; relishing this one canvas was enough for today—there was no need to be greedy.

It was time to head off to the other side of the museum to visit the Henry Moore sculptures, some of which I knew from books or documentaries, and I was most curious to see the "Draped Seated Woman" up close. I had read in a guide book that she was considered "monumental" and weighed close to 1200 pounds. The figure was seated with legs stretched sideways on a multi-level white platform, staring off into the distance.

Except she had no eyes.

Quite suddenly I couldn't bear looking at this statue I'd admired for years in photographs in books and online. Her face felt like some sort of grim warning. It terrified me and I didn't want to decipher its meaning because I could feel sweat breaking out across my face. Blushing furiously, I stumbled out of that gallery and hurried from the museum, shoving my way through more than one startled and angry group of tourists to sit down on the stairs outside and compose myself.

Breathe. Breathe. Breathe.

When I calmed down enough, I called an Uber and despite that horrible painting and whatever was wrong with my flat, I somehow felt safer when I got back there than I had felt at the museum. But it didn't last. I kicked off my shoes, pulled off my socks and padded up and down the stairs to calm myself, but the movement only made me feel more agitated and there was something grotesque and punishing in the rough feel of the carpeting under my feet.

I couldn't get the image of the statue's blank face out of my head. In photographs I'd thought the statue beautiful; in person it was a nightmare.

Desperate for relief, I poured myself a few fingers of whiskey even though it was barely 4:00 and settled onto that torturous couch, closing my eyes between sips of the whiskey whose intensity seemed, finally, to clear the haze in my head.

That's when the phone chirped and I had to put my drink down. It was my therapist Dr. Fetterman calling from Grand Rapids.

"How are you doing, Paul? You missed our scheduled phone session, so I called. Are you getting out at all before your classes start? Remember, isolating yourself can be problematic."

"Yes! I went to a museum today. And I go shopping for groceries."

"Are you eating regular meals?"

"Oh, for sure, and there are a bunch of good places to have dinner or lunch around here and the neighborhood is very nice." I didn't mention the sinister mountains of trash across the street.

"And are you taking your Thorazine?"

I said "Of course," since I knew that had to be the right answer, but I wasn't really sure—was I? Best to change the subject. "My sister called and we had a great talk. She's so happy now, so calm. I'm really proud of her."

There was a very long silence and then Dr. Fetterman said slowly, "Paul, we've discussed this before. Your sister died in a car crash two years ago. She killed herself by driving into a tree. You had to identify the body at the morgue."

"But that's not possible, I just talked to her, like, yesterday—I think."

"Paul, she's *dead*."

"Are you sure? Are you really sure? You wouldn't be making that up, would you? You're lying! Why are you lying to me? There's a dog under my bed!"

Photographs of Falling Objects Blur
Andrew Darlington

Shadows flick the rim of vision both left and right. Shapes advance in luminous menace, then skip furtively back into invisible holes in space-time. They grate at his tiredness, infusing it with phantom presences.

Two screens.

A small portable TV slotted into a self-assembly shelf-unit. Sound-down it strobes local news in sharp bursts — wettest October since '58, shimmers of flooding, yellow inflatable dinghy undulating down main-street, people wading through front rooms — female newsreader. Then a Management Spokesperson in suit and determinedly patronising logic, dismissed assembly-line worker in tracksuit and sullen anger — male newsreader. And another sex murder, red-light Chapeltown, police cordon of cones, and streamers flagging dismally, fingertip search, alleyways where garbage blows.

Norman Straiker blinks down hard. Normal Norman. Norman Normal. Shadows leap forward, then back. In the other screen, the VDU in front of him, a blue-line head turns through three dimensions. Contours ripple. Columns of figures scroll around it, reading out specifications clear on down from cellular to the molecular level. From skin tissue through skull and into each whorl of cortex. Memory. Reasoning and language. Taste and smell. Spatial co-ordination and libido.

'Can't you get enough?' a voice from behind him. Female.

Norman jerks back up through epidermal stratum. 'Huh?'

She smiles from the door, her face — he thinks, too long for good symmetry. 'Are you on overtime?' she asks, 'or are you free for some heavy fraternization?'

The strip-light in the corridor pulses tetchily. The floor is worn parquet that echoes. 'It's all in there' he begins.

'What's all in there, Norman. What Norman, what? Pray do tell.'

'Baines. He's in there. *Baines* I mean, obviously. Mr Personable. Mr Brilliant. Mr Popular. Reduced to byte-size, and stored in memory-files. He's in there.'

The rattle of her heels on the steps down. 'So now that's established to our complete mutual satisfaction, where to now...?'

The Bar carries a background blur of CD vacuity and low-level indirect lighting. 'They used to have live Jazz here Friday nights. Before they lowered the ceiling to create a more intimate ambience, and replaced the stage with video-games and the CD jukebox. Did you know that? They had a Trad band, all ageing local no-hopers. It was pretty terrible. But at least it was *REAL*. This music is digitalised into nothingness.' Norman Straiker is mid-thirties, in an ill-fitting suit. His hair receding at the temples.

'You've been here *that* long?' Trace is younger. Deliberately teasing him by emphasizing the fact. 'How far back are we talking now, Norman? Five, ten years?'

'Someplace between the two I suppose,' missing the humour-bite completely. 'It seems like forever. Around the time I first washed up here, under Baines...'

Liz and Alan slouch down into cushioned rattan chairs across from them, laughing loud and stupidly. His stupid Hipster beard. Her nose-stud and mindless laughter. Much later, back at the flat, they all eat microwaved ratatouille and drink supermart Liebfraumilch. The decor is dark. Rossetti prints heavy on the wall over the low bed. Lines of books, medical and psychological textbooks, chess and conceptual art. Electronics, the theory of narcotics dependency, and third-hand SF paperbacks, E.C. Tubb, 'Nebula SF' magazine.

Norman. Normal Norman. He blinks down hard as things cant and interact in his gut. Waves of cold sweat and nausea crawl and gooseflesh his spine. In bed beside him, breathing hard, her head seems to be made up of patterns of blue lines that turn through three dimensions with contours that ripple clear on down from cellular to the molecular. Tracy. Trace, lost without 'trace'. She sleeps, breathing heavily in darkness. He lurches up, bare feet cringing at the slap of October-cold floor. His stomach a Chernobyl of foul vapours. He throws up into the toilet bowl in seismic spasms of shock that hit him mercilessly. Then the perfect calm and mental clarity that inevitably follows. He holds himself moveless, slimed with sweat. The toilet system trickles deep inside itself. A glassy shimmer of trapped tide swim across the circle of water.

Outside, a car hisses past through damp dead leaves. 'This is stupid' he telepaths his distorting reflection. 'I hate the way I'm living. My life is hurting, and out of control. It should *not* be like this. Not now...'

He trudges to Storrs Hill corner for a 'Guardian' while she makes coffee. It drizzles in fine grey curtains of wetness. A cold chill that makes Leeds a more tactile city. A place that helps thought crystallize. Sometimes Trace annoys him. She's useful, good at what she does, which is fraternization, rest and recuperation. But at times of insight like this he knows he deserves more.

Mrs Patel — he assumes that's her name, doesn't speak good English. Her daughter does. So does her son, a man his own age, but in better shape, who speaks with an eloquence that intimidates him. But Mrs Patel smiles in her usual nervously apologetic way. 'Bad thing, Doctor Straiker,' she says, 'bad thing.' He nods. The front page carries the Chapeltown sex-murder down below the trade deficit figures. It's made the nationals now. **'SIXTH RIPPER-STYLE SLAYING'**. It derails his thought-train irritatingly. The drizzle freezes back to a blur of haze around the dull copper stud of morning sun. Cars shunt up at the intersection awaiting green, left to the city, right for the M62 Pennine M-way. Badly choreographed direction lights flash out of sequence. A recent model Accord. Metallic silver glimmers wetly. A wash of baroque from its in-car stereo as it glides forward... while he has to walk.

He imagines he smells coffee from the gate of no.84. Coffee and other less appetizing aromas. He's been here too long. He can even remember the 'Cobourg' when it had live Jazz. He deserves better than this. A fully featured Accord at the very least. Too old for flat-shares too. Liz towelled her hair as he enters, pulling a face at him as she grabs the newspaper. She gets into a huddle with Trace around the coffee. Alan making ludicrous noises from the bathroom. The radio jabbers phone-in inanity. 'Do we *have* to have this station on?' Trace looks up at him oddly, snatched from whatever silly intimacy she was sharing. 'Do we *have* to have the Pop station on' he repeats, 'there's some Rameau on Classic FM.' She shrugs.

In their bedroom he tries to read 'Clinical Dependency', but re-reads the same passage over and over without it making any sense. After a final attempt he hurls it angrily across the room where its pages fan themselves still.

The block is abuzz when they get there. Baines is dead. Nocturnal heart attack. It was in the morning paper, but he'd failed to notice it. A shuttle of incidents jostle him through to mid-morning before he gets chance to check it out. There's always a heavy therapy schedule and insufficient personnel to fill it out. An overworked cliché. A cliché of overwork. Disk files on the screen document depressingly familiar case histories of substance abuse, sexual dysfunction, narcotic dependency, irrational phobias, eating disorders and behavioural abnormalities. Inadequates incapable of controlling their own lives. Then micro-fine brain scans and figure columns. And interviews, damned interviews. Not good in interpersonal situations. But they have to be done. And yes, yes yes, it's not good to come across brusque and uncaring, but it's like that, that's the way it is, change is not an available option.

He reads Baines' newspaper obit over coffee. There's a photo. A hawkish fifty-year old in diplomatic suit and a bow-tie. He despises Baines even in death. Personable, brilliant, popular. All the areas in which Norman Normal, Normal Norman has so obviously failed. 'Professor Baines whose research into psychological dependency led to the revolutionary 'BAINES TREATMENT CENTRE' that proved so successful in helping so many people into new lives... and balhdy blah fuckitty fuck...' Details are vague. The bio-file obviously hastily pieced together by journalists who know nothing about the techniques involved.

Norman prefers afternoons. Better suited, as he is, to dealing with sedated patients, even though they call for more demanding concentration and responses. And the people he works with, and lives with, make a good team, even though he hates acknowledging the fact, even to himself. He and Alan-of-the-stupid-Hipster-beard monitor the blue-line 3D heads as they turn slowly, focusing, recording, keying in where necessary through electrode irradiation, superimposing healthy sampled behavioural patterns onto deviant ones. Editing and redefining where required...

'Are you alright, Norman?' Is that genuine concern detectable in Tracy's voice? Traces of concern? He resents the way she crops her hair. Why does she have to do that? Why does she have to wear it that way?

The night glistens wetly all the way up from Leeds to the Hebden Bridge Wine Bar, by way of the 'Old Malt Shovel'. A dripping grey fog hangs back way behind the sudden lunge of headlight-white trees where blackness dissolves into holes of space-time. Lakes of running water spume beneath the tread as they climb the Pennine slopes, rivers leaking down from high open fields and through rough stone walls. He drives dangerously fast, aggressively hard. The car lights like cones of brilliance around which the night revolves. She sits tense beside him. He enjoys her fear and her sharp nervous intakes of breath as he brakes too abruptly.

Should he risk honesty? Does she *really* care, or is her concern just a routine dig? A 'Hey, Snap-out-of-it you Bastard'. 'No, I guess everything is *not* alright.'

The whole point of coming here tonight is to get away from distractions. To talk. But she's been sullenly silent as they drive, as though this intimacy is something she dreads. 'Wrong between *us* you mean?'

He catches traces of cigarette smoke on her breath. She knows he hates her smoking. Perhaps she does it deliberately? A long pause. 'Why do all these places wind up looking the same? Low black beams. Horse brasses. Glass cases of cigarette cards of 'Sporting Heroes' from the late-fifties to provide a genuine illusion of character.' He finally meets her eyes. 'Yes. No — not wrong with *us*. Not exactly. It's more the whole thing. I thought I'd never get stranded. I guess I did. What I laughingly refer to as my so-called life's not moving as it should. And my so-called career...'

'There'll be changes now though, won't there? With Professor Baines dead. There'll be opportunities for advancement.' Her voice drops to a conspiratorial whisper. 'You know he was found in his car, pulled into a lay-by a good half-mile from his home. Doesn't that strike you as odd?' Then back to a normal conversational tone. 'But you've got the seniority. You'll be a shoo-in for promotion now.'

'It's not that easy. I know my limitations, and seniority in itself isn't enough.' It all comes sluicing out now, as if once begun it no longer matters. The meal sits rich in his gut radiating warm complacency. The Italian Spumante lubricating his confession. 'I'm not up to it, Tracy. That's why I'm still where I am. Written exam work, information retention... that's where I louse up.'

'But you're good. You are bloody good, Norman.'

'At what I do *now*, yes. But that's precisely *why* I'm still where I am. It's fucking obvious. Can't you even see that...?'

She falls silent. A silence that extends uncomfortably.

'...but there *is* a way, Tracy. There is... with your help.'

She's scared of his darkness. Scared of the implications that lie behind it. His is an intense dissatisfaction that means she might lose him. So she agrees. Her support will be pivotal. Alan will be more difficult. But his involvement is essential. They are the 'team'. Liz will fall in behind him. She always does. Her and her stupid nose-stud and irritating laugh. She'll do it alright, if he does. But the lines of persuasion will have to operate within different parameters.

Shadows flick the rim of vision. Two screens. A small portable TV provides visual white-noise from the shelving. While within the VDU Baines' blue-lined head turns through three dimensions.

'He's all in there, don't you see?'

Alan smirks unpleasantly, slouching back on the wall units where shadows move in luminous menace. 'What are you driving at, Norman?' His green lab-coat hangs open untidily. His Hipster pose. Why can't he smarten himself up?

'It's the next logical step in the programme. And since Baines has a prior engagement with the void, it's up to *us* to carry it through.'

'But why does it have to be *you* that gets the jolt?'

He smashes his hand down hard on the curved unit housing. 'It has to be someone. Why not me? Baines used himself. The evidence for that is here. He's sampled his entire cerebral topography, broken his complete psyche down into easily assimilated ready-to-operate bytes. He mapped himself and stored it in *here*. All we've done so far is condense down from what he learned. Isolate one small area of his research. We sample behaviour patterns from screened donors — right? and use them as matrices to reprogram junkies psychological habits and re-shape anorexics dietary needs. So why not extend that principle to implant other qualities? To enhance memory retention. To programme pre-learned information and skills directly into the memory. The process is the same. We can do it. We can sample direct from Baines' undoubted and well-respected genius.'

He'd stopped off at Chapeltown. And can't remember why. There's an hour of lost time. It's annoying, but everything else has gone so well it doesn't seem important.

The rain falls forever. A dismal thrumming that gives the city an aquatic blur and the atmospheric pressure of an alien heavy-water planet. Traffic on Storrs Hill corner sets up riptides that surge and ebb across the pavement rim. He turns his collar up. James Dean style. His shoes are drenched, but he's barely aware of it. Instead, he's rifling through his new memories. And it's incredible. Figures, equations, names, entire texts are there. Things he's laboured to learn but been unable to understand, techniques he's never been capable of, facts he's never even suspected. Procedures, they're all there, instantly available... just as they had been when Baines had used them! Not quite so normal, eh Norman?

Mrs Patel smiles her nervous apologies. 'Very very bad Doctor Straiker.' He nods. The 'Guardian' carries the Chapeltown sex-murder higher up the page this time. The block letters say **'SEVENTH VICTIM'**. Squelching back, watching the cars. A layer of wet November leaves ooze beneath his footfall. That same silver Accord. Soon, soon. Not much longer. He counts his paces. Counting out the number of times he's made this journey. But now it's almost over. All the things he's longed for are now so near his grasp. He has Baines' technical memories and skills. Soon he'll use them to get Baines' prestige and position too, and all that comes with it. So close he can taste it.

Scuffing back into 84 Liz is there in kimono-style bath robe. She's been showering. The slut. She pulls a face as she becomes aware of his attention. She's taken the nose-stud out, leaving the smallest of dimples. He can smell the wetness of her hair, and other less appetizing aromas. Perhaps in the months to come, when he's got out of here, he'll have Liz as well? She has the shape of a Tanagra figurine. The idea of possessing it is appealing. She'll do all the things for him she probably does for Alan. He turns the image over in his head. It's never occurred to him before, but the more he thinks of it the more he likes it.

The block strip-light in the corridor throbs like a wound.

'We should do some tests.'

Norman switches his attention sharply. 'Tests? — why? Everything is fine.'

'Because it's standard procedure. You know that. There are things we need to check out.'

He pauses at the centre of the worn parquet space, turns to face Alan with an expression of infinite patience. 'You did well, Alan. I'm grateful for your co-operation. I've watched the tapes of what happened while I was under, and I'm totally satisfied that everything you did was absolutely in accordance with my wishes and with the established medical guidelines. I've signed the release forms so you in no way carry any responsibility for the decision. And as you can see, I'm fine.'

'But that's not the point, Norman. And you know it. What we did, we did as a joint project to further the technique of memory implantation...'

'And it's one hundred percent. I'm functioning as never before. You can see that. I appreciate your concern, but I honestly don't have the time for games. So, if you've nothing else...?'

Alan stares hard at Norman Straiker's receding back. As if he's seen a ghost.

Soon after the promotion he suddenly finds himself driving his new Accord towards Harehills. Baines' old address. It's understandable. Things have moved fast. The new flat, the car, the break-up with Tracy. Tracy now lost without trace. The wipers slick a sheen of rain from the windscreen. Baroque music plays in smooth eddies around the upholstery. Trace would've stunk the car out with her foul cigarette stink. He's outgrown her. He always deserved better, now he can afford it. To get home he has to cut across Storrs Hill corner. He reverses into a drive opening, and doubles back. The evening is already oppressive, heavy with storm. Jurassic Leeds. His headlights gleam in a lancing dance of moisture. Other headlights set like baleful eyes in the dark loom of amphibious monsters. He hits the lights as they change to amber, pulling around the intersection just as the local news interrupts the radio, the Police Ripper-Hunt appeal, travel warnings of increased bad weather conditions.

He slows to a halt, parks outside 84. Lights sling long shadows across moist grass.

Liz lets him in. 'Oh, it's you.' Cold. No welcome.

She's alone.

'I've got things to pick up. Some books, stuff like that.'

'So go ahead, no-one's stopping you.'

He rummages around the room he'd shared with Trace. The dark decor, the Rossetti print, the heavy floral duvet. Things from another life. He thumbs through the books. Medical and psychological textbooks. He sneers. The tome on 'Clinical Dependency', its spine broken where he'd hurled it across the room in frustration. How strange it all seems now. The contents of all these books, and his total understanding of them, is now intact in his memory, sampled direct from the subject's greatest (deceased) authority. He eases out a copy of 'Nebula SF'. The only thing he retains affection for...

'It's all there. Take it. Trace wants nothing from you.' Liz stands up against the door. Her long hair flared angrily around her face.

He rises slowly. 'So why the hostility, Liz? Things change. You must learn to grow with the changes.'

'Bastard. You used us all. I don't care for myself, you can go to hell for all I care — but I'll never forgive you for the way you treated Tracy.'

So close now he can smell the scent of her hair, the moistness of her body. 'I was fond of Trace. I still am, in a way. She's a nice kid. But things are going my way now, as I always knew they should. I'm taking it all the way, Liz.' He reaches up, his fingers trace the curve of her cheek. 'You could do a lot worse...'

As she moves, he sees her head made up of blue-line contours that turn through three dimensions, patterns rippling clear on down from cellular to the molecular.

Her nails come up, talons scoring his face. Bright sharp pain. Breath catches at his throat, where it stays. For no longer than a second he rears back in shock, like in a frame from stop-motion photography. Then he hits her. Sees her face crumple. And the other faces. In silence, in explosions of blood. An alley. A cool chill that makes it all seem more tactile. A dingy room. Open wounds. Bare white flesh. Patterns of gore. Faces screaming. Female bodies spasming as he slashes at them. Sluts. Tarts. Whores. A fine drizzle of rain. Handfuls of hair sodden with rain and blood. Sound roars in, he hits her again and she goes down. Waves of cold sweat and nausea crawl and gooseflesh his spine. His mouth fills with the taste of blood where her nails have torn him.

Then he remembers how easy it is. How those other sluts had died.

She's mewling in an untidy heap when he returns from the kitchen with the laser knife. So Baines was the 'Ripper-style' killer. Who'd have thought it, eh? Genius has its dark side. And the Dark Side has its genius. Norman can hardly keep from laughing out loud as he arranges the floral duvet cover in a way that will minimize the spray of blood. And now Baines is inside his head, his memories, his logics, his reasoning, his impulses. Pity if blood traces leak from the body in the duvet, marking the car upholstery. But that can't he helped.

Norman carefully removes the nose stud and puts it in his pocket. A keepsake, for what might have been. Then he begins his grotesque work with the knife. The actions come so easily. A practiced ease.

Smooth

Nick Young

The dirtiest deeds are always done by night, are they not? The acts that men want to remain in the shadows, their nature too vile, too depraved for the light of day. The deeds that bring shame, that promise ruin, that no man would want another man, not one of any decency, to know. Those are the deeds shrouded in darkness.

*****

It had been raining most of the pre-dawn hours — squalls, driven by fitful winds which whipped and moaned under the elevated tracks. Light sifted through the morning mist, falling between the skyscrapers and onto pavement that reflected a dirty, oily sheen. The street lamps cast a dull glow. A world in shades of gray. Even the nine-to-fives hustling along the sidewalks looked like they had all the color washed out of them.

It was that kind of Monday.

And my mood matched it. Not that I felt a big letdown because the weekend had been a dizzying whirl of soirées with a glamorous blonde on my arm. That was somebody else's life.

Mine was a bit less scintillating. The highlights?

On Saturday there had been the lunch-counter stop at Kresge's where, thanks to the astute recommendation of my favorite waitress, I had dined on the day's special — an open-face hot roast beef sandwich with extra gravy and two sides. Tasty enough and filling. And, along with a couple of cups of passable joe, at a buck-fifty, you couldn't shake a stick at it.

Three blocks away, I was just in time for the matinee at the Royale. *Citizen Kane* it wasn't. Instead, a Wild West potboiler. Six-guns and Audie Murphy. But with the newsreel, a cartoon and one or two forgettable "coming attractions," it was good enough to kill a couple of hours.

Around the corner, I dropped in at the neighborhood smoke shop for a fresh carton of Pall Malls. Then it was back to my third-floor flat for a supper of warmed-over chowmein rescued from the icebox before it turned into a science experiment.

The rest of the evening I spent with Mingus on the tune set in the company of my favorite relative — Old Grand-Dad.

As for Sunday, well, not much remained by the time I came around and, I have even less to say about it.

So, back to Monday.

As I sat smoking in my office on the fifth floor of the Andiron Building, I reflected on my situation. Looking down at the street through the dirty rivulets of rainwater that had streaked the window, I felt a twinge of envy for the scurrying figures below. Regular jobs, regular hours, regular paychecks. Thirty years and out the door with a "bon voyage" and a gold watch, off to join the shuffleboard set at Happy Valley.

These moments weren't new to me. They'd come before, and they always passed quickly. I'd done fifteen years of regular as a beat cop and a homicide detective. That was plenty enough regular. So, pushing the high side of thirty-five, I rolled the dice and walked away. No more kowtowing to the brass. No more punching a time clock. I would do it my way. Not always a smooth sail, but it was *my* way, the only way I ever wanted it from here out.

As I took a last drag of my smoke, the inner office door swung open and Doris swung in. Tasteful white polka dots on navy blue rayon. Nice dress. Just right for the July heat. And, like everything Doris wore, it fit her tight five-three frame to a tee.

With a blonde bob haircut and blue eyes, she was still girlish at twenty-eight. But make no mistake — she was no kid. Not the way she handled herself. When she wasn't cracking wise, she was working on a stick of Wrigley's. Juicy Fruit. Damned good description of her rose-red lips, I thought. Not that the observation meant I had designs on her, mind you. Not that at all. Not my type, for one thing. For another, she had a very intense romance going with the maitre d' of one of the city's swankiest eateries across town. An Italian, with the oily good looks of Valentino and a temper like Vesuvius.

I had hired Doris on her references — efficient, trustworthy, professional. She was all of those, alright. The fact that she was a treat for the eye was icing on the cake. Especially when male clients came calling.

She entered bearing coffee, steamy wisps curlicuing up from a large white mug.

"Fresh from the pot," she announced.

"Friday's?" I said, stubbing out my cigarette. Doris stopped chewing her Wrigley's long enough to cast a half-smile of derision my way. "I am badly in need."

"I could tell," she replied, as I took the mug from her.

"That obvious?" I said after the first sip.

"If you have to ask, what's obvious is that you haven't bothered to check a mirror lately."

I set the mug down on the desk, slid open a large drawer and drew out pint of rye. Unscrewing the cap, I doused the coffee.

"It's got to be noon somewhere," I began.

"If we were in the Azores," Doris shot back. Like many of her jibes, I ignored this one, choosing instead to shake a fresh cigarette from a half-empty pack on the desk, snap open my Zippo and light up, drawing a deep lungful of of smoke. "How was your weekend?" she asked. "Do anything exciting with Lana?"

"We did not." My reply was curt and my look sour.

"Oooookay," Doris replied. "I'll say no more." There was a brief awkward moment before I cleared my throat.

"Sorry. Shouldn't bite your head off. The love life is rather a sore spot at the moment. What about you and Alfredo?" I asked.

"*Pietro*, Drummond, Pietro."

"Yeah, sure, Pietro. I was just pulling your pinky."

"As a matter of fact, we had a lovely weekend. After he got off work

Saturday night, he took me dancing at Club Maroc. And since yesterday was so beautiful, we went to the zoo." I froze with the coffee mug at my lips, then lowered it slowly.

"You went to the zoo?"

"We did."

"You and... Pietro?"

"Yes."

"The zoo?"

"*Yes*, Drummond — you know, the place with all the animals? The place where many of our clients belong?"

"Guess I didn't figure you were the zoo type. Guess I figured you and lover boy would have spent your Sunday locked away, far from the madding crowd." Doris smirked.

"In your fevered little brain." With a smirk of my own, I turned my attention back to my coffee.

"My fevered little brain would like to know how the schedule looks today."

"Let me think a moment," Doris said, wrinkling her brow and tapping the side of her head in mock concentration. "Well, this morning you're clear. Then this afternoon, there's nothing until we lock up." I leaned back in my swivel chair, drew on my cigarette, exhaled and regarded my secretary through a haze of smoke.

"When was the last time we had a client?"

"I believe Mr. Truman was still President."

"Seriously, Doris."

"A week. Maybe ten days. Since the Crawford bail bondsman business." I rolled my eyes up toward the ceiling. "Not exactly cover material for *True Detective*," Doris continued. I snorted.

"Did we get paid?"

"Still waiting."

"The story of my life," I said, finishing the last of the coffee and sliding the mug across the desk with an imploring look.

Doris swiped up the mug, and within a quick minute was back.

"Thanks."

"You're welcome. Now, if you'll excuse me, I've got some filing to do."

"Explain to me," I began skeptically, "how you have filing to do when we haven't had any clients beating down our door." Doris smiled, raised a hand and wiggled her fingers.

"My nails, Drummond." I had to shake my head. That one was too easy; I should have seen it coming.

Doris closed the door behind her, and once she did, I turned to the pressing matters at hand.

Pulling a ballpoint out of the desk drawer, I opened the morning paper to the crossword, folded the page, leaned back in my chair and got to work. It didn't take long. Never did on Mondays when the clues weren't very taxing — a four-letter word for "La Scala solo" — that kind of thing.

After I dispensed with the puzzle, it was off to the sports pages to peruse the box scores. It was my daily exercise in masochism, so poorly was my team playing. Halfway through the '54 season, Stan Hack had the Cubs wallowing at the bottom of the National League barrel. And they had lost again the day before to the equally hapless Phillies.

Enough self-inflicted pain for one morning, so I laid the paper aside, threw one more look at the gloom out the window, then kicked back, put both feet on the desk, folded my hands and got down to what would turn out to be the most productive part of my morning. I closed my eyes and caught forty winks.

*****

By just after noon I had come around and so had the weather — big sky scattered with dazzling white clouds, spun confections across an azure dome. With plenty of time on my hands, I decided that a stroll was in order, so I stretched and nipped my homburg off the coat rack.

"And you are going?" Doris asked as I stepped into the outer office.

"Out to get some lunch. What's your pleasure — I'm buying," I replied.

"Well," Doris began with mock surprise, "let me mark this event on the calendar."

"If you're going to be a wise-ass, I'll rescind my generous offer."

"Oh, no, I'm deeply grateful. Really. But fetching food is one of my official duties isn't it?"

"It is, but you're relieved today. I need to perambulate. So what are you in the mood for?" Doris hesitated for only a moment.

"A little Greek, I think." I arched my eyebrows.

"Better not let your big Italian find out," I said reaching for the doorknob. Doris returned a wan smile and lifted a middle finger in my direction.

After a morning in the quiet and relative gloom of the office, the bright sunlight and noise hit me like a slap in the face when I stepped out into the street. I paused for a moment to let the warmth on my skin seep in and allow my ears to adjust to the cacophony.

My destination was Kriti, two blocks over, a humble hole in the wall with only room enough for couple of sorry tables and chairs and the stolid figure of Mother Elektra behind the counter. Still, it offered up the best Greek carry-out in the Loop.

Half-a-block away, my eye was caught by a display in the window of Gold's, a bookshop I frequented, so I slipped in under the merry chime of the small brass bell attached above the door and picked up a copy of Ian Fleming's latest James Bond adventure.

Paperback safely tucked inside my jacket, my stop at Kriti was a quick one, long enough to pick up two gyros, make a fruitless attempt at a joke with Mother Elektra, pay the dollar-sixty tab and get back to the office.

"Famished," Doris said as I opened the brown paper bag and set the sandwich on her desk. "And did you remember --"

"Extra tzatziki? Do you think I'd dare return without it?" I replied, producing a small container with a flourish.

"Oooh, you're good at this. Maybe you should make the lunch run every day."

"I wouldn't get my hopes up," I answered drily.

Inside my office, I quickly shrugged out of my jacket and loosened my tie. The day had turned hot and the room was stifling, so I pushed open the only window, set a small fan on the sill and turned it on. *One of these days, if I ever make enough goddamned money, I'm going to buy myself an air conditioner,* I groused to myself as I settled in behind the desk to eat my lunch and get caught up in 007's newest intrigue. One bite and two pages in, the intercom buzzed.

"What is it, Doris?" I was slightly annoyed by the interruption.

"There's a fellow on the line who says he knows you. He sounds *real* nervous."

"He give you a name?"

"He said 'just tell him it's Smooth.' Mean anything to you?"

"It does. Put him through." I reached for a crumpled handkerchief to blot the perspiration from my forehead. The fan seemed to shudder as it cut through the oppressive air. I slid a Pall Mall from the pack on the desktop and lit up, exhaling twin ribbons of smoke through my nose as I lifted the telephone off its cradle.

"This wouldn't be the city's best damned bass player, would it?"

"We need to talk, Drummond."

"Whoa, man — not even a 'hello-I'm-fine-how-the-hell-are-you?'"

"Ain't got time for that. We need to talk."

"Okay, you got me, so talk."

"Not on the phone."

"Why don't you come to the office?"

"Naw, man, I ain't comin' up there. Tonight, at the club, after the first set. We break about 11:30. And it's gotta be *tonight.*"

And just like that, he hung up. I drew on my cigarette, frowning. Melvin "Smooth" Dobbins had earned his nickname, both for the way he played and how he carried himself. He was always so self-possessed, the most laid back cat in the room, and that was why I was troubled by his tone. Not the Smooth I knew. Whatever was up with him, it must be plenty serious.

*****

Percy's Hideaway wasn't on the tourist maps. Deep on the South Side at 79th and Cottage Grove, it was neither the place nor the neighborhood most folks would seek out. Not white folks, that is. But jazz aficionados knew all about Percy's. To them, white or black, it was Mecca.

Mine was a familiar face at the club. During my time on the force, it was a haven where I could kick back, drink and get lost in the music. And I stayed a regular, making a special point to take in Smooth's quartet whenever they were booked.

That night I arrived in time for the first set, ordered up a bourbon and water and settled in near the bandstand. It was a small room with a dozen or so tables. Intimate. I liked that.

Smooth's combo, the Take Four, was solid as always, whether breathing fresh life into one of the standards or laying down original material. The house was full and appreciative, giving the musicians their due as they took their first break. Smooth wasted no time, approaching me with a hard face that bore no trace of its usual openness.

"Hey, man," I began.

"Come with me. We ain't got much time." He took the lead, behind the bandstand, down a dimly lit, narrow hallway past the dressing room to a staircase. We climbed to the second floor, then through a steel door leading out onto a fire escape. Once there, Smooth seemed to relax, but only a little, shaking out a cigarette. I did the same, lighting both our smokes.

"Never seen you tense like this," I said. "What's going on?"

"Some serious shit, man."

"I'm listening."

"Last night after the gig, I slipped up here, and while I'm smoking my j, the back door opens and Percy and two white dudes walk out and start talking. Now, they don't know I'm up here, so I just mind my own business and listen."

"You recognize the white guys?"

"One of them, a cop. Detective. Dude with a Polack name."

"Senkewicz?"

"Yeah, that's it. I seen him around. Seems pretty tight with Percy."

"And the other one?"

"No idea. Had his back to me, so I never got a look at him."

"So what was the palaver all about?" Smooth took a deep drag off his cigarette.

"Okay. You know that Percy has more going on here than a nightclub."

"Of course — the 'gentlemen's quarters'."

"Percy works with a cat who runs some very fine women. High class, you know? White dudes with plenty of jack don't mind coming downtown for a little taste of the chocolate, you dig? Percy provides the space for entertaining and gets a nice cut of the action."

"Not exactly a secret," I said. "Percy keeps his nose clean, greases the right palms and everybody's happy."

"Yeah, right. But last night he and the other two were talking about something new — *underage* girls, man — bringing them in from over in Indiana, maybe Calumet City or Gary."

"You sure?"

"I'm sure. But that ain't all of it. The whole deal is a special setup for some very important people."

"Like who?"

"I didn't hear no names, but there's supposed to be another meet-up here tonight to finalize the plans, so I'm going to do just like you do, Drummond — keep my eyes and ears wide open. Come back tomorrow night, same time, and if I got anything, I'll pass it along." Smooth paused and looked away into the night.

"You're taking this pretty personally, aren't you?" I asked, noting my friend's distress. He turned and looked hard at me.

"You're damned right," he said. "I never told you, but I got a fifteen-year-old daughter lives with her mother up in Detroit."

*****

The next day was a long, drawn out affair. Fry-an-egg-on-the-sidewalk weather without much to show for it but an afternoon visit from a middle-aged woman in a purple dress and matching hat adorned with a pheasant feather that preceded her by at least two feet. It was clear by her accoutrements that she had a few shekels in the bank and was prepared to spend them, she said, to find out for certain if her husband was carrying on with "a little tramp" who worked as a cigarette girl at one of the city's tonier nightspots. I didn't much like getting into these domestic entanglements — and I'd been in the middle of many — but they helped keep the lights on, so I agreed to take the case. As the aggrieved woman departed, Doris looked at me and rolled her eyes.

That wrapped up the day. After an early supper, a couple of stiff bourbons and an aimless hour in front of the television, I napped on the couch before it was time to head downtown.

When I arrived just before 11:30, there were two police cruisers and an ambulance at the curb, lights flashing and radios crackling. The front door of the club opened and a pair of medics wheeled out a stretcher bearing Melvin Dobbins.

"Smooth — hey, man, can you hear me? What happened?" I said at the side of the gurney. My friend's eyes flickered open and he grasped me weakly by the arm. His lips moved, but what he was trying to say was inaudible, so I bent low, putting my ear to his mouth.

"Dressing room...picture," was all he could whisper before slipping into unconsciousness.

"C'mon, buddy," one of the attendants said to me urgently, "we've got to get him to the hospital." I stepped back and watched as the medics swung the rear doors of the ambulance wide and loaded the stretcher.

"Well, well, what brings you to the neighborhood?" The voice was raspy, cocky. I turned as Frank Senkewicz exited the club followed by Percy Warren.

"What's going on, Frank?"

"It's a terrible tragedy," Percy said, mouth dry, voice pinched, eyes darting quickly to Senkewicz and then away. I cocked my head at the cop.

"Frank?"

"Your boy Dobbins. Bad accident."

"What *accident?*" I snapped.

"Looks like he fell from the fire escape out back, hit his head. Poor bastard." There wasn't a shred of feeling in his voice. "I guess it's a good thing you saw him last night."

"What are you talking about?"

"You were here, right?"

"And if I was?"

"I just mention it, that's all," Senkewicz said nonchalantly as the ambulance pulled away from the curb, siren wailing. "A shame. Accidents, I mean. You just never know." He threw me a thin-lipped smile before he and Percy moved away, leaving me standing, numb.

Smooth had found out too much. And he had told me where to find it myself.

I went to the alley behind the club and made my way to the back door. From there, it was only a half-dozen steps to the club's dressing room.

It was a small space, just enough room for two or three folding chairs, a place to hang a few clothes and a lighted mirror with a lacquered makeup table beneath it. That's where I saw a small gold-framed photo. It was of Smooth, younger, smiling, with his arm around a pretty girl. I guessed she was about ten.

His daughter.

I lifted the picture, running my thumb lightly over the glass, turned it over, moved two small clasps to the side and removed the back of the frame. When I did, a slip of paper fell out. On it, in small, nervous print, there was a date and two names. I read them, and as I did, I let out a low whistle.

*****

I knew just where to find Tony Pugliese on a Wednesday afternoon. At fifty-two, Pugliese had been a cop for twenty-seven years. Still trim and well-muscled for his age, he was also the senior middleweight boxing champion of the police athletic league. Every Wednesday, he and his sparring partner went a few rounds at West Side Boxing on South Kedzie, just down the street from police headquarters.

"How's life among the civilians?" Pugliese cracked as he stepped between the ring ropes, jumped down to the floor and shed his oversized sparring gloves.

"Living the dream, Tony," I replied. This elicited a wry snort from Pugliese as he picked up a towel and draped it around his neck.

"Purely a social call today?"

"Business." Pugliese looked me up and down.

"Give me a few to shower and change."

I liked Tony Pugliese, always had, though our paths hadn't crossed that often when I was on the force. I appreciated his sense of humor, his take on the world. That was part of it. The rest was the respect and trust I had for him. He was a straight-shooter. His slate was clean. That was saying a lot in a town where there were cops so crooked they couldn't walk a straight line if they had a gun to their heads.

Once Tony had cleaned up, we went around the corner to the Shangri La, a misnomer if one ever existed. The lounge was a shadowy hole in the wall that featured faded photos of the town's sports heroes from bygone days and a very large Maine Coon cat that had his run of the place and took a dim view of the clientele.

Toward the back of the room Tony and I found a worn booth, slipped in and ordered beers.

"What's so earth-shattering you had to corral me at the gym?" I shook a cigarette free.

"Do you mind?" I asked.

"You want to kill yourself with those, it's your life." I lit up and took a deep drag.

"How long have you been running the vice task force, Tony?"

"A little over eighteen months."

"Do much business on the South Side?"

"On occasion."

"With Percy's place?" Pugliese wasn't known for his patience.

"You want to cut to the chase here?"

"Percy's got a scheme cooking with Frank Senkewicz — "

"That sonofabitch," Pugliese spat out.

" — to bring in underage girls from Indiana for the express purpose of entertaining some big shots."

"How do you know this?" he demanded.

I reached into the pocket of my suit jacket and removed the slip of paper Smooth had left. I laid it on the table and slid it across. Pugliese's eyes narrowed as he read, then looked up at me.

"How did you get this?"

"A friend of mine, a musician at the club, overheard talk and did some nosing around."

"You convinced it's solid?"

"I am. It was important enough to my friend that it cost him his life, Tony."

"And Senkewicz is in on it?"

"Up to his eyeballs." Pugliese looked across the table at me with a tight smile. He raised the piece of paper.

"You mind if I hang onto this?"

"That's why I brought it."

*****

Three days later I sat smoking in my office, nursing my second cup of coffee The night before, Tony Pugliese and his vice squad had hit Percy's, with the results splashed across the front page of the morning paper on my desk:

SOUTH SIDE SEX RAID NETS BIG FISH
SONS OF MAYOR, CITY COUNCIL PREZ ARRESTED
UNDERAGE COLORED GIRLS

Beneath the glaring headlines were four pictures — the two young scions of the powerful, Percy Warren and Frank Senkewicz. The story fleshed out the details of the raid, with numerous quotes from Pugliese about cracking the case with "inside information," that even "the well-connected were not above the law" and the importance of "putting away rotten apples" who gave good cops on the force a bad name.

It was shaping up to be another scorcher of July day. I looked outside — not a cloud on the horizon. The clamor of the city rose up from the street and through the open office window. The fan, perched on the sill, seemed to be fighting a losing battle against the heat.

I sat back and drew deeply on my cigarette, slowly exhaling as I thought of my friend.

For you, man.

Going to California
John Kojak

They were on their way to California. A fresh start, his wife said. But he knew it was a mistake; they weren't going to make it. In California, or anywhere else.

He tried to focus on the road, and enjoy the low, rumbling growl his 1967 Camaro's 350 cubic inch engine made as it chewed up the miles. But as soon as he managed to forget about her, there she was.

"Why did we get off the freeway? There's nothing on these back roads, it looks like the ass end of the moon out here." Jessica whined.

"The Interstates ruined this country. They killed its soul, and a lot of small towns too. These old highways are the only way to see the real America," Dale said as he adjusted the rear-view mirror. The dark outline of the road stretched out behind them unbroken to the horizon.

"The real America?" She fanned herself with her phone, even though the air conditioning was blasting in her face. "Like that motel last night."

"That's right."

"It didn't even have a name, the sign just said 'Motel.' "

"It had a bed. What more do you need?"

She gave him a disgusted look. "It was probably full of bugs…"

"Oh please, spare me the princess routine." He could feel the anger rising in his chest. "Why don't you just enjoy the scenery. There are no shopping malls or chain restaurants, it's beautiful out here."

"It's all desert, there's nothing but rocks and sand."

"That's your problem, Jessie. You don't see the beauty of taking the road less traveled. You never have."

"Oh God. Here we go." She reached into her purse, grabbed a cigarette, lit it. "Have you ever considered that there might be a reason no one else takes these roads?"

He reached down and turned up the radio, hoping she would take the hint. She didn't.

"Where are we?" She shouted over the distortion saturated chords of a Smashing Pumpkin's song.

He turned down the music and replied as calmly as he could mange, "We crossed into Nevada a few hours ago…I told you that."

"I know we're in Nevada, but where *are* we? I'm hungry."

"There are some chips in the back."

"I don't want any more greasy-ass potato chips. I need to EAT." She slumped down into her seat and let out a long, exaggerated sigh.

He gripped the steering wheel tightly, like it was a rope he was hanging on to for his life. In many ways it was. If he loosened his grip, one of his hands was likely to fly off the wheel and smack Jessica right in her face. "What the hell happened to you…"

"Me? What the hell happened to YOU!" She put her feet up on the dashboard. She knew he hated that.

His knuckles turned white. This wasn't the same girl he married. That Jessica had platinum blonde hair with lime-green bangs, and tits that pointed straight up to the moon. She liked to party, and go to Toadies concerts.

But that seemed like a lifetime ago. Before she stopped dying her hair and her tits began to sag, and before she got caught banging her boss at Lecher & Wolf, the overpriced chop shop they called a law firm, on the conference room table. He should have left her, but there was still a part of him that was in love with the faded memory of the woman she had been. That's why he agreed to move to California and try to save what was left of their marriage, but any love he still had for her died somewhere on the road outside of Albuquerque.

"There's something," he pointed toward a crude wooden sign on the side of the road ahead. The word *Food* was painted across it in big sloppy red letters. A broken board nailed beneath the sign exclaimed *1 mile*.

"What's with the one-word signs, are these people retarded?"

"What more do you need to know? You said you're hungry, they got food."

She rolled down her window and flicked her cigarette out. "I need to know my dinner wasn't chained up out back before they threw it on the grill. That's what."

He pressed his foot down on the accelerator, trying to close the distance before it was too late—for both of them.

"This has to be the place," he said when the old, tattered diner finally came into view. It wasn't much. A small rectangular wooden building that sat back off the highway behind an unpaved dirt parking lot. The outside of the structure, really little more than a shack, was painted in the same fire engine red paint as the sign. A faded powder-blue Ford pickup truck sat slouched beside the building, and a white Lincoln Town Car was parked in front under a long dirty window. He pulled off the highway and parked on the far side of the parking lot, away from the door.

"Seriously…you expect me to eat here?"

"What do you want, a Denny's? Besides, these old greasy spoons have some of the best food anyway."

"I think I am going to throw up," Jessica said. Her words dripping with disgust.

He turned the ignition off and reached under his seat for a small metal tin. There was half a joint he had been saving inside. "Order me a cheeseburger and some fries, babe. I'll be in in a minute."

Loser. That's what he was. It was written all over her face. "Order it your damn self." She threw the car door open, climbed out, and slammed the door so hard the car rocked back and forth on its springs.

He watched as she walked, swinging her arms like an angry gorilla, across the dirt lot to the unmarked red door and went inside. Any grace she ever had was gone.

Who the hell is she to judge me, he thought, lighting the joint, inhaling deeply. She was the one who had been screwing around. He met the guy once; at a holiday party a couple of years ago, back before she was too embarrassed to take him to those sorts of things. He could tell Tim Lecher was a snake as soon as he laid eyes on him. Metallic grey suite, greased back hair, a huge friggin' pinkie ring. Scumbag. She thought that asshole loved her, that he was going to take care of her. She was wrong. He took another hit.

He looked up just in time to see a shiny new silver Dodge Challenger turn quickly off the road and come to a sliding stop in the dirt parking lot. A huge wall of sand and dust drifted swiftly toward his car.

"What a douchebag," he muttered, looking out into the dark orange haze. The cloud quickly consumed his vision, preventing him from getting a look at who was driving, but he told himself he would say something to the guy when he went inside. He took another hit. Definitely.

He had just snubbed out the roach when he heard the shots. A loud *Boom* that sounded like a cannon, followed by several *Pops* that came in rapid succession. He threw himself down across the seat. A few seconds later he heard the roar of an engine, the whine of spinning tires, and the rapid machinegun like metallic clinks as hundreds of little rocks banged off the sheet metal of his old Camaro.

A bitter brown cloud of dust masked everything around him. It didn't matter. He threw the car door open and ran blindly in the direction of the small diner.

Thud!

He found it. He rubbed his shoulder with one hand as he worked his way down the wall feeling for the outline of the doorframe with the other. There. He reached for the knob, turned it, and walked from the hellish opacity of the parking lot into the bright fluorescent lights of the restaurant. It looked about as good on the inside as it did on the outside. There were six stools along the counter and a row of four tables against the window. An ancient green cash register sat on the end of the counter across from the door. Its drawer was open. Empty. The place smelled like the Fourth of July.

A fat old man with a long gray ponytail was lying on the floor beside the cash register. He was a wearing a grease-stained white apron and holding a meat clever in his right hand. A large pool of dark brown blood was spreading slowly out from underneath his sagging belly. Halfway down the countertop a waitress in a pink polyester top was splayed out like a rag doll. Her face was gone, but she was still clutching a sawed-off double-barrel shotgun in her arms. An elderly couple sat at the first table nearest the door. The man was wearing a captain's hat, the kind with the crossed anchors on the front, and a light tan jacket. A small hole and trickle of blood above his right cheek. Pieces of his brains and skull littered the table behind him. An old woman with a beehive hairdo was face down in a plate of eggs. He looked over the counter into the kitchen. No one.

Where was Jessica?

There was a small sign hanging above a door at the far end of the room that said, "Water Closet." He walked quickly to the door and kicked it open. Empty.

Where was she?

"Jessie!" he shouted, walking back toward the kitchen.

"Jessica!"

He looked around the side of the still smoking flat iron grill, and under the ramshackle shelves lining the walls. He even checked the small freezer. Nothing.

Maybe she ran out the back? He flew out the sagging screen door in the back of the kitchen. There was nothing outside but rocks and sand in every direction as far as the eye could see.

"Jessica!" he yelled as he ran around the building, stopping in front, next to the powder-blue pickup truck. She was nowhere.

He walked quickly out to the edge of the road. A dark streak of freshly laid black rubber swung angrily out across the asphalt. It was the Challenger. They were headed east.

He figured whoever was in that car had must swerved off the highway to rob the diner thinking it would be a gravy smash and grab. But then the fat bastard in the apron must have come running out of the kitchen with the meat clever, and the waitress pulled that scattergun out from under the counter. Things must have gotten ugly in there real quick. He had heard the shots. The first, and loudest, must have been from that sawed-off. How the waitress missed anyone with that thing he would never know. But she must have, because they waisted her, the cook, and those mummies in the booth in rapid succession. Four of five shots and they were out of there. But what about Jessica?

Did they take her? Was that even possible? It seemed like there were only a few seconds between the sound of the shots and the roar of the Challenger's engine as it sped off. The dust clouds had obscured everything. He couldn't see who was driving, or even how many people were in the car. It had all happened too fast.

But that must be it. They must have grabbed her, as a hostage, or for God knows what, and taken off. He raced to his car, dived inside and checked his cell phone. No signal. He turned the key, punched the gas, and spun the car around until it faced the road. If he turned east he could try to catch the Challenger, try to save Jessica. Or…

He slammed the pedal down hard. Swinging the wheel toward the plum-purple outline of the Sierra Mountains rising low against the western sky.

"Jessica can go to hell. I'm going to California."

A Smith & Wesson with a Side of Chorizo
Andrew Welsh-Huggins

Then, for the first time in months — in years?—Daniel found himself dreaming of Hannah. A real dream, not a waking reminiscence flaring in his brain when he could least afford it. Those sudden daytime memories so taxing they stopped him in his tracks and rendered him as useless as the dirt-flecked fifty-pound sacks of potatoes he hauled twice a week from the back of the truck, down the hall, past the bored CO and into the kitchen. Debilitating moments, not to mention dangerous. Any perception of laziness and the guards on you like a ton of bricks, and not always figuratively. But this was different. A dream while he slept, playing out like a movie in his unconsciousness. Hannah as real as he remembered her, laughing as she ran ahead of him in the yard. Shrieking as he sped up and then scooped her up in his arms, tagged her it and started the game all over again....

He awoke with a start. He blinked twice in terror, with no idea where he was or how he'd gotten here. Was he even alive? He closed his eyes, slowly reopened them, and remembered. The bus. Rolling along at 70 miles per. Farther and farther from Ohio. Closer and closer to Chicago. Still night, with nothing to see through the window but his own reflection. He tried to remember the dream, to summon Hannah's sweet face, but it was already fading back down into the black well of his memory. She always faded. If only he'd slept just a little bit longer. Had her by his side again for just a few more moments. But something had awakened him. Brought him back to the bus and the rush of the last twenty-four hours. Not something, he realized. Someone. Someone had been calling his name. He shifted in his seat and looked at her looking at him.

"What in the hell?"

"You were having a nightmare. It's okay now."

He sat up. "What are you doing here?"

"I got on in Dayton."

"What?" Not comprehending. Wide awake now, the dream vanished like mist burned off by a hot August sun. Nancy staring at him, her pixie face just visible in the shadows, hazel eyes wide with concern. Swimming in the oversized Ohio State sweatshirt she showed up in at the gas station where they agreed to meet.

"I drove to Dayton and bought a ticket there. After I dropped you off in Columbus."

"What about your car?"

"I parked it on the street."

"They'll tow it."

"It's a piece of crap anyway. And you said we're getting one in Chicago. Once we get there."

He stared at her in disbelief. "I'm getting one. Once I'm there."

In the seat in front of them a woman stirred. Cleared her throat.

"You shouldn't have done this," Daniel said. "You shouldn't be here. I told you."

"You didn't tell me nothing. That's what's got me worried. I ain't quitting on you just because you said to." She reached for his hand but he pulled it away. Instead he rocked forward, making two fists and balling them into his eyes. Tried to process what was happening. Nancy, on the bus with him. Ignoring his promise—his lie—that he'd see her again. Threatening his plan. His mission less than eight hours old and already shot to hell.

"Excuse me," he said, pushing himself up.

"What are you doing?"

"Bathroom," he managed.

"You okay?"

Jesus Christ. Did it look like he was okay?

"Yes," he said.

Getting his balance in the aisle, he looked down the bus toward the front. Less than half full. But fuller now with Nancy on. He stumbled his way into the can, slammed the bolt shut, sat on the seat. He didn't really need to be in here but he couldn't be out there just now. He had to think. This threw a wrench into everything. Chicago. Kelly. The fully loaded special. Just when he thought he had it all figured out. Just when he'd finally taken control. Just when....

Hannah's face swam before him, unbidden as always. Gap-toothed smile. A hundred hundred cinnamon freckles riding her cheeks. Hair the color of straw, pulled back into a My Little Pony scrunchie. Daniel pressed a fist into his forehead, feeling the headache moving in. What was Nancy thinking?

Yet if it hadn't been for her he wouldn't be on this bus at all. He'd have missed his chance altogether. The moment he'd waited for all these years would be wasted. He had to acknowledge that. But did that give her the right to jeopardize the back half of the plan? Did it?

Hannah's face again, sunny as a May day. He squeezed his eyes as tight as possible, trying to drive her away. Trying in vain.

"You're right," he whispered at last.

He unlocked the bathroom door and walked back to his seat. Nancy looked up at him, her sweatshirt off and over her lap. He glanced at her blouse, slid past her and sat down.

"Listen—"

"No, you listen." She took his hand and this time didn't let him take it away. Pulled it under her sweatshirt, placed it between her legs. Nothing between his hand and all of her.

His eyes widened. "What are you doing?"

She pressed a finger on his lips. She reached down and slowly slowly slowly undid his zipper.

"Stop." He looked in panic at the seat in front of them. But the woman was gone. Nancy followed his gaze.

"She's up front. I gave her twenty bucks to move." She tugged at his pants and reached inside his shorts and held him with her right hand. "There now," she said, stroking gently. "There now."

"Don't," he whispered. "This is crazy."

"Ain't it?"

"The driver — he'll see."

"He's not gonna see nothing. And ain't his business if he does. C'mon now, darling. Help a girl out."

Not entirely believing what was happening, he helped Nancy out, pulling his pants to his knees. When he was ready — it didn't take long — he watched her reach into her backpack and a moment later felt her small, cool fingers as she pulled the condom on. When she was finished, she turned herself around, nimble as a gymnast, to face him. She reached around her neck, raised her beaded lariat leather necklace, the one he'd admired the first time she visited, the one her brother made for her, and looped it around his head so it held their faces close. "Just you and me, now," she said, putting her tiny mouth on his, reaching down and drawing him all the way in. He wanted to fight it, to tell her to stop. Just like he tried to stop her from visiting him at first, him not knowing her from Adam. Or Eve, more like it. But now it was too late. It had been too long. He reached for her and brought her close and gasped in rhythm to the rocking. Nancy paused and placed her hand over his mouth.

"I gotcha, darling," she whispered. "I gotcha."

Afterward, they sat together holding hands.

"Ever done it on a bus?" Nancy said.

"Can't say that I have."

"I done it lots of ways. Hope that's okay?"

He squeezed her hand, his mind already drifting elsewhere. To the North. To Kelly.

"Never done it behind, though."

"What?" he said, confused.

"I've never done it behind. Like a dog. You know?"

He turned to stare at her, make sure he'd heard right. It might have been the oddest thing she'd ever said to him. And you could take a ticket in that regard.

"You've done it on a bus but never from behind?"

She nodded innocently as if confessing she'd never watched TV or had a pet bigger than a gerbil.

Nancy said, "Would you do that with me?"

"If you want."

"I want," she said, hand rising unconsciously to the leather necklace.

Daniel looked out the window, the countryside still cloaked in black. Nothing to see and still so far to go. And now this new complication. He wondered idly if he could pull it off, the thing with Kelly, then dismissed the thought at once with the force of slapping a fly on the chow hall table. Did he have any choice? It was just a matter of waiting. He only had this long ride to make it through first. He closed his eyes to help the time pass with no expectation of rest.

When he opened them again the bus was pulling into the Harrison Street depot. They were in Chicago.

*****

"I still don't get it," Qualls said, studying her computer screen.

"What's not to get?" Heintz said, leaning back in his chair. "He's a mope. Mopes run."

Qualls rolled her eyes, not caring if he saw. And how couldn't he, the two them crammed into her cubbyhole of a prison office. For a statie he wasn't a bad guy, but Jesus, the arrogance sometimes. As if God died and made him boss.

"What?"

"Nothing," Qualls said. She scrolled down the screen, back to reading O'Connor's file.

"Sure, some guys run," she continued. "But with one week to go? With a job lined up and housing approved? Why throw all that away? It doesn't make any sense."

"Maybe he got a better offer."

"Har har. And maybe you're full of shit."

Heintz laughed, dropped his chair back to four legs, and picked up the printout Qualls handed him fifteen minutes earlier. "I just don't think we should overthink this."

"Why am I not surprised."

Qualls ignored the middle finger Heintz presented as he pretended to scratch his cheek and focused on the file in front of her. Daniel Brian

O'Connor. Forty-one years of age. Caucasian male. Tail end of fifteen to life for felonious assault out of Franklin County. Not a blemish on his record once he was inside, not even mouthing off to a CO, which took some doing. Which explained his presence at the work camp at the Marion prison just north of Columbus. Which further explained how he'd been able to just walk away, but not why he did so with literally seven days left before his scheduled release. Facing a minimum of ten years, and not at a work camp, once they grabbed him and dragged him back inside. She went over all this again with the patrol investigator.

"So who'd he assault?"

She checked the file. "Carl Boles. Cellmate at Franklin County Jail."

"Why was O'Connor there?"

More scrolling up and down. "Looks like he was overnighting on a DUI."

"So he's a drunk."

"He might be a drunk but that was his first offense. Nothing else in the system on him."

"Any deets on the assault?"

Deets. Jesus. These patrol guys.

"Beat him six ways sideways, according to this. Smashed his head on the toilet seat multiple times. Permanent brain damage. Only thing that saved Boles was another inmate shouting for a guard."

"What was Boles's deal? Wouldn't share the covers?"

Qualls read farther on. "Here we go. Awaiting trial on multiple counts of rape and sodomy." She made a face. "Two nieces, eleven and nine. Repeatedly, over a period of at least two years."

"Sounds like he got what was coming to him."

"Might not disagree. But putting that aside, it makes you wonder about O'Connor."

Finally, Heintz looked interested. He rubbed his hand up and down his pale, pink chin. "Wonder what?"

"Maybe he had a thing about child molesters. Boles wouldn't be the first perv to taste jailhouse justice. I mean, O'Connor has no record, squat, and then the first thing he does when he's inside on his very first collar is pound the living daylights out of this particular guy? Out of all the other guys on the unit?"

"Decent theory. Any chance O'Connor decided to finish the job?"

Qualls pulled up the OHLEG database, typed for thirty seconds, waited a minute, and studied the results.

"No such luck. Says here Boles died inside. Convicted and then spent most of his time on the medical wing."

"Hope he died a miserable death. So, I guess we do it the old-fashioned way. Start with O'Connor's people. Where's he from?"

"Lived in Columbus, far as I can tell. Nothing in the system from before the DUI, so it's a little hard to tell."

"Visitors?"

"I'm having the office pull the logs now."

"Sounds good. I'll have one of the girls in Intelligence work up a profile just in case."

"One of the girls?" Qualls said, raising an eyebrow. "What are they, in elementary school?"

"Sorry. One of the 'women,'" Heintz said, making air quotes and not sounding sorry. "I'll probably ask Altagracia Rodriguez. You know her?"

Qualls summoned up an image of the pretty young analyst. It didn't take long. It also didn't take a job as an in-house prison investigator to know why Heintz would select her out of all the other analysts.

"I know who she is."

"Figured you would."

"Fuck you. That's puppy breath. Your wife know you're thinking dirty thoughts about her?"

"Does yours?" Heintz said.

"Keisha doesn't care because she knows how good she's got it with me around. Can you say the same?"

"I got four kids and one on the way. What do you think?"

"I think a clothes pin would do you some good," Qualls said, reaching for the phone. "Go take a cold shower and call Rodriguez while I see where they are on those visitors' logs."

✶✶✶✶✶

Edgerton paused for a second, raising his fingers from the keyboard. He rubbed his eyes. He reached for the two-liter bottle of Mountain Dew beside him, lifted it to his lips and took three long gulps, draining the remains. He tossed it behind him where it bounced off the other empties gathered on the carpet. Good thing he'd stocked up. Three for five bucks at the Northbrook Aldi's. He needed a cart to haul them all to his car. He blinked, realizing he was having trouble focusing his eyes, as if someone — some bitch — had draped a filmy cloth over his face. He'd lost track of time. No light penetrated the black cloth he'd duct-taped over the basement windows. He squeezed his eyes tight, waiting for the constellation of lights filling the darkness in his brain to dissipate.

A moment later, back in control, he glanced around the bedroom. The bag and the pipes and the chanter were neatly laid out on the table. The kit — the kilt and the vest and the jacket and everything else — lay on his bed. The cardboard box and its valuable cargo were tucked under the bed. Everything safe and sound. Satisfied, he resumed work, returning to the long, unbroken paragraph scrolling down the screen.

... false empress straddling the city between your legs the stolen election the hot cum you don't deserve but will beg for BEG FOR when the time comes (cums) and the time is now if you understand anything in that tiny fem brain the one BETWEEN YOUR EARS not your legs but that brain will understand too finally AT LAST when it's too late for the whores and the sluts and the SLITS unleashed on us but no more because when I ....

Edgerton paused again just long enough to glance at the clock in the corner of his screen. Almost noon. He needed to pick it up. He'd only written 10,000 words so far. Less than twenty-four hours to go and there was still so much more to say.

✶✶✶✶✶

They each had a backpack and nothing else. They walked stiffly off the bus and out of the station and stood on the street and blinked in the early morning sun. They zipped up their jackets, shielding themselves from the mid-March chill. The matching blue parkas a gift from Nancy — "Shoplifted them from Walmart; hope that's okay?" — when she picked him up behind the Speedway when he snuck off from highway trash duty. Here and there short ragged ridges of snow, grimy with dirt, still hugged curbs and trashcans and hydrants. Daniel took a breath and got his bearings. Fought off dizziness as the unanticipated weight of freedom bore down on him: the buildings looming like mountains, the streets wide as rivers, the hordes of people like an army let loose on the city. Steadying himself, he reached into his right jeans pocket and pulled out the used prison kite he'd written the address on. He studied it — pointless, like he hadn't memorized it within the first five seconds — and tucked it back in his pocket.

"You ever gonna tell me what we're doing?" Nancy said.

"Let's find something to eat."

"I packed granola bars."

"I need something hot."

They walked a couple blocks north, Daniel leading the way, then turned east, toward the lake. Low gray clouds bunched at the horizon, gulls wheeling in the near distance, crying like cats. Just before Michigan Avenue Nancy pointed across the street at a McDonald's. Daniel shook his head. Too close to the shit he'd eaten inside. In you and out of you in less than two hours. A block farther on he spied a Greek diner at the corner. He took Nancy by the arm and they ducked inside. Daniel turned his head to the wall while Nancy ordered them breakfast.

"We only got a hundred dollars," she said apologetically when the waitress left.

He blinked. "What?"

She repeated herself.

"You gave me three," he said, fumbling inside his backpack. "At the Speedway, just after I got in the car. I counted it out. You watched me."

"I'm sorry, darling. We needed gas. And then the bus ticket...."

"When?"

"When what?"

"When did you take it back?"

"In Columbus, at the station. When you went to the bathroom. I didn't think it was that big a deal. Since I'd, you know, be seeing you again so soon." She fingered the leather lariat around her neck nervously.

Daniel fought off the panic building in his stomach. "You shouldn't have come along. I told you I'd meet you when I was done."

Nancy made a face, hazel eyes narrowing. "You seemed happy to see me in the back of the bus, I recall."

She had him there.

"But you took my money," he said, trying again.

"My money. That I loaned you. And I didn't take it. I borrowed it back."

"I told you I needed three. *At least* three."

Ask for the special. It's gonna cost you, too, so come prepared.

"Can't we get more?"

"From where? Do I look like somebody who can just walk into a bank?"

"I just wanted to be with you," Nancy said, wiping her eyes. "Like we talked about. When you told me no I just couldn't handle it. My mind sort of went crazy. After everything I did for you. It didn't seem fair. So I thought I'd surprise you. Try to make it right in my head. I'm sorry, okay?"

Flat out bawling now, shoulders bobbing up and down like someone was shaking her. Like the way he should be shaking her. She reached for a napkin and wiped away snot and tears and a dark smear of mascara and balled it up and threw it down on the table and stood.

"I was just trying to do the right thing," she said.

Daniel stood too, his right arm reaching out almost of its own accord. He felt dizzy again, as if he was floating above himself watching the scene unfold. He couldn't afford a ruckus like this. One slip and everything gone to hell. A single nervous customer takes her side, calls a cop.... Done for. He took Nancy's arm as gently as he could and steered her back to her seat.

"I just need more money, is all," he said. "I didn't mean anything bad by you. I appreciate what you did. You know I do." Squeezing the words out one at a time, taking nearly all his energy to keep an even keel.

"Funny way of showing it."

The special ain't cheap, is what I'm saying. And Jessie's not one for negotiating.

"I'll show you the right way soon. I promise."

"Oh yeah?" Still sniffing. Red blotches up and down her cheeks like she'd missed three times trying to slap a bee away.

He tried to think fast. "What you said on the bus."

"I said a lot of things."

It came to him. "Behind?" he whispered. "Arf arf?"

"Fuck you," she said. But with a grin.

"Promise?"

The waitress arrived with their food. Took in Nancy's red face and Danny's extended hand, which he realized was still gripping Nancy's arm. Eyed him like she'd seen him before. Slowly, he unfurled his fingers, folded his arms and sat back. Stared straight ahead, watching the door, waiting. Tensed his legs, ready to run for it. No way it was ending here, in a diner, so close to his target. Counting out the seconds. One, two, three....

"Scrambled eggs, sausage, home fries, toast," the waitress said, setting down a plate in front of Nancy and then Daniel and refilling both their coffee cups.

Slowly, Daniel breathed out.

"So, what now?" Nancy said, her mouth already full of egg and toast. Danny stuffed his own mouth with potatoes, suddenly starving.

"You keep asking that."

"Because I don't know what we're doing here."

"We need to get ourselves a ride, I guess." He chewed his food, dragging it out. Carefully, he added, "And some more money."

"okay. Then what?"

"Then I need to go see someone."

"Who?"

"Guy I know."

"Who?"

"Who, who. You sound like a fucking owl."

"I'm just asking, for Chrissake." Eyes bright once more. Fork stabbing at a sausage link. "Why're you being like this?"

Hannah again. Kitten in her lap, fitting a small, yellow, lacy bonnet onto its head. A warm, summer day, out on the front porch. Seven-year-old Hannah. Kitten sacked out, oblivious, her purring a rhythmic drone.

"Guy named Kelly," Daniel said.

"Why do you need to see him?"

"I need to give him something."

"Like what?"

"Like something, okay?"

He used his knife and fork to quickly cut a sausage in half, waiting for the next question. One goddamn question after another. When it didn't come, he raised his eyes to look at Nancy. To his surprise, she was staring at him with terror in her eyes. He was about to ask what was going on with her when he realized the old man in the booth behind her was staring too. And the young couple opposite them. And their waitress, paused mid-aisle with a full pot of coffee.

Only then did he understand that he'd screamed his last sentence. Literally screamed it.

*****

They video-conferenced Altagracia in ninety minutes later. Wavy mass of black hair, round cheeks, red bow of a mouth. Puppy breath, yeah, but still. Qualls snuck a glance at Heintz. He sat ramrod straight in his chair, patrol hard-ass all the way now. Four kids and one on the way. Sure, he never stared at a face like the young analyst's and thought about stuff.

"Thanks for prioritizing this," Heintz said to Altagracia's forehead.

"No problem."

"You know LaShondra? Sorry — Lt. Qualls?"

"Hey Lieutenant. How's it going?"

"Another crazy day. So, what've you got?"

"Some interesting stuff, actually."

"Oh?"

"Yeah. For starters, your guy isn't Daniel O'Connor."

That got both of their attention.

"Say what?" Heintz said.

"His first name's Daniel. That part's right. But when I cross-referenced his SS number, and started looking at associated people, some things weren't adding up. You see it with women all the time. Changing their name to get married. Men, not so much."

"So, who is he?" Qualls said.

"Looks like he was born Daniel Fitzpatrick. Near as I can tell he was adopted by someone named John Fitzpatrick when he was twelve or thirteen."

"And what do we know about that guy?"

"Died ten years ago of a drug overdose."

"Mom?" Qualls said.

"Bridget Fitzpatrick. Sixty-seven." She read off a current address in Columbus.

"We start there, then," Heintz said. "They always run home, no matter how smart they think they are."

"Yeah," Qualls said in agreement.

"Well, just so you know," Rodriguez interrupted.

"Yeah?" Qualls said.

"Looks like he was thirteen when he came to Ohio. But it's not where he grew up. I mean as a kid."

"Which was where?"

"Chicago," Rodriguez said. "Most of his people are still there — aunts and uncles, I mean. You ask me, that's his real hometown."

Heintz turned to Qualls. "Aren't you from Chicago?"

"Southside," she said, nodding. "Couldn't get away fast enough. Thank you, U.S. Army."

"You think he ran there? Chicago?" Heintz said to Rodriguez.

"I have no idea. I'm just saying he's got ties there. Strong as Ohio, anyway. Maybe stronger."

"Can you get us some names up there? Relatives, I mean?" Qualls said. Mind stuck on something, a snag in the fabric of a memory from home. Staying just out of reach as she tried to grasp it, like retreating waves on the beach on a windy day on Lake Michigan.

"No problem, Lieutenant. Just give me a couple minutes."

"We'll check out the mom in the meantime," Heintz said. "Call me on my cell if you get anything more." He recited the number.

"Got it," Rodriguez said. "Talk to you soon."

"What?" Heintz said when the analyst's face disappeared.

"Not sure. Name rings a bell, is all. Daniel Fitzpatrick."

"In Chicago? Isn't that like Joe Smith or something up there?"

"Not everybody's Irish in Chicago," Qualls said.

"LaShondra's not Irish?" Heintz said.

"Not even black Irish," Qualls said, pushing back her chair and reaching for her keys.

*****

The next time Edgerton took a break, to use the bathroom, he realized he needed to slow it down a little. His pale, nearly hairless hands were jittery, shaking as he held himself, trying to keep his aim straight, filling the toilet bowl with three hours of almost continuous Mountain Dew consumption.

Finished, not bothering to wash his hands, he walked past his desk and the glow of the monitor and removed the box from beneath the bed. He set it down on the workbench on the far side of the room, next to the Glock. He pushed that out of the way — no need for it anymore now. He opened the box, removed the rifle and placed it atop the paper he'd saved all these weeks. The front page of the *Chicago Tribune* from the previous November. From the first Wednesday of the month. From the day he first knew what he had to do to make everything right.

Grayson Elected Mayor in Historic All-Woman Matchup

False empress straddling the city between your legs the stolen election....

He shook his head. All-woman matchup. How much disrespect could a man take? A man with needs going unmet day after day, week after week, month after month. So many needs, and so many women, and yet ... nothing.

He picked up a tiny square of cloth, sprayed it with cleaner, wrapped it around the tip of the thin cable and slowly pushed the cloth through the rifle's barrel. He was not surprised when the cloth emerged nearly pristine. The result had been the same that morning when he cleaned the rifle, and last night as well. Edgerton knew it was obsessive, the repetitive cleaning, but better safe than sorry. Nothing lamer in the world than the failures you read about. "A miracle more didn't die .... Thank God the gun jammed ... the assailant appeared to panic...."

There weren't going to be such deficiencies with him. This would be a reckoning the world had never seen. The worst one you ever read about times ten, times twenty, times whatever Carl Edgerton wanted it to be. Because he had given them a chance, given all of them a chance, with their peach-shaped asses and firm tits and inviting eyes and their shorts and skirts and blouses and dresses and yoga pants, traipsing past him night after night, bar after bar, spurning him like a dog. And then to mock him one last time on the first Tuesday of November. Her Honor Ellen Grayson. The last thing any of them needed. Come tomorrow, she might not be the first, second, or even third to go down. But she would be among them all. Edgerton was certain of that.

He picked up another cloth square, sprayed it with cleaner, attached it to the tip of the cable and started it up the barrel. Just to be sure.

*****

Daniel said their first priority should be the extra money he needed. Nancy said better to focus on a ride. Two people taking cash from somebody on foot weren't going very far, she said. Reluctantly, he agreed, still numb from the close call of the scene he'd created at the diner.

It took them a couple of hours until they found the right play. Florist delivery vehicle, a white panel number with a magnetic business sign on the side. *Frank's Flowers.* Driver dropping off bouquets of daffodils at an office building a few blocks west of the diner. Keys in the van which was left running for the in-and-out delivery. Not as many delivery drivers left their keys in running vans as you'd think. They waited thirty seconds and then Daniel walked up to the van, opened the door, got inside and drove slowly up the street. No big deal. He turned the corner and turned the corner again. Three blocks down he parked between another van and a small sedan, got out, stripped off the magnetic sign, climbed back inside and waited for Nancy to meet him as planned. Ten minutes later he heard a sound at the rear. Panicked, he jumped out. Crouched behind the van, Nancy was unscrewing the van's license plate.

"Beat it," she hissed.

"But—"

"Get lost, darling. I mean it."

He did what she said. He sat in the front of the van, slouched down, heart racing. Where had she gotten a screwdriver like that? Always full of surprises, she was, not all of them good.

"Oh, shit," he said, seeing a man in the rearview mirror coming up the sidewalk and then pausing as he saw Nancy. Daniel was about to jump out again when to his amazement he heard the man laugh, watched him smile and wave at Nancy, and then go on his way. A minute later, she walked around and removed the front plate. Two minutes after that she'd swapped plates with the van in front of them and was sitting beside him in the passenger seat, grinning.

"What the hell were you thinking?" Daniel said. "That guy saw you."

"That guy saw a cute white girl on her knees with her shirt pulled real tight, darling." She thrust her chest at him to demonstrate, the curve of her breasts just visible below the top of her blouse. "It's like his eyeballs were stuck to his dick. I see it all the time. I could be committing murder in broad daylight and he'd still smile and wave." She paused. "You don't mind, do you?"

Daniel wasn't sure what he thought so he didn't say anything. He started the van and pulled onto the street.

"What about the cash?" he said.

Nancy turned around and stared at the containers of flowers filling the van's rear.

"Ain't those gotta be worth something?"

"I guess."

"How come they're all green?"

"What do you mean?"

"The flowers. They're mostly all green."

Daniel glanced back. She was right. Bucket after bucket of green bunches of carnations with a few daffodils mixed in. It came to him after a moment.

"Tomorrow's St. Patrick's Day," he said.

"Is that so?"

"What's that supposed to mean?"

Instead of replying she pulled out her phone and tapped at the screen while he drove. A minute later she gave him directions. Halfway there they stopped so she could run into a drugstore. She came out clutching a plastic bag and instructed him to keep driving. A few minutes later they parked half a block from Holy Name Cathedral. She pulled a green marker out of the bag, scribbled on a piece of construction paper, got out and taped it to the outside of the window. *St. Paddy's Day Special — $5 Each.*

"Okay," she said. "Time to go to work."

Forty-five minutes later they finished up and headed west on Chicago Ave.

"Three hundred fifty-bucks," she said, fanning the money. "Is that enough?"

He thought about it. "Yeah. I think so."

"Good to hear," she said, an edge to her voice. "So, where we going now?"

"See a guy."

"Kelly?"

"How do you know that?"

"You told me. Back at the diner. Who is he?"

"Just a guy."

"Friend of yours?"

"No."

"Then why—"

"Because I fucking said so, that's why," Daniel said.

"And I'm fucking asking for a little more information."

"It's none of your business."

"None of my business?" Nancy said, and then the world went to hell for a few minutes. She started hitting him, slapping him, screaming at him, crying, and him trying to drive down the street and keep from having an accident.

"The fuck? Stop it! What are you doing?"

"None of my business? After everything I did for you?"

He pulled over, face stinging from the slaps. He unbuckled and made to take cover in the back of the now empty van, but he wasn't fast enough. She was on him like an avenging monkey, weeping and scratching at his eyes.

"Stop it!"

"You know the risk I took, picking you up like that?"

"I know, I know."

"Do you?" Now she was on top of him, pinning him to the floor of the truck, knees on his chest. Surprisingly strong for someone so small. Eyes bright as her hands slapped his face over and over.

"Stop it," Daniel said, and finally managed to grab her wrists and hold them still.

"Everything I did for you, and you not telling me jack."

"I'm sorry."

"Are you?"

Even with her hands pinioned she managed to thrust her head close enough to his face to bite his upper lip. He yelled as he tasted blood and not knowing what he was doing tried to bite back. Nancy gave a little cry and then their mouths were together and they weren't biting anymore and a second later Nancy's tongue was in his mouth and his was in hers and they were groaning and their hands were free and pushing beneath each other's clothes. He thought about asking if she wanted it from behind but it was too late. Too late for a lot of things. Barely enough time for a condom. One minute more and there they were, fucking like teenagers. A minute after that, spent, Nancy rested her head beside his, still curled atop him.

"I risked everything," she whispered.

"It's almost over," Daniel said. "I promise."

"At least tell me his name."

"Who?"

"Kelly. His whole name."

It took almost all the strength he had left, but he managed it. "Joseph Kelly. Joseph John Kelly."

"Joseph John Kelly," she repeated. "Thank you, darling."

After they climbed back into the front of the van, they drove in silence while he carefully navigated his way. From time to time he asked Nancy to check a turn on the phone. The streets and the neighborhoods looked familiar, but it had been so long he couldn't always remember the streets. The correct intersections. Time was a memory thief that ripped you off again and again. No doubt about that. Half an hour later he found it. The small city pocket park in Mount Greenwood. Half a block up, Donnelly's Pub. Across from the pub, a five-story brick apartment house.

"That's where he lives? Joseph John Kelly?"

Daniel nodded.

"We gonna go see him?"

"Not yet."

"Why not?"

"I don't have everything I need."

"Like what?"

He was going to have to tell her sooner or later. That die was cast the second he woke up from dreaming about Hannah and saw Nancy and her pixie face grinning at him on the bus, daring him to be mad. Set in stone when he came back from the bathroom and she slid his hand onto her everything and then turned to face him and flipped her necklace around his head and drew him inside and brought him home. *I gotcha, darling. I gotcha.*

"I'll tell you soon. No, I'll show you. Promise."

"You better."

They waited out the rest of the day in the van. Enough room to lay down and take a nap. Shadows were lengthening and the temperature dropping when they awoke, late in the afternoon. They had to use the bathroom and they were both starving. Nancy suggested the pub since it was right there but Daniel vetoed the idea straight out. Instead, they drove around until they found a gas station. They used the restrooms and bought ham-and-cheese sandwiches and pops. They circled back to Kelly's neighborhood and parked and Daniel was unwrapping his sandwich, eager to take a bite, when he looked up and saw him. Kelly, crossing the street, headed for Donnelly's. Just like that.

"That's him," he said, unable to help himself.

"Who?"

"Kelly," he said, spitting the word out like rancid gristle.

"Now we gonna go see him?"

He shook his head.

"Why not?" Taking a small bite of her own sandwich.

"Told you. I don't have everything I need."

"When's that gonna happen?"

"Soon, I hope," Daniel said, cramming a third of the sandwich into his mouth and starting the van. A second later, they moved up the street, passing through pool after pool of shadowy light.

*****

Bridget Fitzpatrick swore up and down she didn't know anything about her son, where he might be, why he ran, what he was up to. They stayed an hour, grilling the old lady as best they could, but in the end they had nothing. Afterward, Heintz and Qualls sat in Qualls's Department of Rehabilitation and Correction-issued Chevy Malibu on the street of the tired subdivision on the north side and studied their phones in the dark, trying to figure out next moves. A minute later, Rodriguez called. Heintz put her on speaker.

"We may have a problem," Rodriguez said.

"What now?" Qualls said.

"Remember I told you Fitzpatrick's from Chicago?"

"Yeah."

"Name Joseph Kelly mean anything to you?"

Heintz and Qualls exchanged puzzled glances.

"No," Qualls said, though she wasn't entirely sure that was true.

"Who is he?"

"He's the reason why your guy may not be in Ohio."

"Then where is he?" Heintz said.

"I'm thinking Chicago's a really good bet."

*****

Daniel was starting to sweat, afraid he'd missed it, or worse, that it had moved. But then there it was, several long blocks east of Kelly's, a taco truck set at the back of a vacant lot. Just like he'd been told.

"What are we doing here?" Nancy said.

"I need to get something."

"I don't like Mexican. It gives me the trots."

"That's not what I'm here for."

Nancy glared at him, some of the wildness from their fight earlier creeping back into her eyes.

"C'mon. You'll see," Daniel said, not wishing for a repeat of the battle, regardless how it ended.

Two people were ahead of them in line. Daniel stood nervously, patting the paper bag inside his parka. Full of the money from the flower sales. He had to credit Nancy. It was the easiest cash he'd ever made.

"Next."

He looked up. A woman was staring down at him from the truck's counter. He swallowed. Long, thick, black hair pulled into a tight braid that fell from the left side of her head. Silver stud through her lower lip, the metal glinting from the truck's inner light. Mouth bright with red lipstick. Green eyes set against dark skin. Dangly gold hoop earrings you could almost put your hand through. "Don't got all night."

Daniel cleared his throat. "I'm looking for Jessie."

Green eyes narrowing, studying him.

"Who are you?"

He told her.

"Well, I'm Jessie. But I don't know you."

"You're Jessie?"

"What's it going to be?"

He swallowed again, trying not to stare at her face. Possibly the most beautiful woman he'd ever seen. "I'd like the special, please."

A sound to Jessie's right. Daniel caught a glimpse of a thin, muscular man in a white tank top, spatula poised above the grill.

"We don't got a special."

"I was told you did."

"You was told wrong. Tacos or nothing."

Daniel felt his heart sink. "But—"

"But nothing. Either order or move aside."

Hannah, alone in the front yard. Left by herself not even two minutes while he went inside for a popsicle. Popsicles — one for each.

"Please," Daniel said.

The cook leaned into view. He was handsome the way Jessie was beautiful, but one look at the hardness in his eyes and the strength in his arms and Daniel knew all was lost.

"You heard the lady—"

"Ain't you the cutest thing!"

Nancy, on her tiptoes, looking up into the truck. But not at Jessie or the man. At a little girl, perched on a chair behind Jessie, only visible now that Jessie had stood and shifted toward the man, crossing her arms in defiance. The girl had dark, wavy hair tied back with a red ribbon, wore a pink dress and hugged a gray, stuffed elephant. She stared at Nancy with a pair of huge brown eyes.

"How old are you, honey?"

Solemnly, the girl raised her right hand and showed five fingers.

"Five years old. Ain't you grown up. What's your name?"

Lips moving. A whisper that Daniel couldn't make out.

"What was that, sweetie?"

"Jacqueline." The syllables drawn out like a whole sentence.

"Jacqueline, hush," Jessie said.

"Ain't that the most beautiful name. Jacqueline. Anybody ever call you Jackie, sweetie?"

The girl shook her head.

"They better not," Nancy said. "Name like Jacqueline, they should say the whole thing every time. That your little girl?" The question, forthright and loud, directed at Jessie.

Jessie stared at Nancy, as if she hadn't heard right. "Yeah," she said at last.

"She's the sweetest thing. What a darling. You must be so proud."

"Yeah," Jessie said, her turn to whisper.

"I can only imagine," Nancy said. "I just want to scoop her up!" She gave herself a squeeze to pantomime hugging the girl.

Jessie studied Nancy a moment longer and then turned her attention to Daniel.

"Turns out we got one special left."

"Okay," Daniel said.

"How do you want it?"

"I'd like it fully loaded," he said, repeating the words verbatim just as the man two cells down had instructed.

"A fully loaded special isn't cheap."

"I know."

"It also comes with your choice of meat."

"Chorizo and barbacoa, please."

"Hang on."

"Everything okay?" Nancy said. She was making silly faces at Jacqueline, who was smiling at her shyly.

"I think so."

They waited five minutes, Daniel glancing nervously around the lot that was home to the truck. At the top of the street a white Chevy Blazer slowed but didn't stop. Daniel relaxed as Jessie re-appeared at the counter with three white Styrofoam containers. She dropped them into a plastic bag. Instead of handing them out, she left them on the counter, just out of reach. She stood back and crossed her arms. Daniel nodded, dipped his hand into his parka pocket, and found the paper bag. He handed it to Jessie. She disappeared around the corner. Daniel heard her whispering to the man, followed by his low-voiced response. The girl hugged her elephant and giggled at the faces that Nancy was making.

Jessie stepped back into view. "Here you go," she said, handing him the plastic bag. He took it, feeling its weight. "Also, you gave us too much." She fingered a twenty and made to hand it to Daniel.

"Nothing doing," Nancy said. "You buy Jacqueline something nice with that. Something pretty for such a pretty girl. You hear me?"

"Thanks," Jessie said, stepping back, the bill already vanished into a pocket. "Enjoy the special. Next."

*****

Edgerton started. Was that a sound, upstairs? Impossible. But still. He sat for a moment, fingers brushing the burnished steel of the gun, listening. Outside, a cold March breeze flung tiny ice pellets against the basement's block windows. No, not pellets. Graupel. A cross between hail and sleet. Didn't everyone know that? He'd tried to explain the difference to the fat girl at the bar off Green Bay Road three nights ago. Attempted to elucidate her on the difference between the various types of stinging Lake Michigan winter precipitation that could redden your cheeks and pelt your eyes so you had to squeeze them tight, so tight, until the pain went away. But she wanted nothing to do with it, her eyes drifting down the bar to a guy pretending to study his phone but obviously studying her instead. Her fat ass, anyway.

"Hey, you listening?" he said. Surprised by how loud the words came out. More than a slight slur, that many drinks in.

"Sorry," she said. "What was that?"

"I said graupel's nothing like hail."

"What? Hey — whaddya say?" She nudged her empty appletini glass forward on the bar.

He ignored her and repeated the statement.

"What the hell are you talking about?"

"I'm talking about graupel, you bitch."

"What the hell?"

He reached out and grabbed her above her left elbow, thrilling at the feel of her flesh beneath the fabric of her shirt. "You're not listening to me," he said.

"You're hurting me. Let go."

"I'll let go when you start listening."

"Let go, Jesus Christ," the girl said, pulling her arm free and sliding

222

off the bar stool. "You freak. What do you think you're doing?"

He was about to answer her, tell her — no, *show* her — exactly what he was doing. But things got a little confused after that. A big guy appeared and told him to take it easy. Then there was another guy, just as big, and before he knew what was happening he was on his feet and being drag-walked toward the door of the bar.

"Leave me alone," he mumbled. "It's that bitch you should be throwing out."

"Keep telling yourself that, asshole," the first guy said, pushing open the door and letting in a flood of cold air.

Edgerton shrugged free and spun around, ready to face the both of them. Instead, he found himself staring at the TV closest to the door. And that's when he saw her. Ellen Grayson. Her honor. Her ugly fem face filling the screen, talking a mile a minute in that way she had, always talking down to everyone, every *man*, every time he saw her on the news. Below her on the screen he made out the word "parade." There were so many more useful things he could imagine that mouth and those lips doing than talking talking talking. Always talking. Never listening. No one ever listened to him, Edgerton thought. Least of all the stupid fem hole bitch Chicago mayor.

And that's when he decided on the timing. That moment, piniored by those two guys by the door at the bar off the Green Bay Road, the fat girl he'd bought two — or was it three? — appletinis already sitting at the other end of the bar. Yacking with the guy who'd been looking to horn in on Edgerton's action all night. Yeah—it was time for all of them, starting with Grayson, to stop talking. No one wanted to hear a lady like that run her mouth anymore.

*****

Daniel drove a mile down the road until he found a place to park under a streetlamp opposite the remains of a shuttered convenience store. He nodded at Nancy and they slipped into the back of the van. He reached into the bag and retrieved the top Styrofoam container and handed it to her. She wrinkled her nose but took it anyway. He lifted out the second box and set it beside him. He lifted out the third and set it down on the floor of the van with a thunk. He opened it and removed the two napkins lying over the Smith & Wesson and palmed the gun.

"The hell?" Nancy said, eyes widening.

"I told you I'd show you."

But as Daniel studied the gun disappointment set in. It didn't look in great shape. Dirt smudged the grip and a shiny fishhook-shaped scratch marred the finish of the barrel. God knows the last time it had been cleaned. He removed the magazine and glanced at the rounds. He replaced it and pulled back the slide and confirmed a chambered round. So, an 8 plus 1, and no extra ammunition. A lot of money to pay for an 8 plus 1 with a smudged grip and a scratch on the barrel and no extra rounds. Fully loaded special my foot.

Except how else was a guy like him going to get a gun? And how many rounds did he really need, when it came right down to it? As long as there was one left when he was finished.

Almost finished.

"Danny?" Nancy said.

To this day he couldn't be sure. Had he heard the idling of the car out front, the muffler starting to go, or not? Middle of the city like that, you hear all kinds of sounds. All the way at the back of the house retrieving the popsicles, he couldn't be sure. Part of him wanted to have heard it, to attach some kind of meaning to the aftermath of what happened. But part of him — the biggest part — didn't want to know. Because that would have meant, for a full count of ten or fifteen, there had been something out there he should have investigated. Something that didn't sound quite right.

"Danny?" Nancy said again, reaching out and touching his cheek.

It was time. There was no going back now. Not after the furtive pick-up at the Speedway after he walked away from the work crew. Not after the bus and her brother's leather lariat keeping their faces close while they rocked back and forth. Not after the flower van and selling the carnations by the Cathedral and the fight that turned into a fuck. And especially not after Jessie and the taco truck and twenty dollars to buy your little girl something nice.

Looking not at Nancy but at the rear of the van, where the glow of the streetlight just penetrated the small back window, he whispered, "I had a little sister. Her name was—"

Bam bam bam.

They both jumped as if an electric current had coursed through the steel floor.

Someone was pounding on the side of the van.

*****

"Hang on," Qualls said, interrupting Rodriguez as she answered her phone.

"Yeah," she said, listening, struggling to suppress a yawn. It had gotten so late. She looked around for something to write with. She pantomimed a pen to Heintz and a moment later he produced a Bic and a small notebook. She grabbed it and started taking notes. "Yeah," she said. "One more time? okay, right. okay, thanks." She disconnected.

"What?" Heintz said.

"You guys still there?" Rodriguez said.

"We're here," Qualls said. "Sorry, that was records finally calling me back. They checked the visitors' logs for O'Connor — I mean Fitzpatrick. Other than his mom and a priest, no one for almost his whole time inside."

"Who's the priest?" Heintz said.

"One of the regulars. You're jammed up in central Ohio and you mark down you're Catholic, you're gonna get a visit from that guy. We can cross him off."

"So, what, then?"

Qualls looked at the notes she'd just taken. "About a year ago, Fitzpatrick starts getting regular visits from a lady named Nancy Richter. Once a week, like clockwork. Then, starting last month, twice a week."

"Who is she?"

"No idea. He put her down as a friend. No flags when they backgrounded her through OHLEG so they cleared her to visit. Course you know how that goes." Heintz nodded. The Ohio Law Enforcement

Gateway network was only as good as the information it contained, which was mostly good but sometimes shit.

Qualls said, "We can run her name but it may take a while, this time of night."

"I can check her out," Rodriguez said.

"That'd be good," Heintz said, beating Qualls to the punch.

"Anyway, you were saying?" Qualls said. "About Fitzpatrick going to Chicago?" There it was again, the feeling that she knew something but couldn't put her finger on it.

"Yeah," Rodriguez said. "It's really tragic. And it may explain a lot."

"It better," Heintz said.

*****

Daniel assumed the person on the other side of the van door was a cop. That somehow the actions of the last thirty-six hours had caught up with him. Was it really so unreasonable to think that way? He'd escaped from prison, stolen a van, stolen the van's pricy cargo, and bought the special from Jessie. At this point somebody in uniform had to be looking for him — for them — and in this day and age how long could they run? That line of thinking was his first mistake. His second was ignoring Nancy's whisper to take the gun as he climbed out of the back of the van and went up front, where no sooner was he looking through the windows than the driver's door was flung open and he found himself staring at the barrel of a much bigger gun than his "fully loaded special."

"Out of the van, bitch."

Daniel thinking the man probably wasn't a cop.

"No trouble," Daniel said, carefully climbing out.

"The girl, too," the man said when Daniel was outside and eying the Chevy Blazer with tinted windows pulled up behind him. Noticing for the first time how desolate the neighborhood was that he'd stopped in after paying the visit to Jesse's Tacos. Across the street, on the other side of a small field more dirt than grass, two of every three houses boarded up or windowless.

"No girl," Daniel heard himself say.

"You serious?" the man said, driving the side of the gun against

Daniel's head without warning. He staggered back, pain stabbing his eyes shut, and reached his hand up to his head. He pulled it away, warm and slick, as nausea washed over him.

"Fuck you," Daniel said.

The man was shaking his head and raising his gun hand when a sound from behind interrupted him. The van door opening. Another man's voice and then Nancy, protesting loudly. A second later she stumbled into view, clutching Daniel's backpack, a second man behind her, a gun as big as the first man's in his right hand.

"No girl, huh?"

"What do you want?" Daniel said.

"You're trespassing."

Daniel looked around, trying to ignore the pain from the blow to the head. The trickle of blood down his cheek and jaw and neck. "Don't see any signs."

"Don't have to," said the man who hit Daniel. "Everybody knows that here all the way to Jesse's is ours. You can't just waltz in and buy a special and not pay for the privilege. There's a tax, my friend."

"That's all the money we had," Daniel said.

"Bullshit."

"I'm telling the truth. We had just enough."

"Not our problem, is it?"

"Look, we're sorry," Daniel said, shivering in the cold. "Honest mistake. You can — you can have the van. Just let us walk away."

"Little late for that."

"Please—"

"Shut up and listen, bitch. Get back in the van, in the back, and get on your knees."

"What about her?" Daniel said, looking at Nancy.

"We got other plans for her. Plans that don't involve you."

Daniel traded a glance with Nancy, whose face had turned white as a chunk of sun-bleached cement. He tried to tell her with his eyes what he was going to do. How he was going to rush the man, because if this was how it was going to end, after everything, he wasn't going out on his knees in the back of a stolen florist van. He shut his eyes and braced himself. He expected to see Hannah's face but saw nothing instead.

"Wait."

He opened his eyes.

"Wait," Nancy repeated. "He was lying — we've got money. How much do you want?"

The first man laughed. "How much? We want all of it."

"All of it?" Nancy said, her voice small as a child's. "Please. Just leave us a little."

"*All of it.*"

Nancy nodded and blinked her eyes as if fighting back tears. "All of it," she repeated. "All right." She reached into Daniel's backpack and in one smooth motion retrieved the Smith & Wesson and shot the first man in the chest — *pop pop pop* — centering the shots in a circle no bigger than the rim of a coffee cup. As the man fell forward, grasping at air, Nancy stepped back and shot the second man in the head and the neck and the torso. It happened so fast his gun hand was still by his side. A moment later both men lay on the ground, blood pooling from their wounds. "Oh shit, oh shit, oh shit," the first man said, over and over, his words a little raspier with each passing second.

"Let's go," Nancy said, voice flat and monotone as a bus station announcement.

Daniel drove, willing himself not to speed away, not to do anything to attract attention as they drew farther and farther from the vacant lot and what they'd left behind in the dirt. His mind reeling. Two minutes gone, and he started thinking about how many shots Nancy had fired. Five shots? Six? Nine? Shit. Smith & Wesson 8 plus 1. That was all he had; there wasn't any more. Three minutes out the obvious occurred to him. They'd left two perfectly good pieces behind, each of the slain men sporting guns much bigger and with many more rounds, and that wasn't even considering what might have been inside the Blazer. The Blazer. Four minutes out and he realized they could have switched rides. Ditched the van altogether. But none of that had happened. It had all gone wrong, just when it was about to go right.

"What now?" he said, more to himself than anything else, as he slowed for a red light.

"Oh, Danny," Nancy said.

"What?"

"Why didn't you tell me?"

"Tell you what?" He turned and saw to his surprise that Nancy was crying. In her hands, the packet of articles he'd carried with him over the years, keeping them safe even on the inside. Tucked safely inside his backpack until this very moment. Almost every word ever printed in the news about what happened to Hannah.

"I'm sorry," he said. "I was going to."

"Oh, Danny," she said. "That poor little baby."

*****

Edgerton had never seen the attraction. Even as a kid, watching his dad in the parades, proud member of the Exalted Order of Chicagoland Hibernians, he felt there was something a little bit off about the pastime. Starting with the sound. The droning of the pipes so loud that he clamped his hands over his ears as the marchers passed. Making little howling sounds until his mother, bundled up in a thick, ill-fitting woolen coat, told him to shut up. Which only made him angrier. He lost track of how many cold, windy, wet days he sat on an uncomfortable folding chair to watch his dad march and play the pipes. The expense was also an issue. No mystery there. He heard the arguments even through his closed bedroom door every time his mother found out his father had bought another one of the bizarre accessories he always seemed to have to have. A tuner, a bag cover, another chanter. A kilt pin, a kilt brooch, another cape, a sharper dubh. It added up, as he discovered when he was old enough to go online and see the prices for himself. Holy crap.

He sat back in his chair and examined the bag in front of him. Was this irony? He wasn't really sure, nor did he care, exactly. Not like he listened much in English class since no one listened to him. But it was kind of interesting, when you thought about it. The way things in life turned out. He parted the slit he'd cut down the long end of the bag —

the slit! — held it open with his left hand and picked up the rifle with his right. Wrinkling his nose at the smell of the bag's interior, still rank even after all the Febreze he'd used, he tucked the rifle inside. He closed the slit and tightened it shut with the tan-colored Velcro strips he'd affixed, matching the shade of the bag almost perfectly. You'd have to be very close to notice something wasn't quite right. And nobody was getting that close. There wouldn't be time. He stood, hoisting the bag onto his shoulder, and practiced ripping the Velcro off and slipping the gun out. The rifle snagged the first couple of times but eventually he had the rhythm down. He only had to do it once, of course, so a glitch or two didn't really matter. But that wasn't the point. The point was that he wanted everything to be absolutely perfect. A perfect day for Her Honor. Her last, after all.

*****

The inside of Qualls's DRC-issued Malibu grew silent as Rodriguez talked. Qualls's phone pinged. She looked down. Keisha, texting, wondering where in the hell she was. She punched out a quick reply, then placed the phone on silent and returned her attention to the state patrol analyst.

"...his sister was seven," Rodriguez was saying. "Looks like they were latch-keying it after school. Fitzpatrick was nine, or maybe ten. Hang on. Yeah, ten. They were playing out front, and it was hot, apparently, and he went inside to get them—"

"Popsicles," Qualls said.

No one said anything for a moment.

"That's right," Rodriguez said. "Did you look this up already?"

Qualls looked again at the message from her wife. She said, "I just remembered the case. I knew it sounded familiar. Even with all the shit going down back then, you couldn't not hear about it."

"Okay," Rodriguez said uncertainly. "Should I stop?"

"No."

After a second, Heintz said quietly, "What time was this? Time of day, I mean."

"Four o'clock, thereabouts. Mom was usually home by six, so they had two, two-and-a-half hours alone."

"Go on," Qualls said.

"The girl, Hannah, isn't by herself more than two minutes. That's according to what Fitzpatrick told police later. But it was just enough time for Kelly to pull up and take the girl."

"Just take her?" Qualls said, trying to recall what she knew of the case. "Snatch and run?" The parents' worst nightmare. Why she and Keisha kept eagle eyes on the girls, even now with them fifteen and thirteen.

"Not quite," Rodriguez said. "He opened the door, called out to her, and then told her that her mother had been in an accident and she needed to come with him right away. According to what he said later, I guess."

Heintz shifted in his chair. "Called her by name?"

"Apparently."

"Did she know him? I mean, beforehand?"

"He was a neighborhood guy. So, yeah. At least a little. He knew her name. The cops speculated she recognized him."

"What then?" Qualls said even though she knew this next part.

"He drove her to a warehouse about a mile away, walked her inside, threw her on a mattress, repeatedly raped her, then strangled her."

"The body?"

"Dumped in a forest. Place called Beaubien Woods. A hiker found her two days later, off the trail a few yards. Looks like it's a popular place up there for disposal. The Chicago cops found articles in Kelly's apartment, afterward, about other bodies found out there."

"How'd they get onto Kelly?" Heintz said.

"One of the detectives wasn't sold on the idea of a random snatch. He came up with the idea of running all the traffic stops for the girl's neighborhood going back a month, on the theory she'd been stalked ahead of time. Turned out Kelly got dinged for rolling a stop sign two weeks earlier. Probably wouldn't have merited a stop normally but there'd been a couple kids hurt bad in accidents that summer. Mayor ordered a crackdown. It took a while to go through all the tickets, but once they did and found Kelly, they came up with a prior for him. Ten years before that he'd been caught in a hotel room with a 14-year-old girl. The manager called police after the guest next door complained about the noise. Never made it to trial because the girl recanted. Anyway, that was enough to knock on Kelly's door. He didn't give anything up but he sweated so much they finagled a warrant. They found Hannah's underwear in a box under his bed."

"A trophy," Heintz said.

"What it looks like."

"Didn't they find other things in that box?" Qualls said.

"Good memory, Lieutenant," Rodriguez said. Qualls scowled, not caring to be reminded that she recalled any of this. "There was a blue hair tie, and a ring that would fit a girl's hand. Kelly swore he found them on the street. They didn't fit with any other cases and Kelly wouldn't crack no matter how much they leaned on him. In the end, he went down just for Hannah."

"What'd he get?"

"Death penalty, reduced on appeal to life with no chance of parole. Then he came down with cancer."

"Let me guess," Qualls said. "Out on compassionate release."

"That's right," Rodriguez said. "Taken out three days ago in a wheelchair. He's not supposed to live long."

Qualls shook her head in disgust. The humanitarian gesture always looked good on paper, as if the prison system was doing the right thing. But nine times out of ten the real reason was the chance to stop wasting precious agency dollars on the cost of care for a low-life end-stage cancer patient.

"He may have even less time to live than he thinks," Heintz said. "I'm guessing this explains Fitzpatrick's walk-away?"

"What do you mean?" Rodriguez said.

"If he found out Kelly was getting out early, and was that sick, he figured he didn't have any time to waste," Qualls said. "Even a week could be too late."

Rodriguez interrupted. "You want me to get a number for Chicago PD? A direct number, I mean? So you can let them know what's going on? That Kelly could be in danger?"

A second passed. Two. Ten. Almost twenty. Qualls thought of her girls, decked out for soccer practice. For ballet. Laughing at the number of boxes sitting under the Christmas tree last winter. Glanced at Heintz. *Four kids and one on the way.* Watched him as he studied his shoes in the footwell of the Malibu, avoiding her glance. Hannah Fitzpatrick, seven years old. A blue hair tie and a child's ring, unaccounted for.

Thirty seconds.

"Lieutenant Qualls?" Rodriguez' voice, staticky and disembodied. "You still there?"

"Yeah, I'm here," Qualls said.

"What should I do?"

"Go ahead and get us a number."

*****

Ten minutes later they found a commercial strip and spied an all-night CVS. Nancy went inside while Daniel stayed in the van, slouched low in the passenger seat, holding one of his socks over the gash on his face, the blood drying but the wound beginning to burn. As soon as she was out of sight he climbed into the back and retrieved the gun. He checked the magazine and pulled back the slide. Only three shots left. Just as he feared. Hardly enough, but it would have to do. On the drive from the vacant lot to this plaza, as his breathing slowed and he calmed down, he found himself almost feeling sorry for the men whose bodies they'd left behind, cooling in the dirt and gravel. He couldn't shake the look on their faces as Nancy executed them like dogs at the rear of a pound. A mixture of surprise and regret that made you think they'd been little kids like everyone else once upon a time. But now, adrenaline fully dissipating like a retreating tide, he realized he was furious at the strangers. Furious and unmoved. Their actions — their greed — had jeopardized everything. Now he had just three shots left and no chance of acquiring more.

He started at the pounding on the door. Not again. But it was just Nancy, her errand done. After he let her in, she told him to get in the back. She sat him down, his back leaning against the side of the van, and removed bandages, a tub of baby wipes, and a tube of ointment from a plastic bag. She used the wipes to clean the gash, rubbing the scented cloth in small circles, up and down the wound, left and right, pausing whenever he gasped at her touch.

"We need to go to the hospital," she said. "I got these butterfly bandages, but they only do so much. They can do that superglue thing on you. Close it up real neat."

"No hospital."

"We'll tell them you were in an accident. Fell down the stairs or something. They're not gonna care."

He shook his head. No money, no ID, a stolen van, a bad gash of vague origin. A recipe for a receptionist's quiet call to the security officer on duty. Game over.

"No hospital," he repeated.

When she finished cleaning the wound, Daniel said, "Where you'd learn to shoot like that?"

"What?"

"Back there. Those guys."

She paused before replying, pulling the plastic strips off a bandage and carefully stretching it over the top third of the gash. Her small, pale fingers so cool to the touch as she worked. "My brother taught me. We grew up in the country. Everybody had guns."

"You never told me that."

"You never asked, darling."

It occurred to Daniel there was a lot he didn't know about the woman who'd befriended him in prison, who'd moved from pen pal to visitor to conspirator in his need to cut his sentence short in order to arrive in Chicago in time to deliver a sentence of his own. She'd just sort of shown up in his life one day and visiting with her, as quirky as she was, sure beat sitting around the pod playing cards or watching TV.

Nancy applied the second of the bandages, pinching the wound closed as she affixed the adhesive on either side. "You never told me about Hannah," she said quietly. "Is she why we're here?"

He shook his head. "Hannah's long gone. We're here for Kelly. He's all that matters now." He stopped and corrected himself. "I'm here for Kelly."

"You weren't coming back, were you? Like you said you would after I dropped you at the bus station."

"I don't know. I wasn't thinking that far ahead."

"Kelly's dying?"

"Did he look like he was dying?" Daniel recalled the sight of Kelly crossing the street to Donnelly's bar. Hardly the stride of an old man, let alone an old man with cancer. He'd walked with purpose, with a touch of bravado even. As if he knew how completely he'd hoodwinked people up and down the state of Illinois. "I don't know how he managed it, but he got himself out somehow."

"It's hard to fake cancer."

"Maybe. But it's not so hard to fake symptoms. To make them think it's worse than it is. To disguise yourself as someone you're not. I saw other guys do it."

Nancy applied the third bandage, which hurt the worst, as if someone were probing the wound with a hot needle.

"So, what now?"

"We go back and wait, I guess. Wait until he crosses the street again."

"And then what?"

"Then I do to him what should have been done a long time ago."

Nancy placed the tub of wipes and the box of bandages back into the CVS bag. "I mean what happens to us after that? We do that, and then what?"

"I do it."

"You know what I mean, darling."

Daniel did know what she meant. He just couldn't think of a way to answer her. To explain why the number of bullets in the Smith & Wesson 8 plus 1 mattered so much. The one, to be exact. Because he had thought about what happened afterward, a lot. He'd done the math and it was simpler than you'd imagine. Even best-case scenario with Kelly, Daniel knew he wouldn't get far once the deed was done. He wasn't going back inside, that's for damn sure. But where would he go on the outside if he somehow walked away after putting Kelly down? All the doors in his life had been shut years ago and he'd long ago stopped trying the locks to see if there was any way out.

"We'll figure it out. I promise," Daniel said, just to have something to say.

"You sure about that?"

"I'm sure," he said.

"So where to now?" Nancy said. "Morning ain't for hours."

"We'll wait."

"Here?"

Daniel considered it for half a second. He bet theirs wouldn't be the first car to spend the night in the drugstore parking lot. But he knew it was too risky, even as he felt exhaustion wash over him, competing with the pain on the side of his face like two giant hands holding him down, keeping him from moving.

He climbed back into the driver's seat, started the van and pulled out. He made his way back to Kelly's neighborhood, taking his time, watching the speed limit every second. On the outskirts of Mount Greenwood they found a Circle K and went inside to use the restrooms. They spent the last of their money — six dollars and twenty cents — on muffins and bananas. They ate as he drove. It wasn't until he reached Western Avenue that he realized something was up. All along the street, block after block, white hoods masked the tops of the parking meters like tiny rigid ghosts. Finally, his curiosity overtaking him, he pulled over and rolled down the window on Nancy's side. Frigid air filled the van. Nancy shielded her face as tiny pellets blew sideways inside. One fell into Daniel's palm and he examined it closely. Not sleet and not quite snow. There was a name for this, he thought, something weird, but he couldn't recall it.

"What's it say?" he said to Nancy.

"Parade route. Parking prohibited 5 a.m. to 2 p.m."

"Parade?"

"What it says."

Of course. How could he have forgotten — all the flowers they'd sold at the cathedral. St. Patrick's Day tomorrow. No — today, he realized, looking at the clock on the van dashboard. The Southside parade. The biggest St. Paddy's Day celebration in the world, though who knew, or cared, if that were even true. What mattered now was how it might affect what he had to do in a few hours, once it was light out. Crowds couldn't help his cause, but would it really matter in the end? He told Nancy what he was thinking — about the parade. Not about the lack of a getaway plan or rather, the fact that he didn't need one.

"Kiss me, I'm Irish," Nancy said.

"What?"

"You know. What they say."

She rolled the window up and shifted in her seat toward him. She tilted her head to raise her left cheek, tapped it with her forefinger and smiled. Against his better judgment, he leaned over and kissed her, her skin cool after the blast of outside air. A peck as chaste as something he'd have given his grandmother. Yet the slight gesture emptied out his heart more suddenly, and more thoroughly, than either the ride in the back of the bus or the fight that turned into a fuck.

Nancy felt it too, pulling away sharply as if he'd delivered a shock. She stared at him for a long second, reading his face. "Let's go, darling," she said finally, turning away and staring out the front window. "Time's a wasting."

*****

Edgerton wrote until 3 a.m. when at last his brain ran dry. He knew that was only an expression, but for just a moment he imagined the organ as a desiccated lump rattling around in his skull, drained of all liquid. The only thing remaining now was to replenish it.

This is your punishment but it is our salvation and that's all that matters after everything you've done to me and to us and now you will understand why this is the beginning of the beginning of the end.

That was his final sentence. That was all he had to say. The last of twenty thousand words that would set the record straight once and for all. He squeezed his eyes shut as a wave of dizziness overtook him. He tried unsuccessfully to remember the last time he'd eaten anything besides Mountain Dew, if that even counted. He saved his work, single-spaced, not a single paragraph indentation to spoil it. He opened his email and created message after message, attaching the document to each one. *The Chicago Tribune. The Northbrook Daily Herald.* Northbrook police. Chicago police. His counselor. The counselor before that. The mayor's office, of course. Time-releasing each one for 11 a.m. Ditto for Twitter and Facebook and Instagram. More than enough time. He wasn't going to be one of those clowns who telegraphed his actions beforehand in some kind of desperate cry for help. A tease hinting that he could still be stopped. That was as pathetic as the ones whose weapons jammed. Edgerton wasn't making that mistake.

He turned his computer off and waited until the monitor blinked and went dark. He checked the bag and the rifle one last time. He sat down heavily in the recliner at the end of the couch, not bothering to turn off the lamp beside it, and shut his eyes. Whether he slept was beside the point. The point was to recalibrate his brain — replenish the dried-up crusty sponge it had become — which now was humming like the buzz of a florescent light that no one ever switched off. Maybe if he'd learned how to switch his brain off — if someone had shown him how at any point in his life — things might have turned out differently. Or maybe not. It didn't really matter anymore.

★★★★★

Qualls rolled over in the middle of the night, restless and unable to sleep after arriving home so late. Jittery with caffeine and a nagging sense of pending disaster. Keisha snored softly on the other side of the bed. No need to worry about disturbing her; if there was something Keisha couldn't sleep through — earthquake, plane crash, cat hairball hack — Qualls hadn't found it yet. Though she knew she shouldn't, she picked up her phone and checked her messages. She blinked and was instantly awake. Heintz had texted at 2 a.m. She held the phone close and scrolled down the long note. After their initial conversation with a Chicago shift commander, someone had finally gotten back to Heintz late and reported testily that they'd tried to complete a welfare check but Kelly wasn't answering his apartment door. They couldn't promise more at this point because it was all hands-on deck in that precinct with the St. Patrick's Day parade the next day.

We did what we could, Heintz concluded.

She almost didn't reply, then typed out a quick *okay thanks* at the last moment before setting the phone down on her nightstand. It was hard to disagree. They still had lots to run down, starting with Nancy Richter's connection to Fitzpatrick, but all that would have to wait until the morning.

By which time, she thought, lying back and staring up at the ceiling, it might be too late.

*****

The parking ban wasn't universal, but Daniel didn't want to risk positioning themselves near Kelly's apartment in case some overnight crew decided to tow cars at the last second. Instead they found a space at the beginning of a residential street three blocks over and just down from a gas station and hair salon. They crawled into the back, pulling the hoods on their parkas tight, and settled down front to back, Daniel spooning Nancy as best he could. She whispered something he couldn't make out.

"What?"

"You're behind me," she said softly, snuggling close.

Even through the parka he once again felt how muscular she was. He thought about what she said, about growing up in the country and learning to shoot from her brother. Just before dozing off he looped a strap of his backpack, the one holding the Smith & Wesson 8 plus 1 — down to three shots now — between his feet for safe-keeping. Really, a 2 plus 1 at this point. Two for Kelly, and then the one....

Daniel awoke to the sound of thunder and a drawn-out, high-pitched wailing. Gray light filled the van's interior. He sat up quickly, heart racing. He realized he could see his breath, tiny puffs forming like quickly evaporating fists in the cold, morning air.

"Shit. What time is it?"

"Mmm?"

"We slept too long. It's light out."

Now it was Nancy's turn to sit up, but not as quickly. She rubbed her eyes, her small face buried inside the parka hood. She fumbled for her own backpack and retrieved her phone.

"It's eight o'clock," she said. "Oh shit."

"No kidding."

"Not that. Someone's been calling."

"Who?"

"Hang on."

Daniel stretched as best he could while he waited. He needed to open the van door, stand on the sidewalk and get his bearings while he readied himself for his final act.

"Well," he said, impatience in his voice.

"Some cop."

"What?"

"Some cop's been calling. Heiss or Heights or something."

"What's he want?"

She listened to a message without responding, then disconnected and studied the screen. Daniel made out a string of text message balloons scrolling upward. She closed the messages and powered the phone down.

"So, what?" Daniel said.

"He wants to know if I know where you are."

*****

Edgerton dressed slowly but deliberately in the still dark basement, his efforts illuminated only by the glow of his monitor, the screen still on after he checked the morning traffic reports. Kilt, jacket, vest, hose, belt and belt buckle, dubh tucked into the top of his right hose, shoes. His father's entire kit. Everything a little snug on him but not intolerable. When he was finished, he assembled the pipes, making sure that when he held the instrument the Velcro tabs that opened and closed the slit on the bag were easily accessible. Satisfied, he picked up his keys and wallet, tucked them into the rabbit fur sporran, and headed upstairs. Pausing in the living room, he adjusted the framed watercolor of a choppy Lake Michigan that had tipped unevenly to the left in all the

240

commotion. He stepped carefully around the body of his father, coagulated blood pooled onto the carpet from the crater in his chest, and of his mother, collapsed on the couch as if struggling to rise from a nap. Half her left hand missing from her final, misguided effort to protect herself — or persuade him to stop. He couldn't be sure. He glanced at the TV, which was still on from their news-watching the day before. A live shot from the parade route, a blond girl reporter bundled up against the cold, babbling about tradition and pride and history. Pretending to care about the story she was telling when it was obvious from the way she was standing, all hips and tits and lips and ass, that she was just waiting for her next lay. Edgerton passed into the kitchen, glancing at the clock as he headed for the garage door. Eight-oh-one. Still plenty of time, Your Honor.

*****

They locked the van and started up the street, backpacks slung over their shoulders. Daniel patted his right front pocket every few steps, the solid frame of the Smith & Wesson assuring him as they walked. He wondered if Nancy, easily keeping pace beside him, knew what was about to happen. He felt bad for her, after all she'd done for him, but there was nothing he could do about that now.

He felt his spirits rise as they turned the corner onto Kelly's street, his quarry so close after all this time. The disaster of the night before, the attempted shakedown, Nancy's marksmanship, the bodies collapsing onto the ground — *Oh shit, oh shit, oh shit* — fading quickly. He stopped, his spirits falling just as fast, and looked on in dismay. People filled the street. Loud music, a recorded jig of some kind, poured from Donnelly's. The bar's door swinging open and shut as people streamed in and out for an early morning nip.

"Danny?" Nancy said.

At least fifty people stood between him and Kelly's apartment building, milling around, several holding clear plastic cups of green beer. Cheers went up as a troupe of bagpipers strode past, headed for the parade route. At the corner, a cop, his cheeks red from the cold, laughing at something a man said to him. After all this time, and now this.

"There," Nancy said.

"What?"

"Kelly. Over there."

He looked in the direction she was pointing. He couldn't believe it. Amidst all that was going on, Kelly, in plain sight. Emerging from Donnelly's, smiling broadly as he pulled a black watch cap from his leather jacket. He tugged it over his cream-white hair and headed up the street, in the direction of the bagpipers. Three men beside and behind him—two young, one about Kelly's age, all big as longshoreman. Grandsons? Nephews? A brother? All three the worse for it after a stop inside Donnelly's first thing, to judge by their hoots and hollers and back-slapping. But also all on their feet and not exactly stumbling.

"Come on," he said.

"Like this?" Nancy said. "With all these people around?"

"Like this."

Daniel took off quickly, his eyes never leaving Kelly's bobbing, black cap, which today stuck out like an airport beacon amidst all the green hats. He tried to shrink the gap between them, even started jogging at one point. But the crowd was just too dense and getting thicker all the time as people emerged from cars and other bars and side streets and joined the fray. He lost sight of Kelly for a moment as a passing bus blocked the next street up. The barrier drawing the drunken ire of the crowd and making him think he'd blown it again. Then he caught a glimpse of the cap once the bus moved on. He hurried forward. He reached into his right pocket and found the grip of the gun and held it, hidden, as he walked.

At last, as they turned toward Western Avenue, the movement of the crowd slowed. A rushing river curling into a series of quiet eddies as people maneuvered for the best positions along the route. Applause erupted as the first floats rolled past, followed by the tinny blast of a school marching band. Out of the corner of his eye Daniel saw girls in sequined tights waving flags. Kids in matching red and white uniforms holding instruments before them. A trio of frozen drummers bringing up the rear. He started to maneuver through the crowd, eyes pinned to the black watch cap a few dozen yards away.

"Excuse me. Thanks. Pardon me. Excuse me."

Daniel looked to his left, hearing Nancy's voice, then felt her hand in his a moment later as she pulled him along. When they paused a few yards farther down, their passage blocked by a pair of bulky women yelling and clapping at something on the route, she pulled him close. "You do this right, all this noise, nobody's gonna hear anything. You time it right, you know?"

He nodded, indicating he understood.

"We get separated, we meet back at the van. Okay?"

He nodded again. Satisfied, Nancy turned and led them around the women and back in pursuit of Kelly. Daniel swallowed, feeling a hole in his stomach. Or was it his heart? How could he tell her that getting away with it, allowing the noise of the crowd to muffle the sound of the shots, wasn't the point? That none of it mattered if he couldn't look Kelly in the eyes at the last second so he knew what was happening — and by whose hand.

A new sound from down the street. A crescendo of shouts and applause with one or two boos mixed in. Something big was rolling towards them. A marquee float, no doubt, with a celebrity aboard. This might be his best chance, the attention of the crowd drawn to the spectacle and away from his confrontation. He picked up the pace, surged ahead of Nancy now, pulling his hand free. Better for all concerned if he lost her in the drunken throng beforehand.

"Danny — wait."

He ignored her, moving fast, the black watch cap drawing nearer and nearer. His focus spiraled into a tight cone of attention directed at the sight of his quarry forty yards away, now thirty-five. Now thirty. Dimly, he heard the sound of the crowd rise even more as whatever big deal display rolled closer and closer. Nancy's voice pleading for him to wait fading behind him. Twenty-five yards. Twenty. Now to his left, a distraction as an exchange of angry words momentarily interrupted his quest. He glanced over and saw a lone bagpiper wading into the crowd.

Pushing his way to the front, to the edge of the parade route. "The fuck are you doing?" a man yelled, his words slurred, as the piper shouldered past. "Cool your jets," a woman screeched in return. "I love me some pipes!" Daniel continued forward. Fifteen yards. Ten. Five.

There.

He reached out, placed his left hand on Kelly's shoulder, and roughly spun him around.

And stared into the eyes of a man he'd never seen before.

"'Scuse me?" the man said, eyes bloodshot, breath a gin mill, as he smiled uncertainly at Daniel.

It wasn't Kelly. He'd lost track of him somehow, distracted by so many people along the route. Followed a different black watch cap through the crowd. What were the odds? After all this time and now this. Daniel pulled his hand off the man's shoulder and looked around, searching faces wildly, like a man in a burning jungle trying to find an opening to flee through. The applause around him grew louder and louder as the headlining float approached. A second later Daniel saw the object of the attention roll past the edge of his vision.

A woman aboard, bundled up in a long green coat, waving at the crowd. A banner — something about the mayor. Seated beside her, a dozen or more children, all races and ethnicities, also waving at the crowd as they dipped into buckets at their feet and flung fistfuls of candy into the air. A frenzied excitement filled the children's faces as they fed off the energy of the enthusiastic, amped-up crowd. A beautiful sight, Daniel supposed. But he no longer had eyes for it. He'd found Kelly.

He was standing three yards to Daniel's left, directly on the edge of the crowd, the trio of men who'd accompanied him from the bar safely out of reach. Kelly standing just behind the bagpiper who'd now emerged onto the parade route after clearing the throng. Daniel barged ahead, shouldering past the people in his way. Ignoring the cries of protest and scarcely registering the splash of cold beer soaking his pants as his progress upended someone's filled-to-the-brim plastic cup. He heard his voice called from behind but didn't turn around. In what seemed no time at all he stood before him at last.

"Joe Kelly," he said, and cursed the dryness in his mouth. The way the words emerged in a half-formed mutter. He cleared his throat and repeated himself.

"Joseph John Kelly," he said loudly.

Kelly turned and trained his watery blue eyes on Daniel.

"And who in the hell might you be?"

Daniel pulled the Smith & Wesson from the parka's right pocket, pointed the barrel at Kelly's chest, directly at the miserable son-of-a-bitch's heart, and said, "I'm—"

"Oh my God! Danny!"

He felt himself jerked back. He turned and saw Nancy, clutching at him, her mouth open in horror. He pulled himself free, furious, then heard a sound like firecrackers and froze in place. A moment later he realized he was the only person standing; the crowd around him had sunk to its knees as screams filled the air. He stared, trying to process what he was seeing. The bagpiper, the man who'd pushed his way through the crowd, was standing in the middle of the street, a rifle in his hands, pointing it at the mayor's float as shredded green bunting floated slowly upward in the cold breeze.

"Danny," Nancy cried. "Do something!"

He looked around for Kelly. Found him beside him, crouched low, those watery eyes now filled with fear. In Daniel's hand, the Smith & Wesson 8 plus 1, transformed now to 2 plus 1. Only two shots for Kelly and one to finish the job, but it would be enough. *The special ain't cheap, is what I'm saying.* He lowered the gun, squaring the barrel between Kelly's eyes.

"Danny — there's children. Oh Danny, Danny!"

Nancy's voice shattered his concentration, piercing his focus like the crack of a falling tree branch heard above a punishing gale. He turned and stared dully at the mayor's float, saw the children flinging themselves off in terror, adults rushing toward them, arms outreached. The bagpiper raising his rifle. At the end of the float, a small child, a girl, head bare despite the cold with her blond hair pulled back in a ponytail, sitting with her legs dangling free, eyes round as saucers, alone and unable to move.

It's so hot. Can I have a popsicle?

Another one?

Please, Danny?

"Danny!"

He looked a final time at Kelly and stepped into the street. He raised the Smith & Wesson and fired at the bagpiper's head but hit his right shoulder instead. His aim lousy, the shot spinning the man around to face Daniel. As blood bloomed from the wound the bagpiper lifted his rifle but Daniel fired again, this time hitting him in the chest, where he'd meant to shoot Kelly a moment earlier. The man staggered back, nearly fell, but somehow kept his balance. He started to turn toward the float, still clutching the rifle. Daniel fired a last time without hesitation, the third shot, his last, the one he'd meant to hold back. He hit the piper square in the head, sending him to the asphalt in an arcing spray of blood.

Daniel dropped his arms to his sides, breathing heavily, and turned to look for Nancy. A moment later he found her in the crowd, tiny pixie face framed by her parka hood, and despite everything he made to wave at her when suddenly a flame erupted in his chest, and then a second, and a bouquet of hot colors exploded in his brain, and something sharp stabbed his neck, and then his shoulder, and he heard more firecrackers. As Daniel tottered and lost his balance he managed to turn and see two men and a woman in blue uniforms crouching before him, guns gripped in their hands, firing again and again. Firing at him. Beyond them, another uniform, man or woman he couldn't tell as his vision dimmed. The officer running up the street with the blond girl from the float tucked safely in their arms. In the fog swarming his senses he thought he heard Nancy — "No!" — but then there wasn't anything left to see or to hear.

✶✶✶✶✶

"So much for tracking him down today," Qualls said, studying her phone.

"No shit," Heintz said, peering at his own phone, sitting in the extra chair beside her desk. Back in the small prison office. "Just our luck. Unless ..."

"Unless what?"

"It has something to do with Fitzpatrick?"

"You make him as an active shooter?" Qualls said. "Nothing points that way. Besides, city that size? Could be anyone. Anything."

"I guess."

"Miracle, no matter what," Qualls said, scrolling down the AP article she was reading. "They're saying just two dead even though the guy had an AK. Float full of kids and none of them hit. Cops must have put the hurt on him fast."

"One good thing, anyway. Hello?" Heintz held a finger up as he answered his phone. "Hang on." He put it speaker and set it down. "Rodriguez," he mouthed.

"Morning, Altagracia," Qualls said.

"Morning, Lieutenant. You guys have a second?"

She told her that they did.

"I was looking into that lady? Fitzpatrick's girlfriend? Nancy Richter?"

"What about her?" Qualls had already received three all caps emails from the director that morning demanding to know why Richter hadn't been vetted better as a visitor.

"I poked around a bit, looked her up on Facebook. You're never going to believe this. But she has—had—an older brother named Danny."

"Please don't tell me Fitzpatrick is her brother," Qualls said. If they'd missed a connection like that, literal heads were going to roll.

"Nothing like that. And I said 'had.' Her brother died in a farm accident about five years ago. Tractor rolled over on him, big soybean spread outside Marion. Judging by her posts, Nancy kind of lost her mind for a while."

"For a while?" Heintz said.

"She hasn't posted anything for months. But it looks like she got religion along the way, or something, and somebody suggested she try some volunteer work. Helping others."

"You mean—" Qualls said.

"She started writing inmates at Marion. And somehow she hooked up with Fitzpatrick."

"Because he was a Danny, too?" Qualls demanded. "Because if so, that's weird. Really weird."

"Not sure, Lieutenant. All I can tell is that she was broken down, she started going to the prison, started to visit Fitzpatrick, and it seemed to fix her. She found life worth living again. At least according to Facebook. I've got a number for her parents, if you want to call them."

Qualls was about to respond when a knock at the door interrupted. She looked up. The director stood there, her face stony as a cinderblock as she glared at Qualls and Heintz. All the way up from Columbus with no warning. So. It was going to be that kind of a day.

"Sure, Altagracia. That's a big help. Thanks."

"No problem. Such a strange case."

"Such a strange case," Qualls repeated, and stood to face the door.

*****

Donnelly's was more crowded that evening than Nancy anticipated, though the mood was somber. The line of men seated at the bar silent as they fingered glasses of amber reflecting the lights of the overhead TVs. As one they stared at the screens, listening to the latest recap of the parade tragedy. Whether by luck or something else, a seat sat empty beside Kelly. Nancy pulled her blouse down, straightened her necklace, and sat down beside him. When the bartender approached, she made to accidentally bump Kelly's elbow. Catching the bartender's attention, she pointed at Kelly's drink as he looked down at her.

"So sad," she said, nodding at the TV.

"A real tragedy," Kelly said, eyes lingering at his glimpse of the milky skinned v-curve of her breasts hiding just below the top of her blouse.

Two drinks later they left the bar in a hurry, a couple of the other patrons sending them off with ill-disguised guffaws. Nancy pretended not to notice the grin on Kelly's face as he flipped them a good-natured bird. Five minutes after that they were across the street and Kelly was fumbling for the keys to his apartment door while Nancy stood beside him, brushing her hand on his back in a slow, sensuous circle.

"The world's so scary," she said once they were inside and he had her pinned against the door. She did her best not to recoil at the stink of whiskey and bar nuts and something oniony on his breath as he snaked his tongue into her mouth.

A minute later he excused himself and went into the bathroom, not even shutting the door all the way in his haste. Nancy beelined for the bedroom, where she took in the shabby furnishings as she undressed down to her bra and panties and leather necklace. Kelly didn't take long. When he emerged and walked into the bedroom he stared at her and licked — actually licked — his lips.

"Come here, darling," Nancy said, patting the bed. "A girl gets so lonely."

He undressed quickly, his eyes never leaving Nancy. After a moment he stood there in nothing at all. Pale, hairless legs. His junk shriveled up and ridiculously small, even aroused. Belly like he'd swallowed a helmet. Concave chest lined with wisps of curling, gray hair. Not a lot of signs of cancer.

"Let's make this special," Nancy whispered, putting her arms around his neck as he climbed into bed. "Let's do it from behind."

"Not a good Catholic girl, I take it," Kelly grunted, his eyes glinting with anticipation.

"No darling, I'm not," Nancy said, flipping herself around, nimble as a gymnast, as she rotated herself onto his back. In one smooth motion she removed the leather necklace, flipped it around his neck, and pulled back, hard.

"What now—" Kelly grunted, but those were his last words. His hands clawed at the necklace, seeking space between its tightly woven braid and the flabby wattle of skin below his chin, but Nancy's grip was too strong. Three times in a row she whispered the name of Daniel's sister in his left ear. Kelly grunting as she jerked the necklace tighter with each whisper. He groaned and gasped, bucking to throw her, but she clung to him, clamping her thighs hard against his ribs as she tightened the lariat over and over again. Once, toward the end, just for a moment, she thought he might free himself so violent were his struggles, so raspy his choking. But she shifted her knees onto his back and braced herself by pushing down with all her might as she pulled back harder and harder. Her arms trembling with the effort. She pulled so hard that she lifted Kelly upward, and as he rose, tongue protruding, phlegm-specked spittle dripping from his mouth, she saw his reflection in a mirror above the small chest of drawers opposite the bed and watched as the last thing he looked at were his own eyes bulging from his head like a pair of cold, pale, freshly peeled grapes.

"Sorry about that," Nancy said, letting his body drop forward when it was over. "It had to be. There just weren't no other way."

She waited until she caught her breath, then reached up and lifted the necklace over and off Kelly's head. She tossed it onto her clothes crumpled in a pile at the base of the bed. She wasn't sure if she would keep it or not. It was one of those decisions that took time. She had a few other things to think about first. She decided to make up her mind when she figured out what she might be doing, where she might be going, next after this.

The Usual Unusual Suspects

Brandon Barrows is the author of several crime and mystery novels. His most recent, The Last Request, was published September, 2023 by Bloodhound Books. He has also published over one hundred short stories and is a three-time Mustang Award finalist, as well as a 2022 Derringer Award nominee.
Find more at http://www.brandonbarrowscomics.com and on Twitter @BrandonBarrows

Anthony Regolino was a Finalist in 2020's 1st Quarter of the L. Ron Hubbard's Writers of the Future Contest, and he has had fiction and poetry included in various anthologies devoted to fantasy, horror, science fiction, crime, and comedy. He worked as an editor in the book publishing field for over a dozen years, has been a ghostwriter, a contributing writer, and composed blogs professionally for major companies' websites.
Check him out at https://anthonyregolino.weebly.com.

Madeleine McDonald finds inspiration walking on the chilly, windswept beach of her Yorkshire home. As a former precis-writer, she enjoys the challenge of writing flash fiction. Her short stories have been broadcast on BBC radio, and published in various anthologies and journals. Her historical novel, *A Shackled Inheritance*, is available from Amazon Kindle. Madeleine's *Not the Dog* appears in *Crimeucopia — One More Thing To Worry About*, and *I Can See Clearly Now* in *Crimeucopia — Tales From The Back Porch*, and *Murder at St Botts* in *Crimeucopia — Rule Britannia – Britannia Waves The Rules*.

Nikki Knight describes herself as an Author/Anchor/Mom…not in that order. An award-winning weekend anchor at New York City's 1010

WINS Radio, she writes short stories and novels, most recently *Wrong Poison,* from Charade Media. Her stories have appeared in Crimeucopias, *Alfred Hitchcock's Mystery Magazine,* and other magazines, podcasts, and anthologies. As Kathleen Marple Kalb, she writes the *Old Stuff* and *Ella Shane* mysteries for Level Best Books. She's Vice President of the Short Mystery Fiction Society and Co-VP of the New York/Tri-State Sisters in Crime Chapter. She, her husband, and son live in a Connecticut house owned by their cat

Michele Bazan Reed's short stories have appeared in *Woman's World* magazine and several anthologies, most recently *Detective Mysteries Short Stories, Mid-Century Murder, Malice Domestic 15: Mystery Most Theatrical, Masthead: Best New England Mysteries 2020, The Fish that Got Away, Crazy Christmas Capers* and *The Big Fang* (2022).

A member of Sisters in Crime and its Guppy Chapter, Private Eye Writers of America, and the Short Mystery Fiction Society, she won a 2017 Daphne Award in the unpublished mainstream mystery category.

Michele's Crimeucopia appearances have been in *The I's Have It, Tales From The Back Porch, We'll Be Right Back – After This!* and *One More Thing To Worry About.*

Lyn Fraser currently resides in the U.S. but has also lived in London and Brighton. At present she teaches a course in crime fiction for the adult education program at Colorado Mesa University and has served as a hospice and palliative care chaplain. Publications include short fiction in literary reviews, a mystery novel, and an academic textbook.

Lyn's first appearance was with *Hallowed Odours,* in *Crimeucopia – The Cosy Nostra.*

Michael Wiley is the Shamus Award-winning writer of two series of PI novels – the Joe Kozmarski and Sam Kelson mysteries – and two other crime series – the Daniel Turner and Franky Dast novels. His short stories appear often in magazines and anthologies. Michael is also a frequent book reviewer and an occasional writer of journalism, critical books, and essays. He grew up in Chicago, where he sets his PI stories, and teaches creative writing and literature in North Florida. His kids accuse him of being as disinhibited as Sam Kelson.

Eve Fisher has been writing since elementary school, and her mystery stories have appeared regularly in *Alfred Hitchcock Mystery Magazine* and other publications, and her *A Time To Mourn* received an Honorable Mention in *Best American Mystery Stories 2012*.
She's part of the mystery writers' blog, *SleuthSayers*, at www.sleuthsayers.org (every 2nd Thursday!), and a fan in Shanghai is translating her work into Chinese. She's been volunteering at the local penitentiary with the Lifers' Group for over a decade, which gives her interesting acquaintances. A jack of all trades, she also writes historical articles, fantasy and science fiction. She lives in South Dakota with her husband and 5,000 books.
Eve's *Collateral Damage* appears in *Crimeucopia – We're All Animals Under The Skin*, her *Truth & Turpitude* in *Crimeucopia – The Cosy Nostra*, and her *Nude with Snow Geese* in *Crimeucopia – Tales From The Back Porch*.

John M. Floyd's short stories have appeared in *Alfred Hitchcock's Mystery Magazine, Ellery Queen's Mystery Magazine, Strand Magazine, The Saturday Evening Post, Best American Mystery Stories* (2015, 2018, and 2020), *Best Mystery Stories of the Year 2021, Best Crime Stories of the Year 2021*, and many other publications. A former Air Force captain and IBM systems engineer, John is an Edgar finalist, a Shamus Award winner, a five-time Derringer Award winner, and the author of nine books. He is also the 2018 recipient of the Short Mystery Fiction Society's lifetime achievement award.
His last Crimeucopia appearance was with *The Florida Keys*, in *Strictly Off The Record*.

Michael Cahlin started his career as a newspaper reporter and later contributed to developing a vast array of software whose DNA can be found in today's desktop publishers, word processors, spell checkers, file managers, backup programs, and system utilities. He co-created *The Official XTree MS-DOS & Hard Disk Companion*, one of the blueprints for the successful *Dummies* Series. His non-fiction articles have appeared in *Basketball Weekly, Family Circle, PC World, Tom's Guide* and *The Writer*. Dean Krystek at Wordlink.us represents his mystery thrillers, *Wicked Problems* and *The Right Regrets*. His short stories have appeared in *Mystery Weekly, Black Cat's Mystery Megapack*, and *Down & Out Mystery Magazine*. Michael has a Master's degree in Education from Pepperdine University and is a member of The League of Vermont Writers. He is currently working on a sequel to *The Right Regrets*.

Kevin R. Tipple reviews books, watches way too much television, and offers unsolicited opinions on anything. His short fiction has appeared in magazines such as *Lynx Eye, Starblade, Show and Tell*, and *The Writer's Post Journal* among others. He's also online at such places as *Mouth Full Of Bullets, Crime And Suspense, Mysterical-e* and others. *Mystery Weekly Magazine* published his story, *The Damn Rodents Are Everywhere*, in May of 2021 and soon had to change their name to *Mystery Magazine*. His short story, *The Beetle's Last Fifty Grand* appears in the 2022 anthology, *Back Road Bobby and His Friends*, and everyone involved seems to have survived the experience unscathed. He hopes the same for *Crimeucopia*, which features his *Sweet Dreams Are Made of This* in the *Strictly Off The Record* anthology..
Fully trained before marriage, Kevin can work all major appliances and, despite a love of nearly all sports, is able to clean up after himself.

Martin Zeigler writes short fiction, primarily mystery, science fiction, and horror. His stories have been published in a number of anthologies and journals, both in print and online.
Every so often (okay, twice), he has gathered these stories into a self-published collection. In 2015 he released *A Functional Man And Other Stories*. More recently, in 2020, a year we will all remember with fondness, he released *Hypochondria And Other Stories*.

Besides writing, Marty enjoys the things most people do. And besides those, he likes reading, taking long walks, and playing the piano. Marty makes his home in the Pacific Northwest.

Lev Raphael Ten of my twenty-seven books are mysteries set in academia which I escaped many years ago. I've had mystery fiction in Crimewave and other journals, taught mystery fiction as a guest at Michigan State University, and was the crime fiction reviewer for The Detroit Free Press for over a decade before switching to radio.

Andrew Darlington has been regularly published since the 1960s in all manner of strange and obscure places, magazines, websites, anthologies and books. He has also worked as a Stand-Up Poet on the 'Alternative Cabaret Circuit', and also has a phenomenal back catalogue of published interviews with many people from the worlds of Literature, SF-Fantasy, Art and Rock-Music for a variety of publications (a selection of his favourite interviews have been collected into the Headpress book *I Was Elvis Presley's Bastard Love-Child*).
His latest poetry collection is *Tweak Vision* (Alien Buddha Press), and a new fiction collection *A Saucerful Of Secrets* is now available from Parallel Universe Publications, and a Scientifiction novel *In The Time Of The Breaking* (Alien Buddha Press) was published in January 2019. Catch up with him at http://andrewdarlington.blogspot.com/.

Nick Young is a retired award-winning CBS News Correspondent. His writing has appeared in more than thirty publications including the *Pennsylvania Literary Journal, The Garland Lake Review, The Remington Review, The San Antonio Review, The Best of CaféLit 11* and Vols. I and II of the *Writer Shed Stories* anthologies. His first novel *Deadline* ("I read it in one sitting...I could not put it down!") https://www.amazon.com/dp/B0CGGFR5YY was published in September. He lives outside Chicago.

John Kojak is a graduate of The University of Texas and a US Navy veteran whose short stories have appeared in numerous books and magazines of a dubious and independent nature, including *Bête Noire, Pulp Modern, Switchblade, Serial Magazine, EconoClash Review,* Blue Room Book's *Stories of Southern Humor and Southern Crime Anthology, Mystery Weekly, Pulp Adventures,* HellBound Book's *Road Kill: Texas Horror By Texas Writers Vol 5,* and *The Toilet Zone: Number Two* among others.

Andrew Welsh-Huggins describes himself as a writer, a reader, and a veteran pet feeder. Shamus, Derringer and International Thriller Writers award-nominated author, you can find his latest adventures and also sign up for his newsletter by visiting him at https://www.andrewwelshhuggins.com/.
You can also follow him on: BookBub – GoodReads – https://www.facebook.com/awhcolumbus – Twitter and Instagram: @awhcolumbus
Out now: *The End of The Road,* from Mysterious Press:
"A crackerjack crime yarn chockablock with miscreants and a supersonic pace." (Kirkus)

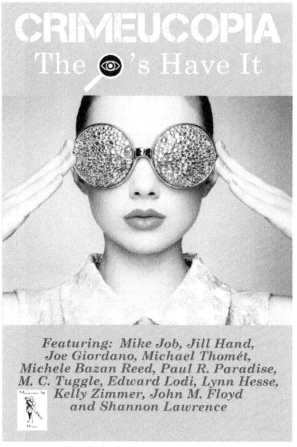

CRIMEUCOPIA
The 👁's Have It

Featuring: *Mike Job, Jill Hand,*
Joe Giordano, Michael Thomét,
Michele Bazan Reed, Paul R. Paradise,
M. C. Tuggle, Edward Lodi, Lynn Hesse,
Kelly Zimmer, John M. Floyd
and Shannon Lawrence

Investigators and investigations are the mainstay of most Crime fiction sub-genres. Everything from the original *Golden Age* of country houses and the amateur sleuth, through to the high tech ultra-modern 21st Century – a place where the cyber investigators sometimes appear to be baffled by old-fashioned motivations of power and greed, and human foibles such as love and revenge.

So is there any real difference between the Private and the Public Sector investigators? Not much, if writers are to be believed, and the two can often be found straddling both sides of the 'what's legal procedure?' fence.

Of the twelve authors contained within, eleven are voices new to the world of Crimeucopia - and although the theme is *Investigators*, the material ranges from Cosy, through to not too Hardboiled - and most are touched with a vein of humour, be it light or dark. Rather like a box of chocolates…

Paperback ISBN: 9781909498327 eBook ISBN: 9781909498334

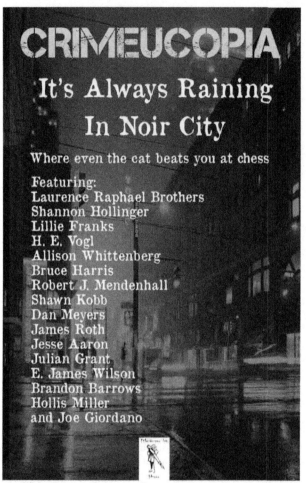

CRIMEUCOPIA

It's Always Raining In Noir City

Where even the cat beats you at chess

Featuring:
Laurence Raphael Brothers
Shannon Hollinger
Lillie Franks
H. E. Vogl
Allison Whittenberg
Bruce Harris
Robert J. Mendenhall
Shawn Kobb
Dan Meyers
James Roth
Jesse Aaron
Julian Grant
E. James Wilson
Brandon Barrows
Hollis Miller
and Joe Giordano

Is the Noir Crime sub-genre always dark and downbeat? Is there a time when Bad has a change of conscience, flips sides and takes on the Good role?

Noir is almost always a dish served up raw and bloody - Fiction bleu if you will. So maybe this is a chance to see if Noir can be served sunny side up - with the aid of these fifteen short order authors.

All fifteen give us dark tales from the stormy side of life - which is probably why it's *always* raining in Noir City....

Paperback Edition ISBN: 9781909498341
eBook Edition ISBN: 9781909498358

CRIMEUCOPIA

Tales From The Back Porch

Telling tales are:
Penny Hurrell, Teresa Trent, Wendy Harrison, Maroula Blades,
Tom Sheehan, Jan Christensen, Bryn Fortey, Michele Bazan Reed,
Carol Willis, Madeleine McDonald, Adam Meyer, Nikki Knight,
Regina Clarke, J. W. Wood, Deb Merino and Alison McDonald

Small town, big city, watercooler or the back of that 1950s beat-up
Chevy Bel Air with the leather back seat that your parents told you
never to get familiar with. It doesn't matter where you hear it, gossip
is 100% pure ear addiction – and knowledge is, after all, power when
all's said and done.

So why don't you settle down, get yourself comfy, and pour yourself
a drink – long and tall, or just short and nasty, the choice is yours –
and let these 16 story tellers spin their tales as only they know how.

Paperback Edition ISBN: 9781909498365
eBook Edition ISBN: 9781909498372

CRIMEUCOPIA

When the theme is no theme at all, you've just got to ask the question

Say What Now?

Featuring:
Peter Ullian,
S. E. Bailey,
N. M. Cedeño,
Edward St Boniface,
Jan Glaz,
Eleanor Luke,
Momodou Bah,
Eve Fisher,
John M. Floyd,
Joan Leotta,
Glen Bush
and DL Shirey

Sometimes editors are forced to reject submissions through no fault of the author. It could be a wonderfully written manuscript, but if the editor cannot place it, then what do they do?

MIP has been lucky in its flexibility and its "Can we start a new project with this?" attitude. Some of the dozen authors contained within are seasoned professionals, having been published in the likes of Alfred Hitchcock's, Ellery Queen's, or other notable publications, while some are making their publishing debuts as Crimeucopians. And while the quality throughout remains exceedingly high, the subject spectrum is the widest we've published so far. But that's only fitting when you consider that the theme of this Crimeucopa is that of No Theme At All.

And in true Murderous Ink fashion, with a dozen authors to choose from, you're bound to find something you'll like, and something you didn't know you'd like until you've read it.

Paperback Edition ISBN: 9781909498389
eBook Edition ISBN: 9781909498396

This is the first of several 'Free 4 All' collections that was supposed to be themeless. However, with the number of submissions that came in, it seems that this could be called an *Angels & Devils* collection, mixing PI & Police alongside tales from the Devil's dining table. Mind you, that's not to say that all the PIs & Police are on the side of the Angels....

Also this time around has not only seen a move to a larger paperback format size, but also in regard to the length of the fiction as well. Followers of the somewhat bent and twisted Crimeucopia path will know that although we don't deal with Flash fiction as a rule, it is a rule that we have sometimes broken. And let's face it, if you cannot break your own rules now and again, whose rules can you break?

Oh, wait, isn't breaking the rules the foundation of the crime fiction genre?

Oh dear....

CRIMEUCOPIA

One More Thing To Worry About

Featuring
Gerald Elias, Bob Ritchie, Michele Bazan Reed,
Terry Wijesuriya, Aran Myracle, Alexei J. Slater,
Nikki Knight, Issy Jinarmo, N. M. Cedeño,
Wendy Harrison, Andrew Darlington, Larry Lefkowitz,
Jesse Aaron, Madeleine McDonald, Joan Leotta,
H. E. Vogl, and Vinnie Hansen

New Crimeucopians *Aran Myracle, Alexei J. Slater, Gerald Elias, Terry Wijesuriya, Issy Jinarmo, Larry Lefkowitz,* and *Vinnie Hansen* smoothly rub literary shoulders with a fine collection of familiar Crimeucopia old hands: *Bob Ritchie, Michele Bazan Reed, Nikki Knight, N. M. Cedeño, Wendy Harrison, Andrew Darlington, Madeleine McDonald, Joan Leotta, H. E. Vogl* and *Jesse Aaron.*

All 17 tell tales that will make you realise there's always going to be One More Thing To Worry About....

With 16 vibrant authors, a wraparound paperback cover, and pages full of crime fiction in some of its many guises, what's not to like?

So if you enjoy tales spun by

Anthony Diesso, Brandon Barrows, E. James Wilson, James Roth, Jesse Aaron, Jim Guigli, John M. Floyd, Kevin R. Tipple, Maddi Davidson, Michael Grimala, Robert Petyo, Shannon Hollinger, Tom Sheehan, Wil A. Emerson, Peter Trelay, and Philip Pak

then you'd better get

CRIMEUCOPIA - Strictly Off The record

by the sound of it!

Boomshakalaking is a variant of the expression Boomshakalaka, currently recognised as a boastful, teasingly hostile exclamation that follows a noteworthy achievement or an impressive stunt — the meaning similar to *in your face!*

Which is why this anthology is subtitled *Modern Crimes for Modern Times*, because most, if not all, are not your 'regular' crime fiction pieces — in fact some quite happily dance along the edges of multiple genres and styles, while others skew it like it is.

Of the 14 who appear in this anthology, 8 are new Crimeucopians, and even we have to admit that this is one of the most diverse Crimeucopia anthologies so far, and still sits under the umbrella of Crime Fiction.

As with all of these anthologies, we hope you'll find something that you immediately like, as well as something that takes you out of your comfort zone – and puts you into a completely new one.

In other words, in the spirit of the Murderous Ink Press motto:

You never know what you like until you read it.

Printed in Great Britain
by Amazon

37161880R00158